You Are Safe

Russell C. Arslan

BOOKS PREVIOUSLY PUBLISHED

By

Russell C. Arslan

"Those People"

David Russell was traveling in Kenya with his two grown, adopted sons, was there to share his earlier life experiences. Father and sons left Los Angeles on a rite of passage trip.. They encountered all his old friends and a new species in their search for his earlier life.

"HIGHEST STAKES, ALL IN"

Matt Papaz knows nothing about the crimes Homeland Security is charging him with and goes *All In* to prove his innocence. His life depends on the intelligence and strategies needed to win Texas Hold'em or any card game of skill. Going full throttle, *All In,* means take a commanding position, based on odds and the reading of your opponent's hand. Taking an aggressive stance gave Matt Papaz the edge in his life and death situations.

"Leopard Directive"

Matt Papaz was appalled when he saw the email from Frederic Valance. Breaking three year's silence the unexpected shock evolved into a communication with the horrifying prospect of identity exposure for both the president and his Chief-of-Staff.

Drug cartel's business practices no longer perceived as a government threat made possible the use of monies and personnel for the betterment of society.

Roberto Coto, the new democratically elected Costa Rican President with his Chief-of-Staff, Matt Papaz and his old friend, Frederic Valance carefully circumvented usual money laundering techniques, infusing millions of dollars from the notorious Tijuana cartel into the Latin American country. His political and personal persona manufactured after the Porter affair was clean and impervious to public scrutiny. His identity for the entirety of the past four years had been safe.

ISBN: Paperback 978-0-9857695-9-8

Ebook 978-0-9857695-3-6

This is a work of fiction. names, characters, places and incidents either are the product of the author's imagination or are used fictitiously, and any resemblance to any actual persons, living or dead, events, or locales is entirely coincidental.

This book was printed in the United States of America.

Additional copies may be ordered from:

russellcarslan.com

and

russellarslan-booksandarts.com

Forward

After reading an article in the Los Angeles Times about corruption in Nairobi Kenya, a restless Matt Papaz discontented with his opulent and mundane Beverly Hills life plunges into another adventure with his cohorts, The Papaz Group. An investment vehicle created to act as a countervailing agent for change against Nairobi's notorious Mungiki gang and their Chinese benefactors who want to control the mineral trade in Kenya and other underdeveloped nations. Globalization and imperialist methods to obtain resources for China's meteoric economic growth must be stopped.

Papaz, Alvarez, Valance, Guzman, BiBa and the other players of the Matt Papaz group match wits with the Chinese and engage in a deadly battle for heavy and precious metals which will determine the political and economic control of the Third World.

Chapter 1

Matt Papaz and BiBa Lamanas were driving on Beverly Glen Boulevard. She said, "I don't know how to deal with you when you're acting this way."

On their way to a meeting with real estate agent, William Smythe, from Rodeo Realty, Matt and BiBa were looking for Westside residential property near the heart of Beverly Hills.

"Come on, not that look again," she said. "You have everything, more money than God, you even have me! Fess up there's something wrong. What's going on?"

"I don't know," he disgustedly retorted. "I have everything, that's for sure, but I feel empty. I feel like I'm out to pasture. The adrenaline rush after Africa and South America has run its course and I feel like after an accident when you have the shakes. The six months in Toronto were great, but didn't make me feel what I expected. I guess just too laid back. Coming out here to LA, buying a house and setting up a photo gallery supposedly would make me feel better. Well it doesn't. Everything I dreamed of since we've been together seems empty. Maybe I just need time to clear my head and feel sorry for myself."

Looking directly at him she said, "Not on my dime!" Raising her voice she continued, "I told you I would be with you and you didn't have to explain that mess in Africa. I know people died and all. The relationship with your so-called friends is fine with me. That should be enough for you. You know I love you. I probably shouldn't say this, but I actually need you. I just don't need a shell of someone I fell in love with. You want something and I guess it's not me. Either talk to me, and stop the bullshit, or sure as hell, I am going back to Vegas. My job is still there. I can't take this anymore even if it means not being with you. I will go!" she said emphatically.

Matt pushed the telephone key on the steering wheel and said, "Call William Smythe." The phone rang and Smythe answered, "I'll be there in 20 minutes."

Before Smythe could continue Matt interrupted, "Listen Bill, we have to cancel. Sorry for the late notice and your inconvenience, I'll call later and reschedule. We're still interested but something important came up, sorry."

Hanging up the phone, he looked directly at BiBa sitting in the passenger seat. "Okay, you're right; I have been acting like a sniveling piece of garbage. We do have to talk. Let's go to the Glen. It's right up the street near Mulholland Drive. We can stop and get some coffee or something."

She nodded her head in agreement as the rented Mercedes-Benz 550SL pulled into the strip center above one of BelAir's most prestigious neighborhoods. They parked and walked to a Starbucks table in front. The whole scene was surreal. The opulence of the neighborhood and its superficial residences played heavily on Matt. The soullessness of his money and the restlessness of his non-productivity for the last six months were an emotional weight. That was evident to them both.

"I feel useless," he said, "I need something. I'm bored and I feel empty. Truth be told, it's a lot more than that. I feel like a voyeur looking at my new life and it's not what I want. Everybody is doing something, except me. I feel like I'm just watching, not doing anything. Managing our investments isn't stimulating or even the least bit entertaining. This morning was too much for me. I got depressed after reading the paper. You know a real helpless feeling."

BiBa had a way of getting Matt to talk by being quiet and making him feel uncomfortable. She just stared at him. He continued, "The same old routine, the gym, the trainers, the self-defense classes, and the incessant reading. I feel like I'm treading water, especially in Beverly Hills. Do I really want to live here? It's overwhelming! It's not good for me. It must be horrible for you, and shit, I brought you here! Everything is too perfect and easy in this new life.

Everything is in place and nothing is satisfying. I've come to the realization, this is not what I want to do. People envy me but all this is just a bunch of crap. I don't even envy myself; in fact, I don't even like myself! What makes it worse is that I can't even stand hearing about the most important things in my life. You know, the political things, all the international things I live for. I can barely stand watching the news or reading the paper. It all just hits me the wrong way. My life is an escape. I don't participate in anything anymore. This morning it all came to a head."

BiBa continued listening patiently as Matt talked, "There was an article about Uhuru Kenyatta and his Mungiki army. He is the son of Jomo Kenyatta, the father of Kenya, you know, kind of like our George Washington. The article was about how corrupt he is and how brutal his Kikuyu tribesmen are. They are the largest and most violent tribe in Kenya. They've been repressing the Lou and Masai tribes during the latest political upheaval. They've been killing them in central Kenya and even in Nairobi. Mungiki is the name of his personal army, but it is just a huge gang, they call themselves Kikuyu soldiers. They are mostly unemployed teenagers. The leadership of the Mungiki is nothing but thugs and is an offshoot of the 1950's Mau Mau revolutionary movement. I just can't standby, sitting here doing nothing, while they kill innocent people. I have to do something. But, I don't want to put you through all the shit I put you through when I was in South Africa last year. I can't do it to you again. I haven't had the courage to talk to you about it. For the last 6-months, I've been trying to make your life as good as I can. We've been traveling and I've been trying to buy things for you to make up for my not being real. I feel so disingenuous and now I'm afraid of losing you. I've tried to buy you stuff instead of being honest. I haven't had the guts to tell you the truth about my being so unhappy. It is not natural for me to open my soul."

BiBa grabbed his hand and said, "I'm either in or out. If you want, I will go to Kenya with you. I'm in. If you want, we can seek counseling together. I'm in. You know I will do anything except continue what we're doing. I don't want things! I want you. If I can't have you, I want out. If it's Kenya, then let's get cracking. Let's get out of Beverly Hills if that is what it takes. Being here right now is a little too much for me anyway. If you want a home here, it has to be after whatever we have to do to get you through this."

Her directness made him a better man. He knew he would have to discuss his past. It was something he knew he had to do but had wavered about for almost a year. Suddenly it seemed appropriate for Matt to open up, asking her to jeopardize her life by going to Kenya.

He smiled and said, "I know I've been selfish and a little passive aggressive. I just thought I was making life easier for you. I screwed up. I'm sorry. Let's get out of here. I will be as truthful as I can. We need to talk, but not here."

It was clear they both had needed to clear the air. He reached for her hand across the table.

Chapter 2

As they drove down Laurel Canyon Drive to the heart of Beverly Hills and the Montage Hotel, they each had thoughts of their passage. In anticipation of their new lives in California, they took a month's lease on a $1,700 per night apartment in the hotel. It now seemed awkward. Their plans were so shallow and capricious. Thinking a change of scenery would mollify their unhappiness was sophomoric at best. They both acknowledged Beverly Hills would only be a temporary destination. Kenya was in the offing. BiBa seemed more interested in their future than hashing up Matt's past. Conversation led directly to Kenya, nothing about his past. He would summon the strength to change the subject and talk about his past once he had a verbal opening. She said they had to be cautious in their preparation for such a dangerous excursion.

As they pulled up to the valet in front of the hotel, Matt realized the pretentiousness of the last six months. He said, half kiddingly, "Let's look at the last few months as the last vestiges of comfort we will have for a while. Kenya won't be a picnic, that's for sure. I hate to sound like a racist but I'm pretty sure they don't like white people."

BiBa chuckled and said, "You're right. We will be viewed as European devils or colonialists, not the good guys. They hate white people. They won't care that we support their causes. All they'll care about is the color of our skin. I had some clients in Vegas who said Kenya is not much different from Zimbabwe. They blame the Europeans for everything. It's just getting worse day by day. We have to be careful and make sure we are acceptable to them. We have to at least appear as benign. We can't be viewed as white outsiders. If we are, it could put our lives in danger. I know there are big problems in East Africa, but how do we define them and what do you want to do about them? An article doesn't make a cause. I don't really know what you want to do. It's like trying to stop a tank with a peashooter. What are we actually going to accomplish when we get there? You know, it's just not this Mungiki gang and Kenyatta. Corruption and brutality are all over Africa. We have to be specific; we must have a working plan before we go. Just feeling bad and helpless without any direction or strategy will get us killed." She started to get very serious. "I feel like a little kid. If we are impetuous and just go there, we are in big trouble. We could die. So let's not make this a romantic adventure. We have to be very cautious. You have friends and connections. We should start there."

She was doing all of the talking, but Matt was half listening and throwing phrases into the conversation. His mind was on the talk he had rehearsed a million times and put off for six months.

They walked through the lobby to the hotel's manicured gardens and sat at a front table of the Conservatory Grill eatery. Even before they sat, Matt started to open up about the last five years.

"Slow down," BiBa said, "We haven't even gotten our food yet. You can tell me all this stuff later. I know it's very important to you and it's important to me too, but not today. This whole thing about Kenya will take a while to sink in. I know it will be cathartic for you to talk about your past. We have to, but not right now. Sweetie, you know that cliché, cool down those jets? At least hold off on your deep dark past for a while, please."

He had to accommodate her request but it took the wind right out of his proverbial sails. He owed it to her. He would now have to focus on Africa. They ordered drinks and slider sandwiches and talked about everything they knew about Kenya and the plight of its people. It became obvious they were extremely unsophisticated and didn't know very much.

BiBa looked at him and said, "I know it seems we are out of our element, but we are quick learners. As they say, this is not rocket science. There's so much we don't know but we'll figure it out. For a first blush we didn't do bad, did we?"

"Not bad at all," he said. "We have lot's of work ahead, that's for sure."

After 30 minutes of sitting in the sun and talking, they decided to go back to the room. Matt had completely put his talk of the past aside. They walked through the hotel's main lobby to the residence's elevators. As soon as he entered their room, he passed in front of her in an uncharacteristic manner, and grabbed his iPad from the coffee table in the living room. He quickly pulled up the article from the LA Times on the Mungiki gang in Nairobi. He hit the print icon on the iPad and the printer in the office suite spit out the article. He picked it up from the tray and handed it to her. She had not seen him so animated since the Leopard Directive that had taken him to Africa and South America the year before. She felt she had to read the article. She would hear about his past later. It wouldn't be today, but soon she would hear Matt discuss his yesterday.

BiBa was on a high pitch about Kenya after reading the article. Her feelings replicated his passion and desire for action against the Mungiki. She stole his thunder about Kenya. Her reading about the corruption and horror in Nairobi sealed it. There would be no more talk about his past that afternoon. Matt seemed comfortable with that. They started discussing the article and she became even more positive Kenya was their shared destiny. His understanding of events, knowledge of the tribes and

African culture that would send them on their sojourn to Africa was unique.

She told him, "I feel the urgency. Something must be done, not just in Nairobi but also all over Africa. Matt, I'll be honest with you, just to save our relationship I was ready to lie and tell you that going to Kenya is what I wanted. I would do anything to be with you," she said as she waved the article in her hand, "But being in Kenya is what I want, not just for you but for me. When you were gone last year, I was so conflicted. I missed you. I hated you for making me fall in love with you and abandoning me in a matter of just a few days. I hated you communicating with me from all over the world and not knowing when or how I would hear from you again. I just sat in Vegas, clutching my phone, waiting for your call. It was horrible, but more to the point, I was jealous of you. You had a cause and an adventure, and I didn't. I still don't know anything about what you did in Africa and South America. I sat there and dreamed of your adventure and your courage. I was pissed and hurt. Knowing so little made me conjure up so much. It was awful. I said I would never go through that again. Let me get to the point, I need this as much as you do. The reason I'm not pressing you about the last year and all the things you and your friends were into is the truth might diminish what I think of you and who you are. I know that sounds terrible. I know we both have to talk about stuff, but not now. Do you see how important this trip is to me?"

He didn't know what to do with her pronouncement of weakness. She was standing there trembling with an uncharacteristic passion for adventure and a deep carnal thirst for Matt. She grabbed him and held him as tightly as she could. He lifted her onto her toes and slowly walked her into the bedroom. He kissed her deeply on the mouth, gently lowered her onto the bed, and undressed her with the tenderness she longed for. The sex was long and undulating. It was different. The intertwining of their souls almost made it a religious experience. The emotional block of the last year lifted and an unspoken agreement of openness and trust emerged.

Matt woke up to BiBa's supple body draped over his right side. His first response was to still himself and savor the softness of her beauty. She was an unimaginable mix of silken skin and the perfect amount of body fat, layered on an athletic physique. Her softness juxtaposed to her muscularity was an irresistible combination of sensuality and power. He was not only intoxicated by her beauty, but also mesmerized by her sheer femininity and the power of her sex. They had been together for almost a year. He craved her as much as the first time they were together. He kissed her on the top of her head which was resting on his chest and said, "BiBa, BiBa, wake up. It's almost 4:00 p.m. in the afternoon."

His eyes glanced at the alarm clock sitting on the small table next to the massive king-sized bed. "Wake up," he said again. She opened her eyes with a look of trust and security. He held her in a tight embrace and said, "I love you. I hope you know that, I really do love you. Sorry I've been such an asshole."

She lifted her head off his chest and responded, "I don't need an apology. I love you too. This is kind of awkward, this is too serious for me. You don't have to say another word. Let's get up, it's Beverly Hills, we have a lot to do!" and she laughed with deep sarcasm. "Let's go shopping. Maybe I'll start to enjoy spending some of your unlimited financial resources. It's great having a rich boyfriend!" and she rolled on top of him and pressed her body into his.

After making love again, they showered and dressed. The two walked out onto the balcony of their room, overlooking the hotel's garden and Beverly Drive, one of Beverly Hills busiest streets. Sitting there holding hands and sharing the moment, he wondered if she was hungry. Sex always made him hungry. He felt she must be also. Calling room service, he inquired if high tea was still being served downstairs. He asked the operator to tell the café to hold a table outside for them. Matt called Frederic Valance and put the phone on speaker. Three rings were enough for Frederic to reach the phone.

"Hey buddy, how are you and BiBa doing in Beverly Hills? Did you get along with Smythe? I guess the real question is how much is it going to cost us for your new digs?"

BiBa interrupted and said, "Frederic, how are you? This is Matt's wonderful girlfriend, as if you didn't know. We have had a change of plans. It's better if I tell you, than Matt. It's no surprise how ambivalent he can be, so let me just blurt it out. We are not buying a house. We're going to Kenya."

There was silence on the other end of the phone.

Matt interjected, "Listen, this is something I have to do. It's an imperative. You can't talk me out of it. So as usual, I need your help...I really do, big time."

Matt told Frederic about the article in the LA Times and gave him a short synopsis of what he and BiBa had discussed. "I know I'm all over the place. I really don't have a plan or anything, but we have to go. You can't talk me out of it. I don't want to hear anything from you about not going. Don't even think about telling me, I'm crazy, that this is stupid, or that you'll jeopardize yourself, or any of your general BS. This means a lot to me. Maybe I'm not articulate about this, but I will be after I study a little more. You're a better wordsmith than I am, so I'm not looking for a debate. We, BiBa, and I just need your help."

Frederic in his miffed voice said, "You're a little touchy, aren't you? You know, I have never said no to you or not covered your back. Obviously, nothing more has to be said. I think you are overcompensating for something. Don't worry, I'm with you. So will everyone else be. I might sound crass, but this is a shitty way to say hello!"

Matt apologized and said, "Yeah, you're right I overreacted. I know what I want to do is a gut reaction and very simplistic, but it's important to me. You've always been there for me. You are my compass, my starting point for everything. Well not exactly, not women, that's for sure," he chuckled as he looked at BiBa.

Frederic said, "Let me get this straight -- a change of plans. No new life in LA, okay. Toronto was not what you were looking for, okay. Now you think you want to go to Kenya and act as a freedom fighter or something like that, okay? Is that all you want? Now, was that so bad? You didn't have to act like a jerk and bite my head off? You'll get everything you want. Let me make a suggestion. I want you guys to come back to the East coast, not Toronto, but New York. We have a nice property in Chelsea that is part of your investment portfolio. At the moment, it's vacant. You can use it as a base of operation. That way, I will be much closer to you. In fact, I have to be in New York in a couple of weeks. Why don't you stay in LA for another week or so while I get the property fixed up? When I get to New York, I will have a better bead on Kenya and this Mungiki gang, or whatever they're called. Look guys, let me say something. I have a feeling that prosperity and security are too much for the two of you. You have the greatest lives in the world, and the resources to do anything you want, but for some stupid reason it makes you feel guilty. To tell the truth, I understand how you feel. I am suffocating from prosperity myself. I'm actually rather glad about this Kenya thing. I guess someone should just slap the crap out of us. It sounds like we need some kind of adventure to be happy. How sick is that? Let me see, wealth and security versus the possibility of torture and death...well that's easy! We pick the latter. BiBa, close your ears, boy are we fucked!" he said to Matt. "Okay, I will call the guys. You call José." He laughed, "Shit, nothing ever changes."

Then he hung up the phone.

Chapter 3

They left the hotel and walked north along Beverly Drive for a block, turned right on Braxton Way and went north again. They found themselves on Canon Drive. An area festooned with restaurants and exclusive boutiques. BiBa was ravenous even though it was only 6:30 p.m., so yes, sex affected her that way also.

She tried putting on a half-serious face and said, "If you were a little better lover and a little nicer to me, maybe I would not have to charge you for sex. You're going buy my best meal ever, I'm starved after great sex with my man."

Matt smiled, "My pleasure! Great sex and the thought of going to Kenya with you have gotten me a little hungry too. Why don't we find some place to eat? If we have enough time after dinner, we'll go shopping for safari clothes. I have this crazy thought, since we're going to be in East Africa, I want to go to Rwanda and see the silverback gorillas. I've always dreamed of seeing them. We will need some specialized gear if we are going into the mountain region of Rwanda. Photography will be a good cover for us, unless Frederic says otherwise. One way or another we will bring my photographic equipment and take a lot of pictures."

Matt was starting to feel like his old self again. BiBa looked at him and smiled. It was fun to see him bloom.

"Maybe Frederic can use photography as a cover, I don't know, let's at least look at some stuff, shopping should be fun," she shot back in a comedic way and smirked. "It's not as if we can't afford an adventure-type wardrobe, even if we don't use what we buy."

He said, "I agree. Eat first then shop. What a great day. Sex, food, and then spend money and sex again."

She laughed, "You're sure of the sex thing later aren't you? Someone would think we were rich and didn't have a care in the world. They would have been half-right. The rich part for sure but maybe we are a little crazy about Kenya and this romantic notion of saving people."

Matt stopped, looked at her and responded, "Are you second guessing us already?"

"No, no, maybe some sanity but not second guessing," said BiBa. "I would not want to miss this adventure for anything. Even if it's dangerous, and I am positive it will be. I am sure it's the right thing for us. It's what we should do for a whole bunch of reasons and getting new clothes is right up there!" she laughed. "Just kidding, I am positive of all this. My heart and soul tell me its right."

Together they strolled up the street for a few minutes, separating for a bit as she looked into the shops. Matt found himself standing in front of Wolfgang's restaurant, as BiBa came out of a boutique fifteen feet away, he pointed at the front door asking, "Is this place okay with you?"

She nodded her approval. One of the most popular eateries in all Beverly Hills, Wolfgang's, has a reputation in Los Angeles of simple, expensive but the very best. It was early, so there was no problem getting a table at the window, overlooking the busy street. The hostess was typical of all Beverly Hills hostesses; 25 to 28 years old, at least 5'10", maybe 120 pounds, small waist and big fake breasts.

Both BiBa and Matt said plastic surgery was imperative in Beverly Hills. They laughed at the fact that all young girls had to have surgery just to walk around this town. The waitress' legs were extremely long, heightened by her six-inch heels and her too short skirt. Her tight fitting gray sweater and black skirt created a look that could only be called, the 'knock down and fuck me' look, all-too-familiar to BiBa. In Las Vegas, where she had been a personal assistant to the Encore Hotel high roller clients, she saw it every day. Sitting at a table overlooking the street was a treat. These were the best seats in the restaurant for viewing the comings and goings on Canon Drive. The people-watching was amusing.

Looking out the window at the passersby exemplified the insincere plastic nature of this opulent city. All the women looked alike, cookie-cutter types, they must've all gone to the same plastic surgeon. BiBa was beautiful but these women weren't bad on the eyes, Matt thought to himself. The cars were as homogeneous as the people were. It seemed as if everyone owned a Lamborghini, Bentley, Aston Martin, Jaguar, Mercedes-Benz, or BMW. There was no place in the United States that rivaled the over-the-top decadence of Beverly Hills. As the scene outside the window played itself out, it became evident; their decision not to buy a house and hide in this world of glamour and capriciousness was the correct decision for the two of them.

When the waitress came to the table, they decided to order the house signature rib eye steak with thick cut French fries and a wedge salad. Even though they were hungry, they decided to share a meal so they would not push themselves into what Matt called, the mortal sin of gluttony. Drinks did not accompany dinner because they both wanted to be clearheaded when they got back to their suite. Once back to the hotel they would start their investigations of Kenya by going online and pulling up as much information as they could on the Mungiki Gang and the Mau Mau uprising, but shopping came first. Matt decided to pay the bill in cash because it would expedite a quicker exit from the restaurant and give them more time to walk over to Neiman Marcus and Northface where they could look at clothing for the trip.

"This should be fun," he said. "Frederic will set up everything we need once we are in Kenya."

"I would still like to get some of my own clothes," BiBa answered.

They would discuss Frederic's role in all this later. They shopped for approximately an hour and a half, asking both establishments where they purchased safari clothing and gear to have their bags sent to the hotel. Matt's and BiBa's addiction to the internet and thirst for knowledge was like a magnet drawing them back to the hotel as soon as they finished shopping. Matt would use his Mac Pro Air laptop and BiBa would use the hotel's Dell computer desktop in their office. They had an array of smart phones, an iPad tablet, his laptop, and the desktop provided by the hotel. Immersing themselves into research was the second best sex they would have that night.

Chapter 4

BiBa was very forceful in her declaration that she would look into the Mau Mau rebellion. While in college, she had read of the rebellion in African History and her interest had been peeked by the latest activities. Matt took the job researching the present-day offshoot of Mungiki Gang and Kenyatta.

"I think our work should be divided into two parts," she said. "As far as I can see, the Kikuyu domination of Kenya is not just because they are the largest tribe, but it's because they have a history of being the most militant. I'll research the rebellion in the 1950's and the 1960's. You put your efforts into the present day," she said, all business. "I think all of Kenya's problems lay at the foot of British colonial rule. The English were savage and totally immoral in the treatment of Africans. I remember their systematic land grabbing to create an agricultural empire in Africa is the root of Kenya's problems today. You take the present and I will delve into the past."

She opened her laptop computer and typed in a couple of words. "There is so much information. I can't believe all the sites. I'm really skeptical about the reliability of most of these sites and articles. I don't know what the word is, their veracity, I guess, I don't trust what I find on the internet all the time." She was looking at a Wikipedia summary. "If I read enough articles I will get some kind of idea that's fairly accurate."

"I hope that's the case for both of us," he said. "Mining through as many sites as I can should give me some type of information base to be able to start from. I guess we've got the same idea."

Creating a big picture analysis, Matt, with his analytical background in engineering, and BiBa, with her purist attitude towards research, immersed themselves into collecting and synthesizing data. Their work supplemented the work Frederic would present to them. They both jumped into their Google searches, Matt with pen in hand, taking copious notes, and BiBa, more the data retrieval technician, setting up a system of bookmarks. Four hours of relative silence except for the occasional, "I can't believe that," or "Oh, this is just unbelievable," or "Oh man, this is incomprehensible," or just deep groans of disapproval came to a halt when BiBa finally said something. She could no longer contain herself.

"Reading all this is like spitting into my soul," she said. "That's an old Latvian phrase my grandmother used to say. I don't usually get so angry at history or politics but the British were totally out of control. They were brutal, just animals towards the Kikuyu. They were just racist! I know their actions were more acceptable back then, but so racist in every sense of the word." She caught herself, "Can I interrupt your work for a few minutes? I'm frustrated. I need to talk."

He answered her, "It was time for me to take a break anyway. Sure, I am all ears. What's up?"

She took a deep breath. "The British were so repressive. It's no wonder Africans hate their guts. It was not just colonialism and land ex-appropriation. It was their Protestant religion and their deep feeling of superiority that was so horrendous. I thought we were bad towards our slaves here in America but that was nothing compared to the British. They really treated the Kikuyu as if they were animals. They didn't treat them as if they were humans. In the late 1870's they systematically started confiscating the tribal lands and restricted the movement of tribal people. The Kikuyus were the largest tribe but more importantly, they lived on the most fertile land. You had mentioned that when you were younger you went to the Rift Valley in Central Kenya with Frederic. That's where the Kikuyu came from. That area has the most water and the best soil in Kenya. The British took more than 90% of the small farms. Then they broke up the family structure of the so-called savages. They made most of the men indentured slaves. The ones that didn't or couldn't work on the farms were shipped to Nairobi. They even built a major railway line to move farm products, but maybe more importantly, the people. Slaves were the major source of wealth for the British. Once the Africans were deported to Nairobi, the labor laws in the city and the high rates of unemployment created a situation of subsistence level living. Life in the cities was worse than anything the people had ever suffered. At least they had their families when they were on the farms, now they had nothing. Mass poverty, followed by violence and decay of the tribes' authority over its people, was the outcomes of planned migration."

"Some of the Kikuyu men were lucky and were recruited into low-level civil servant jobs. Even though fraternizing with the British, it got them out of abject poverty. The civil servants were the only tribal people allowed any form of education. Effectively the Kikuyu divided into two groups; some with low levels of education who work for the British and the rest with no education used in the manufacturing sector as unskilled laborers or cheap labor for agriculture. The British thought the Kikuyuans were stupid, they tortured them, or killed them, or just subjugated them to the worst possible lives. The English were called white devils, as they fractioned the tribe and created a deep division still existing today. Even when the Kenyans were given independence in the 1960's they didn't have the political sophistication or high enough levels of education for self-rule. Some of today’s troubles, the corruption, the inefficiency in government, the inter-tribal hatred and plain inhuman brutality, all fall on British rule. The indigenous people excluded from the rule of law. My God, Matt, in the 1920s the British set up a network of work camps separating men from the women. They had Pass Laws, like in South Africa, that restricted all movements of native peoples. The women were sex slaves and the men brutalized. Some were not killed, but were mutilated instead. Castration and severing of appendages was widespread. Whippings were public until World War II. It eased up some during the war, but afterwards, from 1952 to 1956, it got even more restrictive for the Kikuyus. The British called a state of emergency in 1952 to quell the native unrest. The Africans wanted their land back after their war contributions, they wanted free education for all tribal people, they wanted higher wages, and what was the most abrasive to the British, they wanted political rights and a voice in self-determination. The British reaction called the Swynnerton Plan set up 804 concentration camps. They arrested and placed in camps more than 1,100,000 Kikuyus and about 70,000 from other smaller tribes were. The militant Kikuyus who escaped the internment camps sought refuge in the forest. They where called Mau Mau. That is where the rebellion started. It started in the highlands. Some of them hid in the ghettos of Nairobi among the workers of the small manufacturing plants. Some of the less militant informed on the more radical for self-preservation and gained British favor. There was systematic torture for information. It created a deep divide between the different tribes and agricultural workers and civil servants. Trying to squash rebellion, thousands of political prisoners were killed. Tribes pitted against each other and those divisions still exist today. It just wasn't Kikuyu versus Kikuyu. The Lous, the Embu, and the Merus all tried to gain favor by informing on the Kikuyus and in some measure informing on the smaller tribes."

"The Mau Mau was fighting on three fronts, one front was with each other, the second was with the other tribes, and finally they were fighting with the British. By 1957, the rebellion was quashed but it shaped the horrible political landscape of present-day Kenya. The military costs of tribal repression and land expropriation were so great for the British that they had to grant independence in 1963. The Kikuyus would gain control of the government but not have the technical expertise to run it. I am not sure, but that might have been a British plan for post-colonialism. Maybe the most important thing causing present day problems was tribal the British exacerbated hatreds. As far as I am concerned, the Kikuyus are no better than the British are. Since they effectively left their colony, the Kikuyu have done nothing to move Kenya from poverty and create equal rights for all tribal peoples. It has been more then a half-century and I think they are worse off. The Kikuyu are just as brutal as the British were, but much more corrupt and obviously not very efficient. The average person is no better off in any area of life except there is less white control. The Europeans, as they are called today, are major players in Kenya because of the vacuum they created when they left. They still have vast holdings in minerals and agriculture, but they let their affairs be run by African surrogates. They still get all of the wealth and their black underlings are the power elite.

The Kenyans still are not ready for self-governance. They don't have the skills for ownership of major industries, or minerals extraction, or mining, or even agricultural production. Kenya will be like Zimbabwe over time. Matt, that's frightening! I'm sorry, I got off track. Let me get back to the Mau Mau. I promise I will be done soon."

BiBa continued, "They were seen as a necessary vehicle for change to get rid of the British but became expendable because of their radical leanings. Jomo Kenyatta, the father of present-day Kenya, was an active member of the organizations' leadership. He disavowed their extremism in place of a more moderate path for Kenya, but everything has collapsed and it is tribalism again. The Mau Mau no longer exists as an organized group, but they do have a romantic following by the most extreme Kikuyu. The Mungiki are the present day extension of the Mau Mau. The gang has its tentacles in the hierarchy of Kenyan government. The Mungiki are Kikuyu and hate all other tribes. The hate for whites can't be overstated and they blame the whites for everything. Haters are what they are, and they have influence on government. They are Kenya's gangster class, young and dangerous. What is worse is their influence. I know what I am going to say is not right, but they are worse than the British are. It is just the biggest mess and I see no solution and no role for us."

Matt just listened as if he were still in school, but he never had a professor with such passion or who was so beautiful. He knew why he loved her and it wasn't just for her incredible body.

Chapter 5

It was Matt's turn. He was exuberant in a strange way. He had been totally engrossed in BiBa's take on the Mau Mau. He was animated.

"Shit, BiBa," he said, "These people are animals," referring to the Mungiki gang. "They have control over all the major slums in Nairobi. The different areas they control in the inner city are almost like personal fiefdoms. The slums run by mega gangs, like our Crips and Bloods, are divided into smaller cells or units. They are like the gangs we have in our major cities on the West Coast. The Mungiki control everything."

BiBa was braced for a long one-way discussion. Once Matt got amped-up, he was hard to slow down.

She was fine with that because she had told Matt of the world of the Mau Mau. Now it was his turn.

He started, "The Munguki is nothing but a present-day extension of the 1950's Mau Mau, deadlier, larger, and much more sophisticated." Matt drew a deep breath and kept going, "When Jomo Kenyatta took power in the mid-60s from the English, he had to become a moderate conservative and a consensus builder. He needed to create a state where tribal differences and all their animosities, were subjugated to populist demands for democracy and equality. Obviously, it never happened, but the radical Mau Mau philosophy was suspended as a political platform, even though it was embraced privately. The Mau Mau were politically sacrificed. As the party moderated its political views, a new competing tribe, the Masai, emerged in the Central Valley as the true revolutionaries and competed with the Kikuyu for power. To protect them in the agriculture region of Kenya and in the city of Nairobi, the Kikuyu recruited disenfranchised teenagers and formed the Mungiki gang. Oppression in Kenya took on another form. No more British colonial rule, but a worse, more violent tribal rule took its place. BiBa, it's the worst, just the worst. When the British were in power they implemented the labor camps and even finalized the land redistribution to the whites. Most of the Kikuyus in the Central Valley were deported to Nairobi, where they had to fend for themselves. Their living conditions in the slums, and their inability to get jobs, forced them into abject conditions. Their nemesis, the Masai, who also had been targeted by the British, was now the Mau Mau major concern in Nairobi. They competed for the same inner-city land and jobs. One of the sites I read called it territorial assertion; tribal hatred raised its ugly head in an urban environment. It was as if someone had placed two reactive elements together, just waiting for an explosion. As in all divided societies, each tribe tried to dominate not only geographical but employment sectors for their own protection. The Masai control the farmer's markets and all poultry and meat markets. The Kikuyu took full control of the taxicabs, small city busses, and all forms of transportation. Both gangs were violent and segregated the worst slums of Nairobi by a rash of kidnappings and killings. The Kagumo Market district and the Fourth Area Project were the Mungiki strongholds. The Masai and the lesser tribes controlled the rest of the inner-city."

Matt continued, "Over a 20 year period the slums of Nairobi became a war zone the government effectively ruled as a hands-off area. By the 1980's the two rival tribes were committing indescribable atrocities, a kind of social cannibalism. Kenyatta politically distanced himself from the violence in public but behind closed doors, he remained committed to Mau Mau philosophy, even if it meant dealing with the Mungiki. By this time, they were animals, but their stronghold on the inner city made them indispensable. The government just let the gangs prey upon each other, until one became victorious. The Mungiki prevailed under the leadership of Martin Mugumba. Their control of the taxicabs, minivans, and communication systems allowed them total sway over millions of people in the slums. They were unsophisticated but brutal, and ruled with an iron fist. Police corruption allowed total freedom for the Mungiki gang, as long as they paid police protection money and stayed out of the wealthier areas in Nairobi. It's estimated the actual gang member numbers today is close to 200,000, with as many as five times that number of sympathizers. Mungiki makes money by extortion, drugs, kidnapping and by taking a percentage of any legal businesses in their districts. BiBa, it's real complicated, but the city is divided up into districts and each district has its own ruler who oversees anything and everything within its boundaries. Today it's like an organization with many equal partners and no apparent CEO. A bunch of unorganized small gangs working together and calling themselves Mungiki, there was no formal structure. The only thing they have in common is they are all vicious and unpredictable."

BiBa listened quietly as he continued, "They are not very sophisticated, but they are powerful, and are used by the major Kikuyuan politicians as an army to keep people in check and divide the tribes. Mungiki has a political wing called the Kenyan National Youth Alliance. It's a stepping-stone into national politics. This organization guarantees hundreds of thousands of votes in an election, through either intimidation or ballot stuffing. In today's politics in Kenya, they can determine who wins or loses. Running up to and during the elections, they are transparent. They can be seen attacking people with shovels and machetes and in some cases have intentionally lit people on fire to express their resolve and terrorize the population. No one can stand up to these thugs. They have total control in Nairobi's poorest areas. Today, because of corruption and sheer brutality, they're the strongest political force in Kenya's major cities. In most African countries, at least East Africa, the Central governments control the gangs. Not Kenya, not anymore. The gangs have considerable control over the central government. The Kikuyu and the Mungiki are simply inseparable. BiBa, it's just unbelievable. We live by the power of civil laws and have traditions that protect us. They have no rule of law in Kenya. It's pure survival of the fittest. It's just tribalism at its worst. The Kikuyus are no different than they were hundreds of years ago, except for the fact they now have guns. They don't have constitutional law or Koranic law, but they do have Kikuyu law. It is primitive and hasn't changed since the first tribal king took power. Some of the more conservative leaders of the Mungiki gang believe in female mutilation, some men can and do actually own women and treat them as property. They are anti-modern and hate Western values. They don't believe in democracy. They only want to subjugate all the other tribes and rule with Kikuyu law. They hate whites in general and the British in particular. BiBa, they are so barbaric they think killing with an ax or machete is honorable. Rape is not only tolerated, it is used as a way of humiliating the other tribes. They are animals!"

Chapter 6

Matt was on a roll, as BiBa described it. "Sweetie," she said, "It's been almost 30 minutes since I got a word in. Come up for some air. I have never seen you so pissed at a political problem. Why are you making this so personal? I read the same article and I am doing the same kind of research. I know how powerful this stuff is. It really hit me, but I just can't personalize it the way you do. My research was so depressing I don't see much chance for change. I feel like crap about all of this, but I can't get into it as deeply you. Why is this such an emotionally high threshold for you? You are almost crazy with anger, I can see it in your eyes. You have to slow down for a second. Is there something I am not getting? Is there more to this than just being bored?"

BiBa got up from the couch and walked over to the desk where he was sitting. The bar area of the suite was next to the office. She stood over his right shoulder and pointed to the round table with six chairs next to the granite bar. She suggested, "Let's leave the office and sit at the table overlooking the garden."

Once Matt was seated, she started to massage his shoulders and neck to calm him down.

"You're not okay," she said. "This frightens me. You are so consumed by this and we are just getting started. What is going to happen when we get to Nairobi? Does this have anything to do with the last time you left me? I have tried to piece together what you did with your friends in Africa. I can only guess, because we haven't really talked about it. Is South Africa affecting your involvement in this? Does this have anything to do with the Leopard Directive?"

He was taken aback by her semi-knowledge of the event that played out in South Africa the year before. He shrugged it off and tried to focus on the present.

"Shit, I don't know. I feel like I'm drowning in quicksand. I told you we should talk about my past, but we put it off for this Kenya thing. I don't even know what to call what is going on with me. I guess I am depressed or something. I don't think there's anything in Kenya that has anything to do with Johannesburg or Cape Town, other than they are in Africa and things are beyond screwed up. Maybe it's the injustice of it all. Maybe it's the arrogance of the Mungiki. I don't think it has anything to do with South Africa. Right now, I'm not rational and I know it. I am so pissed. I am over the top with anger. I know in my heart it's not because we're white. I know I'm not part of what's going on in Kenya. I don't know why it's so important, but it is."

"My blood pressure is up and I feel like the veins in my neck are going to burst. This isn't good for me," thought Matt.

She grabbed his hand. "Sweetie, let's get out of here." She took the jacket that was sitting on the chair and threw it over to him. "Let's go over to the Beverly Wilshire Hotel and have a drink or something. The night air will do us both some good. We need to get out of here. This is supposed to be fun and exciting but I feel suffocated right now. We'll figure it out."

They left the hotel and walked up Beverly Boulevard to Wilshire Boulevard. Within 10-minutes, they had reached the Beverly Wilshire Hotel. They walked through the hotel's lobby into the bar and BiBa ordered for them.

"He'll have a double MacCallum on the rocks and I will have a lite Cosmopolitan, you know light on the Grenadine heavy on the vodka. We will be sitting next to the fireplace," she said.

They slowly maneuvered through the crowed room, crossing the large antique-filled bar and sat. Two large Baroque styled chairs next to a small coffee table were empty. BiBa and Matt felt like they had arrived at an oasis. The table had peanuts and corn chips in Waterford cut glass bowls. The symbolism of two rich white people sitting in Beverly Hills trying to deal with problems in Africa was not lost to BiBa. Matt had not said a word from the Montague all the way to the bar. When the drinks came, he took a long sip of the savory Scotch and swirled it in his mouth. He leaned back and finally started to talk.

"BiBa, I'm really sorry. It's hard for me to express myself right now. I think this all started when I read that article about the Mungiki gang. You know, how they dismembered a man in front of his wife and then raped her in broad daylight in front of their six children. No one came to his or her rescue. No one did anything. I'm sitting reading that article with a deep sense of horror. I felt like I just was sucked into it. Kind of like a dream, when you're running, but never fast enough and you know they're going to catch you."

As his description of the events in the article became more detailed, his voice raised to such a pitch BiBa became embarrassed.

"Matt, Matt, just stop! This is too much. No one came here to listen to you. You're really loud! Please, change the subject. In fact, let's just get out of here." She got up from her chair and placed her half consumed drink on the small table. Then she walked over to the bar and gave the bartender a $100 bill.

"Sorry for the inconvenience." She walked to the large double doors as Matt followed her out to the lobby and then into the street.

She looked at him, "I can't take this. I know this is not what you want to hear, but you have to stop."

Matt felt embarrassed by his behavior and softly apologized. "BiBa, BiBa, I'm really story. I know I'm out of control."

They walked back to the Montage in complete silence. As soon as they got to their suite, Matt walked over to the couch in the living room, sat down and started staring at the walls.

BiBa looked at him and said, "This is the last time I am going to say this. Enough is enough. You are feeling sorry for yourself. That's unacceptable. Let's go to bed."

She pulled off her sweater, undid her bra, and pulled him up by the arm. "Now take off your pants and act like a man."

She smiled, "I know it's real hard for you sweetie, I don't mean that the way it sounds, I don't know, maybe I do. Now get your ass over here."

Chapter 7

Matt and BiBa stayed in Beverly Hills three more days. They got totally absorbed in researching the vicissitudes of strife-torn Kenya. On the fourth morning Matt said, "I feel like a caged animal. I've been cooped up looking at this computer screen for what seems like forever. I can't do it anymore. I need to clear my head. How would you like to get out of here and drive down to La Jolla? We have a few days before we have to go to New York."

"That will be great!" she said.

He called the front desk and asked them to make reservations at the Valencia Hotel. BiBa's mind rushed back to the first time they made love. He had invited her on a road trip from Las Vegas to La Jolla.

It was a little more than a year ago. The trip changed her life.

"La Jolla sounds wonderful, but this time after our little trip, we go to Africa together, as partners. You don't call all the shots and make all the decisions. I mean it; you have to be upfront with me from now on. I am going with you to Kenya. There is no way to stop me. You cannot leave me in the dark about your location or what you are doing with your friends. I'm going to help you. Promise me that going to La Jolla is not a way of running from me."

He shook his head. "I promise you that I will never again leave you out of any decision-making. But, if and when things get tough, just remember why I shielded you from all of this in the past."

She didn't take this as an ominous threat. She just knew he didn't want to replay the tragedies of yesterday. "BiBa, you know once we get involved in Kenya there will be no going back. You have to trust not only me but also my friends. I feel it, I just know it, there will be a lot of violence and death. There is no way to prepare you except to say, you will be safe no matter how bad things look. You will meet my friends soon. We, that's both of us, will have to trust them with our lives. They do this crazy stuff for a living. I promise you we will be safe."

She knew what he had gone through last year was dangerous but the word death was unexpected. It kind of set her back a step. Their conversation seemed like a good segue way for Matt to talk about the past. “I have been holding back on this for almost a year," he said, as he prepared to discuss his involvement in the Leopard Directive.

Before he could say a word she said, "You don't have to be specific. Just let me know the generalities. I do have some questions. I never asked you if I needed to be jealous of any women. I never asked you if there were any laws you broke I have to be worried about. Just let me know what generally happened and how it affects our future."

He felt relieved. This was not going to be the time he must discuss the family that he had left behind, the wife he did not love and not bonding with his children. His year long anxiety of not telling her about his ex-wife Janis and his two daughters could be put on hold. He knew at some point in time she would have questions about his past that might lead to his wife and children, but today would not be the day. He felt lucky he only had to discuss the Leopard Directive. He wouldn't have to talk about anything that had an emotional substance.

"Sweetie, there's no reason to worry about other women. I have never strayed from you, nor will I."

This was true for the present and recent past. He could not deal with his distant past. He knew he had to at a future date. He would have to lie. He could not be totally truthful now. It was beyond his emotional ability.

"I have broken laws. I have done horrible things to people, some really vicious things, but they have all been for self-preservation or self-defense. I have not killed anybody, but what we did as a group led to many deaths."

He tried to hide some of the truths of his role in Johannesburg by treading lightly on the torture of local police and the killing of innocent bystanders.

BiBa sat there motionless as he told her of the six-month period of mayhem and havoc he and his friends participated in to protect their world. She could not believe the love of her life was involved in the global manipulation of illegal narcotics. She could not believe he was part of the world's largest most lethal mercenary army. She could not believe he had hundreds of millions of investment dollars placed through out the world to hide his identity. She could not believe his relationship with underworld activities. She knew of his dark side because he told her things, but the depth of his involvement, even in generalities was hard for her. She did believe his political ties that ran through the highest halls of the European Union and his direct links to the president of the United States because she had seen them. He had only inferred about his relationships in Central and South America, and conveniently did not mention Jose Guzman.

After 30 minutes the only utterances that came out of her mouth were, "You can't be serious about all of this. I don't need to know anymore. In fact, some of this has been too specific for me. This is not what I expected," she sighed, "but that's all right. I can't imagine all you had to give up. I don't really want you to be any more detailed because I think it would really bother me to know how much of a price you had to pay to be here with me right now. I love you, that's all I have to know. I have never seen any of your dark side, but I expected you and Frederic had done things that are best for me not to know. I guess I'll learn to deal with your other friends. I know they're comrades in arms or comrades in circumstances and I know they have been good to you. No more has to be said to satisfy me. What you and your friends have done together doesn't sound like some deep plan for money or power. It seems more like you had no other choice. I can understand that. The only thing I don't understand is, how do we translate who you are and what you are with Kenya? What will your friends want you to do in Kenya? What will they do in Kenya? No matter how powerful you think you are, and how much money you control, change in Kenya seems impossible. Maybe I do not understand something, but even with your friends and all your money and power, this seems crazy. It is like a death wish. For Christ's sake, the British had to leave because they didn't have the resources to control that screwed up country. It's so primitive and so tribal. I don't think there are any solutions except to leave it alone. I am not anywhere nearly as battle tested as you are. I am not as adventurous as you are. I might not have the capacity to be as brave as you are. I think we will be in over our heads if we pursue this. Look sweetie, even with the support of your friends, I don't know what you want to do. I don't know what outcomes you want to bring about. I am not scared. After all our research, I really think I have a handle on the challenges that will face us. Saving Kenyans from themselves seems out of our reach".

She stopped for a minute. "You know, yesterday was yesterday, and you don't have to explain it any further, but this Kenya thing might be too vast. At least it is for me. I don't understand exactly what you want. I love you. Whatever you have to do, you can count on me. The only thing I ask is that you don't leave me in the dark about anything and we have to be careful. That is all I am saying. Kenya is scary. Now let's discuss La Jolla," she said as she changed the subject, "Enough of Kenya!"

Chapter 8

Four days and three nights in La Jolla went by in an instant. They drove back to Los Angeles and collected all their belongings from the Montague Hotel. They brought many of their personal items on the plane and had the rest freight forwarded to New York. Their new residence would be 160 15th St., Chelsea, NY. It was a property Matt had purchased for his investment portfolio almost two years earlier. The 7,500 square foot single-family house was the only building on the street that was not an apartment or cooperative. Their new living quarters were between 15th and 16th Street, nestled near 6th and 7th Avenue. The brownstone was a block from the nearest subway stop, a 15-minute walk to the Chelsea Market and High Rail Park, and a few blocks from Bleeker

Street and its restaurants and shops. On the plane, both felt an anticipation and anxiety for their new lives in New York. Matt found himself saying, "I'm kind of torn. I really don't like New York, but I'll give it a shot after Beverly Hills."

BiBa was trying to read a book on Kenya and wasn't paying much attention to Matt. "I didn't get what you said about New York. Did you get a chance to look at your e-mails since we left the hotel?"

He knew she was in her own world and said, "I wasn't talking about anything important, and no I haven't had a chance to look at my e-mails." He pulled out his iPhone and got onto his Gmail account. He deleted the first 15 e-mails before he got to the one from Frederic. He opened it.

"Well old buddy, simple and plain. I will have somebody waiting for you at the airport, a driver and a real estate person, who will open the house and show you around. In the office, I have left two files. They are for your eyes only. That's you and BiBa of course. One file is some materials on the Mau Mau and the Mungiki gang my staff generated. The other file is a prescription for what you have to do to prepare for Kenya. Most of this is for BiBa. I think you already know. She will have to do a lot of self-defense training and learning her character when she goes undercover. Look over these files and you'll see that you will have to walk her through a lot of the same stuff you went through in the Leopard Directive. I will call tomorrow morning. Have a safe flight. I hope you enjoy the new house. Frederic"

The 45-minute drive from JFK to their house went by quickly. As they arrived at their new house, Elisabeth Arden, the real estate agent who had accompanied them from the airport, came to life. She started by describing the house and all of its functions.

"Mr. Papaz," she said, as she gave him an electronic key, "this house is totally integrated in electronic terms. Let me show you." She gave him a device looking much like a smart key for an expensive car. "No traditional house keys for you. A chip that will identify you and BiBa from up to 75 feet from the front door is integrated with the security system and identifies you every time you enter or exit the house. You can set the lights, heater, air conditioning, music and communication systems, dishwasher, and all other appliances. Anything electrical is controlled by clicking this device. It is very intuitive and easy to use. We call your house an executive property. It not only comes with state-of-the-art electronics, but it comes with a personal butler. That butler is me. I will be at your disposal 24 hours a day. Hit the red bottom on the key."

She was almost finished with her remarks. "A few more things before I leave. Everything electronic is voice activated and very intuitive. I am sure you have heard that before, but in this case, it will be simpler than any device you ever used. It's calibrated to yours and BiBa's voices and cannot be activated by anybody else's. There is no learning curve. If you give it a command it will walk you through it."

"We will see ourselves out," as she pointed to the driver who had carried the last bags up to the master bedroom. "I am your butler but my work is all encompassing. Frederic will fill you in. I am an associate of his and will be at your service. Again, I am at your disposal 24-hours a day. Your house and its needs, your security, whatever you need, I am resourceful in computers and research. He calls me his woman Friday. That should say it all." She smiled and walked out the door.

They were both surprised and smitten by Ms. Arden. The grandeur and sophistication of their new home was more than expected. It was not the country style house in Toronto, but a contemporarily decorated brownstone for a Fortune 500 executive. It was not warm, but it was elegant. Matt and BiBa both loved the house's location, but were a little put-off by its coldness. They felt they would acclimate to the neighborhood, but the house might be another matter. They walked around the house for 15 to 20 minutes before they got to the office on the 3rd floor. Matt noticed the two folders sitting on the Philippine mahogany library style desk. He picked them up and said, "These are the materials from Frederic. Do you want to look at them now or later? It's too late to get down to business, I'm a little hungry. How about you?"

"We're just a block or two from a bunch of restaurants," she said. "Try the voice-recognition; I don't know what to call it, the Siri type thing."

He pulled the electronic key out from his pocket and said, "Nearest restaurant."

Urbanspoon, an app for Apple products appeared on a 40-inch flat screen TV on the office wall. The application was tied to the houses' IT system and a woman's voice responded, "Mr. Matt, Ms. BiBa, what type of food are you interested in? Would you like a review of the restaurant before the directions?"

They both laughed and she responded, "How about Asian food? Thai food?"

The name Qi appeared on the screen with a Google map that showed its address to be 93 14th St. They put on their jackets and walked downstairs to the front door. It opened automatically and said, "Have a nice night. I will lock up and set the alarm system."

It took approximately ten minutes to arrive at the high-end Asian restaurant. They were amazed that it was crowded and busy at 1 o'clock in the morning. The conversation during the meal was no more than small talk: the flight, the new house, Ms. Arden, and Frederic.

BiBa said, "Frederic was correct about leaving Los Angeles and coming to New York. It's not as pretentious. Either you or Ms. Arden said the house is, what, 8 or so million, and it's not even in a great neighborhood. Don't get me wrong. It's fine but in LA for 8-million, we would be in Bel Air. What's good about New York is that it is not pretentious. Its like people have money and they don't have to show it. Everyone knows how expensive things are. It is old money. You had to do something to be able to live here. This place is not like LA. People there are trying to show off their wealth and kind of let you know they have never done anything for it. It's as if they are using someone else's money and are showy and obnoxious because they didn't earn it. This is going to be great. We can hide here. The house will make a great office. We don't need a car. If we get bored, there certainly is enough entertainment and culture. I am fine with this place. By the way, what did Frederic say about tomorrow?"

"Ah, we'll talk about it in the morning," answered Matt. "Nothing important. Some stuff on Kenya and a regimen for us to get up to speed for our trip."

After paying the bill, they got up from the table and walked home.

Fifty-feet from the door he pulled the automatic key out of his pocket and said, "Open the front door. Turn the lights on leading to the master bedroom and set the shallow water to 108 degrees."

As soon as they got to threshold of the four-step stoop, the house's front light went on and the door automatically opened. They went up to the master bedroom, took separate showers and fell asleep.

"No sex that night. An uneventful beginning for an adventure," Matt thought to himself.

Chapter 9

At 10:30 am, Eastern Standard Time, the phone rang and the house's communication system announced, "Mr. Matt, there is a call for you on line 1. It is a Mr. Frederic Valance. Would you like to accept the call or have me gather the appropriate information for future contact?"

Matt acknowledged the call as he and BiBa sat at the breakfast room table. A 40-inch LCD television monitor mounted on the wall in the kitchen turned on. It was in-sync with Frederic's office computer in South Beach.

"Hey old buddy, our good friend, Jose Alvarez will see you and BiBa at Equinox, the fitness club. It is in the Chelsea Market. He will be there at 1 o'clock this afternoon. They have workout clothing there in case you didn't bring your stuff from LA. José will work with BiBa and he has a self-defense guy for you. BiBa how you doing? José is going to push you through a simple self-defense program. I don't know much about it but it is some kind of martial arts thing. It is going to be hard, it will be a big commitment, but it is necessary. Guys, Alvarez is my house warming present for you. Kenya is going to be extremely dangerous and that probably is an understatement. BiBa, I have to be up front about this, you can't be the weak link. For the next three or four months you will have to train to be able to protect yourself. It will not only be rigorous, but it will push you to your limits. We will be forming a team that will operate initially in Nairobi and then later in the Central Valley. I haven't worked out all of the particulars yet, but we will set up an NGO, a non-governmental agency, as a cover. I guess you notice that I said we, that's right I am going too. I will be there to oversee the operations. Excuse me if I seem a little excited. What has it been, 25 years Matt, since we were in Kenya? Wow. That sounds like a long time. Let me get back to the point. Did you get a chance to look at the files I left for you? I know reading the analysis of the ruling party is tedious and complicated but it is an imperative. We will be meeting lots of these folks when we start throwing around money. As soon as you can, that means in the next few days, please have the file read so we can discuss it. I will be coming to New York early next week. Hopefully, by Tuesday night. You should be settled-in by then. That is when we will talk about our cover and the NGO. By the way, BiBa did you get a chance to look at the other file? Most of it is for you. Alvarez is coming out to New York primarily to work with you. He might be intimidating but Matt can tell you he is a good guy."

She responded, "Don't worry about me. I'm sure he's going to be fine. As long as he's up front, that is all I care. I pride myself on being an ex- world-class athlete. After college, I was invited to try out for the US Olympic women's soccer team. I got an invitation to their training center in Colorado. I didn't go for a bunch of reasons, but that should tell you I'm pretty athletic. He can push all he wants and I'm sure I can take it. Everything I heard about him makes me respect him. I will not be the weak link in any group. Whatever it takes, I will do. If we are going to put our lives in his hands, then I'd be crazy if I didn't trust him and do what he asks of me. Frederic, you said you wanted to be upfront with me. Let me respond, I am not high maintenance. I will pull my own weight. How about you?"

She looked at Matt and said, "This is the way it should be. We are all responsible for our own actions and how we impact the group. I will be treated as an equal because I will not be the weak link." She had a bite in her voice. The conversation ended and the screen on the wall went black.

Matt and BiBa walked at a rapid pace for 5-blocks to the Chelsea Market as if they were already starting their workouts. They traveled through the market's food galleries and after ten minutes exited on the Hudson River side of the building. The back end of the market, which was the original production facility for Nabisco cookies, was a retail complex of boutiques and a fitness center. Equinox was at least 40,000 ft.^{2} which was extremely large for a gym in New York City. As they walked into the lobby, Alvarez was waiting for them.

He approached BiBa and said, "It's a real pleasure. I am Jose Alvarez. You must be BiBa. I've heard a lot about you," looking at Matt, "and it is all good. Truly, it is my pleasure. I don't know what Matt has told you, but he literally saved my behind. He is the man as far as I'm concerned. That doesn't mean he can do no wrong, but he is a good friend and has my loyalty. When I was told I could come to New York and see him and be of some help to him, that's all I had to hear."

He looked at his friend and extending his arms gave him a bear hug.

"Great to see you. Man, you look good! It's been too long. That's enough of this reunion mush; we have a lot to do. We can talk later."

He pointed to the boutique inside the lobby of the gym. "You can get some workout clothes in there. BiBa, get some sweats that are tight fitting. Matt, anything will do for you." He put his arm on Matt's shoulder, "You look great. Frederic sent a martial arts guy from South Beach to work out with you. He seems like he knows what he's doing. He's down the hall in room #8. I will be next-door. When you are done, just knock. Oh by the way, his name is Ron."

BiBa purchased her clothing and asked José where she could change. He gave both her and Matt membership cards that Frederic had set up earlier.

He pointed to the woman's locker room and said, "You have your own personal locker. Your name is on it. See you in a couple minutes. I will be in room #7."

BiBa came out of the women's locker area with two bottles of water and walked over to the room where Jose Alvarez was waiting. He looked at her and said, "Sit down; we are going to talk for a couple minutes. Here's our program. We will power train five days a week. It will be very structured and disciplined. Your body needs it and it is my military training. It's not my fault or your fault, but we are a little behind the curve and need to catch up. We will have to condense our workouts. Kenya is a badass place. Real dangerous, especially for a beautiful female like you. It's hard to explain but your looks are your worst enemy. You will stand out like a sore thumb. That is the last thing any of us needs. We will have to do something about the way you dress, the way you walk and your posture. It’s all great for here, but deadly over there. Your greatest asset is your athletic ability. Frederic said you were a world-class athlete and we are going to work with that. Soccer, right, while you were in college? That's a great starting point because you can deal with pain and all of the little nicks you get here and there. You are familiar with hard work and that is real important too. You look like you are still in good shape. We will find out soon enough. Our workout routine will be brutal. What are you, 5' 9" or 5' 10", 125 or 30 pounds? Well you are too light and not strong enough to take care of yourself. So we are going to start you off with a six-week regimen of steroids. You will be eating 5,000 to 6,000 calories a day. We will have food brought in with the proper mixture of proteins and carbohydrates. You're going to be eating 6 to 7 meals a day and drinking a minimum 14 to18 glasses of water. You will be blood tested every 7 days. We have to put at least 40 pounds of muscle on your body. When we get done, your body fat will be less than 6%. I know this sounds excessive, but at 130 pounds, you can't protect yourself. You'll be up against people you're no match to face. Over there carrying guns into an enemy zone might not be acceptable many places. You might need the extra weight to be able to take care of yourself. That is hand to hand. If I can get you to 170 pounds and you have trained well, you might have a chance in a combat situation. I know this extra bulk thing sounds terrible, but trust me, when we get there, your life will be at stake. That extra 40 pounds could be the difference of coming back alive or dead. You don't want anything less than the best chance to survive."

BiBa just listened. She was good at listening. He continued, "After 6-weeks of sessions of five to six hours a day, five days a week, we will evaluate your progress. In most cases, really good athletes who are dedicated and disciplined, take anywhere from 2,000 to 3,000 hours to get to a level of martial arts where they can take care of themselves. We don't have that much time. You have a maximum of 12 to 16 weeks to get it done. We don't have a year and a half like other people have. Look, we have one quarter to one fifth of the time to do this thing right. It is going to consume you for the next few months. I have to be real honest. Expect to break some fingers. As a soccer player, I'm sure you had bruised ribs. Well, expect to get a couple of broken ribs. You will get battered, you might lose some teeth, your feet are fair game. I can't stress how hard this is going to be a physically. You will not look or physically be the same as you are today when we get done. This is the high price to pay for your safety. There is no other way to do it. You will end up hating me during this process. I'm sure you're going to want to kill me at some point or other. I can deal with that, can you?"

Chapter 10

BiBa listened intently, not saying a word, taking mental notes.

Jose continued, "Just a few more things. I'll push you harder than you've ever been pushed. Never, I mean never, lie to me about how you are doing. Never hide any injuries. Are we together on this?"

She nodded her head in agreement.

"Realize this is not a contest. I can always change up whatever we are doing. We're shooting for physical and psychological excellence. Everything we do will be based on my special forces training. I don't want to push you so badly that you fail. This will be the hardest thing you will ever do in your life, but it is doable. Do you understand? If Matt could get through my training, you certainly can. What I have heard from Frederic and Matt tells me that you are twice the athlete he is. You're just smaller by 60 or 70 pounds. Your body mass deficit is what we have to compensate for in our training. You're much smaller than the adversaries you'll meet. I know this is a generalization; most Kenyans are small, but not the guys who will come after us. In four months, with the proper training and the extra pounds, you will be able to take care of yourself. When we're done, don't think you are a total bad ass. That is how you get killed. Your preparation is for defense. BiBa, when we are done with this you will know that you are tough, but it's all relative. To get to my level of aggression it takes years. You have to suppose that the Kenyans we conflict with are going to be large men. Some of them will have had actual hand-to-hand combat training. You will be able to defend yourself from these guys to the extent you will be able to break away from almost any situation. You can't be asked for more than that, especially in such a short time. All we are hoping for is you realize your ability to defend yourself in any situation."

"Our training will get you to the point of being able to defend yourself, but like I said nothing offensive. After the second week or so, it will start to get easier. The first couple of days will be the worst thing you have ever felt in your life. Once you get past the initial pain, you will see incredible results."

She looked straight into his eyes and without saying a word.

"I'm not letting you say a thing, is there anything that I missed?" he asked. "I must sound overbearing and I don't mean to. I hope you can tell how important this is. It's my honor to be with you and Matt on this. Are you ready to get started?"

BiBa finally said something. "Jose, I understand. Matt has told me how much your friendship means and all this makes sense to me. You are a little too nice by not saying I can get all of us killed if I don't carry my own weight. I don't know what lies ahead, but what I do know, in a roundabout way, is that you guys have been through it all. I'm willing to put as much time and effort or whatever it takes to get it done. I won't let anyone down. I won't be the weak link. I do have one question. Matt will not talk about your excursion to South Africa and that's fine. I have this feeling that Kenya can be just as dangerous. Maybe even more so than what you did over there. So here's my question. Will we be involved in any killings? I have to know to prepare myself. Whatever it takes, I can do it, but you just have to fill me in so there are no surprises when I get there. All this self-defense training tells me how serious this can be. But I have to know how far we will go to protect ourselves."

Alvarez responded, "I don't know. These people are violent and unpredictable. Their existence is based on killing, rape and torture. We have to train for the absolutely worst and assume anything and everything will happen. Killing people to defend our position or even executing people to maintain our security is not out of the question. In all honesty, there might be a lot of killing, certainly a lot of blood. There will be four of us directly involved in our mission. Watching each other's backs is part of the training. In East Africa, all bets are off on controlling every situation. It is fluid and unpredictable. The more we prepare, the safer we are. Matt and Frederic think you are formidable, not only physically but also mentally. I am going to work with you to give you combat skills. If I didn't train you to the highest level, it would be a waste of personnel. I will not directly train you to be to be lethal, but it is part of the package. Training and preparation lead to execution. I can't be any more specific. I can tell you we study our intelligence and layout a plan for what we want to do. But honestly, prepare yourself for the worst."

"You have to trust me. I know Matt's capabilities, but I don't know how disciplined he will be if you are in danger. That is why I will never let you out of my sight. He would give his life for you but he is not a professional and civilians always make mistakes. I will not let that happen. As for Frederic, I have no idea of his capabilities. He hasn't been in the field with us. He wasn't in Africa or South America. Let's just say that we will have to take care of him, not the other way around. I think we will have to get some bodyguards for him. That will not stand out because his cover will be that of an executive for an NGO. He will not interact with the Mangiki gang. He is too far up the ladder. They wouldn't expect someone like a CEO of an NGO to deal with them directly. On the other hand, he will be visible, maybe our cover will be donors, or just do-gooder type tourists who want to help the poor Kenyan people. Frederic's organization will be the conduit. In any case, we won't have access to the right people if we have bodyguards. We will have to go in naked. I am bringing in one more person. His name is Malique. He is an old Navy seal buddy. He specializes in explosives and weapons. He is black, but an American black. He can't cover as an African. That would be way too hard. It is easy for Africans to detect American blacks. Our walking gates are different. Believe it or not, we smell different to them because of our diets, and you can never carry out a perfect dialect for any African language, it's just too hard. It seems really easy to create an African cover, but after looking into it, it would be impossible not to be detected. We will create a cover for Malique as an American banker, a black banker from New York. We will give him a mission of trying to help his African ancestors. He is our bleeding heart. They will think they can take advantage of him. Don't worry, we are professionals and preparation makes for successful outcomes. As hard as you and I are going to train, Frederic and some of his associates will be putting equal amounts of time into creating realistic covers for us. Everything we do is based on limiting the unknown and any potential problems. In this business, you are never safe. All you can do is prepare for any eventuality."

Chapter 11

Jose Alvarez stood up. "Okay let's get started. It is balance and your core strength that we have to work on." He showed her the fundamentals of placing her feet deep into the floor. Gripping the innersoles of her shoes with her toes and forcing her heels down flat into the carpet.

"Bend your knees, don't slope your shoulders, push that head back. Do you feel any more balanced by bracing yourself?"

Without saying, another word he lunged at her with both arms extended and threw her to the floor. His body mass was too great for her to maintain her balance. On the floor, she looked up as he hovered over and said, "Get up. We will do it again."

This time she lowered her hips and butt and shifted her feet so her stance was a little wider. He knocked her down again but she showed a little more resistance. This went on for 15 to 20 minutes before she started to understand her body's mechanics well enough to lessen the severity of the knockdowns. She was still not able to stay on her feet, but she held her ground a little more each time he came after her. Every throw-down prompted a competition.

"I will do better the next time," she said to herself.

The hard body blows inflicted by Alvarez started to take a toll. Her arms were tired and fatigue started to settle into her legs. She would not give up. Every time he lunged she tried to hold herself up, but he was too heavy and too strong. The 40 pounds that he said were necessary for her to put on was a truth of the first order.

Alvarez suddenly stopped. While BiBa was getting into her stance, he walked over to the other side of the room and picked up a 2' x 3' body pad. He handed her the black rectangular leather cushion and said, "Hold this as tightly as you can." With incredible force and stealth, he swiped his muscular right leg in a roundhouse maneuver and kicked her to the liver side of her body with enough force to knock her down yet again. She got up with the same tenacity as she did in defending herself against his body lunges.

After ten minutes of the exercise, BiBa finally bent over at the waist, put her hands on her hips, and said, "Jose, can I get some water?"

"No," as he knocked her down again. "I will teach you how to use those bottles," pointing to the plastic containers filled with water. "They are weapons to protect yourself or even kill somebody with. But no drinking in here. In combat you can't stop and say, I'm thirsty."

She was indignant at his treatment of her, but thought to herself that he was right. She was starting to hate him. From that, point on she would use her competitiveness to prove to herself he couldn't break her. Her mentality of hating her competition, as she did in intercollegiate soccer matches, kicked in.

"Fuck him," she said to herself. "Fuck him. This son of a bitch will never make me quit. I will learn this shit and kick his ass. I don't care what it takes; this prick will never see me in pain. I'll never let him have that kind of control. Fuck him."

After every kick, she just got up and stared at him. Jose abruptly called it a day.

He put his hands on his hips, leaned a little forward, and said, "You want to shoot me, don't you? You might not like this, but I have a compliment for you. You took more heavy-duty punishment from me than I ever expected. You are stronger mentally than anyone I have trained. I know this won't make you feel any better, but physically, compared to most people, you can take a lot of punishment and absorb a lot of pain. That's good. You're one tough person. I respect you enough that tomorrow I'm going to push you even harder. You make my job easier by being so angry and so strong. I have a feeling I would have to kill you before you would stop getting up.

Matt and Frederic both told me what a special person you were, and believe me you are. When this training is over, I'll be glad to be standing next to you. You know, a comrade in arms, that kind of thing."

Alvarez always believed in the knockdown and build up style of training, even if it meant lying to his student. In this case, he was being truthful. "I know this wasn't easy. right now I know you hate my guts. I can deal with that, can you? We have no choice but to push really hard and prepare you in a short period of time. So I'm going to push like hell."

She looked him straight in the eyes. "You're right, at this very moment I do hate you. I will be damned if you break me. I respect that you can kick my ass a thousand times over, but when we're done, believe me that won't be the case. Right now, I want to kill you for how you have abused me. I just have to deal with that and understand that this is your job. I don't sense you are doing this because you enjoy dominating me. I know you have to teach me and be real physical with me, but I don't have to like it. I do respect it, but I don't have to like it."

Jose laughed, "Man, you are tough. Has Matt ever seen this side you?" He extended his hand. "You're all right."

He turned and walked away, pointing towards the door and said, "If you think you are pissed off at me for this type of aggressive training, then you're really going to hate me for what's next. Come on, we are going to the ice bath. There is a pool down the hall filled with ice water. It is probably in the high 30s to low 40s, but a few minutes in the bath for both of us will heal all your bruises and start to replenish the blood supply to your muscles. Tomorrow you would be in such pain and not be able to move if we left right now. If you soak in the ice it will repair your body to the extent you can use it again. It is only for a couple of minutes. Your body can only take so much time in the ice bath before it completely shuts down. How bad can three minutes be? There will be no black and blue marks, no welts, and you'll be able to start from scratch tomorrow. Come on let's hit the baths. Now come on, a couple minutes of torture and you'll feel much better. Maybe not enough to like me, but you'll feel better. You would not want it any other way. You're tough as hell and I have never seen anybody so competitive. You are special, that's how you will get through this. Believe it or not all this is going to save your ass someday."

Matt walked out of his training session and knocked on the door of their room.

"Come on in!" Jose said.

He opened the door and took one look at BiBa. She was bent over, pronounced bruises reddened her face and arms. She had a look on her face of determination that he had never seen before. Her hair was a mess. Her tight bodysuit was totally soaked from head to toe. Her makeup was all over her face and her swollen lip had a slight grin.

Matt could only get a few words out of his mouth, "What the hell happened to you?"

She looked at him and said, "One down, 120 to go!" as she tried to smile. He was frozen speechless. "It even hurts to talk," she said.

"Don't say another word. We are going to the ice baths. I'm sure you don't want to come." Her face hurt so much she couldn't even show him her disgust for what she perceived to be his easy workout with the man from South Beach. He looked fresh and relaxed. She thought to herself, he was the complete opposite. of her and what she had gone through.

He begrudgingly said, "I don't know what I am getting into, but sure I will get into the bath with you guys. What are they exactly?" Both BiBa and Jose just looked at each other.

Jose said, "In both of your lockers you will find bathing suits. We'll see you at the baths in ten minutes."

He grabbed Matt's shoulder and said, "Let's go change and meet BiBa."

Matt started to ask him how it went on her first day of training. Jose said, "I mean this, she's just unbelievable. She is as tough as nails. She can tolerate pain better than anyone I've ever met. She's special all right, she's amazing. I don't think she likes me right now, but she'll get over it."

The 10' x 10' pool had a rope affixed to the ceiling, which hung over the midpoint of the ice bath. Jose grabbed the rope, swung over the pool, and released his hands. The shock of hitting the ice water almost stopped his heart and he had to use every ounce of his faculties not to pass out. The freezing 35° water felt like razor blades ripping into his skin. He motioned to Matt and BiBa to follow. It was so cold he could not utter a word. First Matt then BiBa entered the water with the same reaction. They all huddled in the 5' deep pool near the exit ladder for almost 3 minutes before they had to exit. Hypothermia would set in if they stayed in the freezing water for an extended period of time. Once out of the water, trembling and almost unable to speak, Jose told Matt and BiBa, "Make sure when you hit the showers that you don't turn on any hot water. It could be such a shock to your system and create such a burning sensation on your skin that it would be much worse than the ice bath. I'm so cold I can barely talk, but whatever you do, don't turn on any hot water. Just shower with cold water."

Being under the cold shower would take approximately five minutes for their bodies to start warming up. Within 10-minutes, the healing powers of hypothermic hydrotherapy started to do its work. All three dried off, put on their clothes and met in the lobby. The therapeutic process of rapidly bringing down their temperature had begun. Within two hours, there would be no physical attrition to their bodies from their workouts.

Jose said, "I will walk you guys home. We need to talk for a couple minutes and your place is only a few blocks away. The food and supplements I have ordered for you should be at the house by now. I need to walk you through them." He handed them a piece of paper. "The regimen will get old but you can break it every now and then. BiBa, you will feel like all you're doing is eating. But it's important, like I said, you have to gain at least 40 pounds." Matt just stood there dumbfounded. He couldn't believe his ears. 40 pounds seemed excessive, but he didn't say a word. "I will have a list of restaurants for you guys that have okay food that you can eat. Maybe that will make it easier if you go out every once and a while. BiBa, you will be eating small meals all day long. Tomorrow you will start your first course of steroids. I'll give you the shots if you don't want to do it yourself. We can do it at the gym. The insulin size needles are very small. It shouldn't be too bad. No one said this would be a picnic. I am sorry but there is no other way to prepare you. The steroids, the food you are eating, the huge amounts of pasta and protein mix you will be consuming, will drive you crazy. It's more like eating 24 hours a day and it gets boring real fast."

He stopped as BiBa and Matt looked at him. It started to set in how much their lives were going to change. "I better get home. See you guys tomorrow at the gym. 1:00 pm."

Chapter 12

The pace of BiBa's training grew exponentially. Every day Jose added a new element to her program. He added cardiovascular after the first day. She ran 45 minutes at the YMCA on 14th St. every morning at 8:00 a.m. Running included wind sprints as well as long distance training and running on the stairs. José even hired an ex-track and field coach to have her run the woman's 300-meter low hurdles to give her more strength and stamina. She incorporated free weights into her routine to bulk up her 125-pound frame. Nautilus machines were used to supplement the weights. She worked on her lower body four days a week and her upper body five days a week. Training had to be a seven-day a week endeavor because of the limited time to get her to a high enough level of strength and proficiency to be able to protect herself. Cumulatively, the cardiovascular training, weight training, and self-defense instruction took more than six hours a day. It wasn't the time or the physical havoc that was pushed upon her body that bothered her the most. What made her life miserable, was all the food and liquids she had to consume with her steroid regimen. Her goal was 40 pounds of muscle and body fat no more than 11 per cent. During her 16-week training, she broke her right thumb learning how to use it as a weapon to gouge out a combatant's eye. She had a cranial fracture when José kicked her in the head just as her leather headgear slipped to the side of her face. She suffered numerous concussive events that led to blackouts, headaches, and nausea. But it was her beautiful hands causing the most trouble. She suffered broken fingers on her hands that mangled and slightly disfigured them. Her second and third fingers on her dominant right hand were broken at the knuckle with one permanently listing concavely and the other setting in convexly. Her large straight hands that mimicked the hands of an extremity model (someone who modeled their hands and feet for jewelry) were now that of a warrior. BiBa was paying the price for her newfound skills.

Matt's training was equally time-consuming, but his sessions were not as arduous as BiBa's. His program was designed to maintain his cardiovascular integrity and add to his self-defense skills. As the weeks progressed, the difference between their daily routines flattened, and she went from a neophyte to a well-trained athlete with successful defensive prowess. Matt maintained his skill level in self-defense with a minimal acceleration in his stamina. It was all he had hoped to accomplish. Her physical race in catching up with Matt was meteoric. After 16-weeks, her defense skills and cardiovascular development were impressive, but Matt was stronger and faster, and that would never change. His physiognomy dealt him a better hand. BiBa was developing into a welcome compliment to the team of José, Matt, and Malique. She could and would hold her own in Kenya. She would not be the weak link, but the men, for all intents and purposes, were more lethal.

Even though it dominated their schedules, New York was not all training. They became patrons of the arts and ran in the philanthropic circles of the city. Frederic placed them on boards and in the founder circles of the most prestigious charitable organizations in New York by simply throwing around large sums of money. BiBa and Matt became members of Free the Children Foundation, the International Rescue Committee, Save the Children's Foundation and UNICEF. Frederic's strategy was to create a cover as philanthropists that would lead to their support of children in Kenya. They joined the Museum of African Art, the Museum of Contemporary Art, the Metropolitan Museum, and the Guggenheim. Frederic felt if they were well placed in the upper crust of New York's charitable giving, they could incubate relationships with Kenyan and East African communities. Their major target was Kenyan Alliance for Helping Children in Need. On paper, it was a real player in East Africa. It acted as an intermediary between supporters in the United States and the disenfranchised in Kenya. As was the case with most African organizations, it was corrupt. Its real function was to facilitate the laundering of charitable contributions to the Mungiki gang. American philanthropists' monies diverted to Kenya's underbelly. The organization's cover hid the co-mingling of legal and illegal activities from international scrutiny. Funneling money into the criminal/terrorist organization was a way of deflecting rogue-financing actions of the Kikuyus. The Alliance gave the image of working with disadvantaged children, when in fact its expenditures advanced the cause of the Mungiki gang. Because of its relationship with the Alliance, the Mungiki was protected from being classified as a terrorist group by the United Nations or the World Court. The ruling Party of National Unity, or the PNU, could hide millions of dollars of illegal monies from kidnapping, killing, protection or government graft by having it go through the legitimate accounts of the NGO. It could protect its foreign currency balances in international banks by dummying up the books. Frederic always followed the money and in Africa, it always led to the bad actors.

Chapter 13

BiBa and Matt received a call from Frederic to discuss a charitable event staged by the Kenyan Alliance proposing the building of a medical facility in the central Kenyan Rift Valley. He managed to get an invitation for the three of them and José. The purpose of the social event was to solicit funds from wealthy donors. More importantly, Frederic wanted to create a relationship with Martin Arup Moi, the president of the Kenya Alliance. His intentions were to facilitate a trip to Kenya and open the doors, as he put it.

At Frederic's insistence, BiBa accepted a personal shopper luncheon at Bergdorf Goodman, New York's most exclusive department store. At 12:00 pm, she arrived at the store's 58th Street flagship property, and met Timea Eather, who was in her early 40s, shockingly beautiful in an ethnic way and spoke with a British accent. Her national origin was not immediately apparent to BiBa, but she surmised it was somewhere near the Horn of Africa. She was either Ethiopian or Dinka because of the vertical lines of her body and her unique facial bone structure. Her skin was a cream color, not the olive patina of her ancestors.

Timea spoke first, "I feel a little uncomfortable. Mr. Frederic was so direct on what gowns and accessories we should provide for you that I assumed you wouldn't be so beautiful. He said he wanted you to look stoic and refined. His inference was matronly but after seeing you that is not what I would suggest. He wanted me to hide your figure as best I could. May I say, I am not comfortable with his requests? Would you please call him and work it out so I am not in the middle of any potential disagreements. You are elegant and your body is athletic to the point of almost perfect symmetry. It is obvious that you pride yourself on being fit. I would like to accentuate your beauty and your wonderful lines, not hide them."

BiBa called Frederic. He said, "What took you so long? I thought by now you would have called and had a fit over this. Please hear me out. You can't look too attractive and for sure, you can't look physically formidable. These people are dangerous and the last thing we need is for a woman to challenge their masculinity. Every detail of the fundraiser will be sent back to Kenya. The security cameras will be taping the event. Their mode of operation is to get a description and detailed summary of every guest. They are professionals and will be gathering intelligence to send back home. There cannot be a trace of anything threatening to them. I am sorry, but you are too pretty and that body of yours will threaten the hell out of them. BiBa, they are anti-white and fiercely sexist. I hope you understand."

She answered, "Yeah I do, you're right. When I heard what you wanted it just sent me back a little. No big thing."

Frederic replied, "Thanks. I thought you'd understand. Wait until you see the tuxedo I have picked out for Matt. It won't fit him quite right and the pants will be just a little short, just enough so he won't be altogether perfect. In addition, for José, I think he's going to be pissed; he will look a little effeminate. You know the tuxedo too tight and the color will be a little off. You three can't come off as challenging."

She got off the phone and looked at Timea. "Well, it is settled. Do what Frederic asked. It's okay. I don't want to go into it but I'm now on the same page as him. He makes everybody uncomfortable with his bluntness. We are going to an affair where everyone is in their eighties and it is just easier to please Frederic than fight a war with him. I should not upstage the guest of honor. She is excessively controlling and Freddy would never hear the end of it. As he puts it, he doesn't want me to look too glamorous. He says people won't take me seriously. My boyfriend and I seek Frederic's advice; we are new to New York. We pay him a lot of money, so it would be foolish not to listen. So far, he has been right on everything, from where we live, to investments. Therefore, I guess I should take him up on how I should look to be charitable. Like I said, it's not worth the fight."

Frederic had prepared her to always speak in generalities about her and Matt's affairs. He said, “You never know what is out there and who is listening.”

“It's a small world,” BiBa thought to herself, "What were the chances of having an East African personal shopper? Maybe she's not Kenyan, but you never know."

After trying on an infinite number of matronly looking formalwear, as Timea called them, she finally picked out a $16,000 Versace gown that was sophisticated in its own right but certainly not elegant. BiBa was informed that Bergdorf would lend her a chinchilla coat and matching gloves.

"My dear, we only have one thing left," added Timea. She had an attendant bring out boxes of shoes. Within 15-minutes they were done.

Timea thanked BiBa for her patronage and said, "Mr. Frederic has an appointment for you at Tiffany's. It is only a couple of blocks up the street. A Mr. Volker will be waiting for you. It's been my pleasure, thank you."

Frederic had arranged for her to rent some accessories for the night. The Versace gown would be offset by an emerald necklace and matching bracelets. The necklace mainstay was forty-two matching 5-carat flawless emeralds encircled by white diamonds. The 16-inch choker design of the necklace augmented with three 20-carat teardrop shaped emeralds, also encircled by white diamonds, tied together by 2-inch long strands of three-quarter carat diamonds. The necklace looked like a beautiful collar dropping large green, perfectly cut tears into the center of BiBa's cleavage. Volker brought her three diamond rings with a total count of 18-carats to finish off her ensemble. Her jewelry was the epitome of wealth. Frederic was hiding BiBa's beauty and displaying the couple's opulence.

Chapter 14

The black tie event was held at the Hemsley Park Lane Hotel off 59th St. and Central Park Avenue. The hotel grandeur and setting next to Central Park made it one of the most highly respected hotels in New York City. It was a draw for major events, weddings, corporate seminars, retreats, and charitable functions. Matt and BiBa's cover was wealthy Americans, leaving their Toronto lives for repatriation to New York. His wealth came from real estate in the United States and extensive holdings in Central America. José was the acting CEO of their South American division and oversaw farming and mineral exploration for Papaz Inc. Frederic represented Matt and BiBa in the capacity of a financial advisor who was eager to place money into worthwhile causes to promote their acceptance to New York's "A-list." Their cover included Matt's desire of future travels to Kenya and East Africa with the romantic notion of seeding charitable organizations that would foster change for children and promote medical care for the poor. His ears were open to any suggestions of taking money out of his wallet for involvement in any worthwhile NGO. All he wanted was a minimal role in choosing the projects that his money would fund. BiBa's cover was that of a supportive girlfriend of ten years who had empathy for children and a desire to change their plight. Her background was developed to show that she had been an administrator in the field of public health at the University of Texas. José, as the CEO of Matt's South American division, attended because of his expertise in dealing with the abjectly poor farm-workers, of which there were many in Kenya's Central Valley.

"He will be advising us," was the way Matt phrased it to Martin Arup Moi.

Jose's cover was that he had dealt with poor workers and their conditions and his conclusions were, "All poor people suffer a similar fate. It just happens in different places, that's all."

Matt commented, "José has a feel for what we should do to better the conditions of the workers. I trust his experience and knowledge. As for Frederic, he is our conduit for placing any of my money. Martin, if things work out, you will be dealing directly with Frederic."

Matt looked at Frederic at a predetermined time in the conversation with Moi and said, "We have something for you to show our intentions. Frederic please give Martin our check."

It was a check for one hundred thousand dollars made out to the Alliance.

"It is hopefully the beginning of a partnership. We have done our due diligence and comfortable in aligning ourselves with your cause. Take this check and deposit it tomorrow. Hopefully, after you look at us, you will feel the same way."

He held out his hands and smiled at Moi. "No more business if you don't mind. Tonight is for the entertainment of your guests and I am monopolizing your time. If you have any interest in our help, please contact Frederic. He will set up a meeting later in the week. It will be nice to have a place to put our resources and help the Kenyan people. Just one more thing, we only want to participate from a far. We just want the advantage of having you as a shepherd for our money. We will not aggressively seek any position of power in your organization other than that of a donor. We hope you'll find this acceptable. Just to be clear, if you don't want our participation that is fine. The $100,000 is still yours with no strings attached. Look at it as a declaration of our intentions." He clasped Moi's hands and said, "It's been a pleasure."

Then Matt, BiBa, Frederic and José walked off, leaving Martin Arup Moi standing by himself.

Chapter 15

As they crossed the lobby, Frederic noticed a beautiful brunette walking up to the host table to pick up her nametag. He looked at the other three and said, "Excuse me, my date is here."

Matt grabbed BiBa and cut off Frederic as José led the phalanx of three to walk right in front of his intended date. Matt was first to arrive at the table. He extended his arms and gazed at her from head to toe and said, "What a wonderful surprise." He turned to BiBa and said, "I want you to meet my dear friend, Giselle."

BiBa had not heard of her and was put off by a feeling of jealousy. She studied the situation while looking at the anguish on Frederick's face as he tried to greet his date. She realized it was Frederick's love interest making her insecure and was happy she was not facing part of Matt's past.

José approached her next and gave her a big hug. "It's been awhile," he said, "I will be the first to say it, I have missed you. How are you doing?"

Frederic finally worked his way closer to Gisele, "I am glad you are here. Looking at Jose and Matt, you'd think they thought you were their date. I'm really glad you came. I know it took a lot for you to get here on such short notice."

He put his arms around her and gently kissed her on the lips. "Thanks, it means a lot to me."

No one was sure what to make of the two, but Frederic was always full of surprises. Matt felt he knew Gisele because of their relationship in Toronto on the Leopard Directive, but he had never seen this side of her. She was stunningly beautiful and conducted herself with an air of subtle sophistication.

"Beauty and a perfect French accent are a hard combination to compete with," BiBa said to herself. Soon she realized she didn't have to compete because Gisele was clearly there to be with Frederic.

The five stayed at the Kenyan reception for a little more than an hour, engaging in small talk and building up each other's egos. Matt and BiBa were the first to suggest they wanted to leave. José followed suit and the three left the gathering and went outside to hail a taxicab. José's place was closest and he told the cab driver to drop him off in Chelsea at his apartment and then take Matt and BiBa to their brownstone on 15th Street.

Frederic, the ultimate planner for every contingency and detail, had a limousine waiting for himself and Gisele to take them to his suite at the Trump Towers. The cab ride from José's to Matt's house took less than 15-minutes. The three had a nonstop discussion on how well the night went with Moi. Gisele's name was not mentioned, as if almost to say they didn't want to put a hex on Frederick's relationship.

After getting out of the taxicab, Matt and BiBa were in the throes of walking up the stoop of the brownstone and electronically unlocking the door, when Matt's cell phone rang. The electronic butler answered Matt's phone with its perfunctory greeting.

"Yes I will take the call from Frederic," Matt said. "Meet us for drinks old buddy. I know you just got home but we have something to tell you. Don't bother to change. I will be there soon. How about we meet you at the coffee shop on 14th Street right across from the American Eagle store? You know which coffee shop I'm talking about, don't you?"

Matt and BiBa found it strange because they had just left them 15-minutes earlier. "Sure, we are only ten minutes away and believe it or not, we were just walking into the house."

As they turned around, Matt commanded the butler to lock the house. He and BiBa were in silence as they walked down 15th Street to 7th Avenue. Approaching the coffee shop for their rendezvous with Frederic and Gisele, Matt put his arm around BiBa and whispered in her ear, "I don't know what was going on, Frederic is a little eccentric. Maybe he is showing off to Gisele, I don't know."

He kissed her on the side of the face and they continued their walk. Within 15-minutes, the two couples ran into each other in front of the coffee shop.

Frederic leaned over to Matt and said, "I'm sure we were followed. Do you have a read on anyone following you? I'm not sure, but it felt like there were eyes on us. It started. In the limo on the way, back to my place I checked my iPhone and found security had been breached on all my computers. Someone is very sophisticated, and whoever they are, they're trying to hack into my database. Not just the financial stuff, but the personal stuff. That makes me think it can only be the Alliance. It could be run of the mill, they check out all their potential donors, I don't know. But I do know these guys are good and there can't be many people with their skills. We will be able to track them. It will be easy but it will take some time. This is all too fast. They've compromised all the fictitious accounts I have set up for you in our investment funds. They haven't gotten any further, and I know they can't, but they tried to enter all our data systems. They really can't get any further than just looking because of all the firewalls we set up. Let me tell you, they are good and unbelievably fast. We traced their origin to China. It is real obvious that these people are working for the Kenyan Alliance. They only got into the data bases we let them get into, but they are good. We are better than these guys are, but they can be a potential problem. The good thing is we put a cookie into the Alliance's network through their associates in

China. The security system in your house shows that someone already tried to break in. I'm sure they want to place bugs, both audio and visual. The e-butler stopped them. But they will do whatever they have to compromise your security. We can circumvent it, but that will take a few days. On the way here, I called our man at the Trump Towers and he said someone sent for room service to our suite and it wasn't us. I talked to the front desk and people at José's hotel and they said the same thing. I'm sorry I forgot to mention it, but he will be here within the next few minutes. He said he wanted to walk to see who was following him and how professional they were."

"I have already set up some countermeasures for all of us. As far as I can tell, we are not in any physical danger. All they want to know is if you are real and if your money is good. This is just a minor inconvenience in the grand scheme of things. Its better we know who we are dealing with as early as possible. This way we have a better chance of protecting our mission. Tomorrow, once we know who they are, I will let them into our houses. They will try with the cable company or a utilities company, or a grocer that delivers. These are professionals. They won't stop until they're breached our systems. We will let them compromise us as soon as possible. The easer it is, will make them think we are unsophisticated and not a threat. We'll just play into whatever they're doing. I have some preliminary ideas I want to throw at you. I want to put a power communication cell into your house. It is kind of like a cell tower for your phone that AT&T and Verizon put on the rooftops. I am sure by now our phones are bugged. If they haven't done it, yet it is just a matter of time. So tomorrow, when I call you I will tell you that we are putting this communication cell in your house to assist the transfer of information from our office to your house to make sure our financial data can be transferred quickly and securely. Many brokerage houses are doing this kind of thing with hedge funds and their bigger clients. It is not a big thing in the financial world. This will effectively block their surveillance. To make it more plausible and keep them off track I will ask you to shut it off when you're not home because it might affect your neighbors' electronics. I will ask you to keep it on only when you're using it. I will ask you to be sure to turn it off when you're not. I'll make a point never to leave the house with it on. Something else, starting tomorrow you will have a full-time live-in maid. She's ours. She's security but she won't know anything about the cell except what we tell her. So when I call tomorrow I will make sure to tell you to inform her to turn off the electronic device whenever you are not in the house. Whoever these people are, they are going to try to figure out ways to block this data transfer booster. They know it's plausible that you have electronic assistance on the transfer of data. The timing may be questioned and piss them, but they know it happens all the time. For the next few days don't forget you have someone's eyes and ears in your house."

Gisele chimed in, "I don't know how to say this, so I will be blunt. Whatever personal things you do on the toilet or in the shower, they will be watching you. So don't do anything different. These are professionals and they will know if you are uncomfortable and that could compromise us. They are good. You will have to be better and convince them that nothing is going on in your house. Wow, you will even have to let them see you nude. That means the shower, making love, changing in the morning, whatever you do, they will be right there with you. I know it's an incredible violation, but if you don't pass as being yourselves, they will know. This is only for a couple days until Frederic can get everything in place."

Frederic took control of the conversation again. "Don't forget, once you're outside of the house they will try to use every means possible to have surveillance on you. They will use ultrasound, sophisticated microphones, temperature detectors, anything you've ever thought of or heard about, these guys have at their disposal. We know they will use them. They already have. Figure that anything going on inside your house, they have eyes on you. They will try to read your lips and they've got microphones on you to hear even a whisper."

He looked at BiBa. "I'm sorry, but welcome to our world. Right now, this is all manageable and we can control our environment. You are safe. You have Matt and all of our resources. Right now this might be overwhelming, but trust me, we are as good as it gets."

As she started to speak, José entered the coffee shop. Frederic continued laying out the scenario. "I didn't mean to cut you off," he said to her.

BiBa replied, "Its okay. It will take me just a little time to absorb all this. I'm fine with it as long as I can do something and be useful."

José entered the conversation. "These guys are really predictable. They followed me here, two different teams. They don't have a clue I spotted them. They are all by the book. It looks like a real professional operation."

Chapter 16

"Since we're here, let's have some coffee," José said. "What does everybody want? I'll get it," he rose from his chair and walked over to the counter.

Upon arriving back to the table he said, "They'll bring it; I got some scones and cookies. I hope somebody else is hungry besides me." He smiled, "It makes for better cover and of course it has nothing to do with my sweet tooth. I'm going to go outside to see what our friends are up to."

He turned around and bummed a cigarette from the table next to theirs. He took it from a kid with tattoos and piercings and then exited the coffee shop. He lit the cigarette and inhaled it as if he were having an orgasm. Leaning against the building, he looked for trucks, vans, or SUVs, any vehicle large enough to carry surveillance equipment.

"They'll be here soon enough," he said to himself. It would only be a couple of minutes because the men who followed him from Chelsea were sitting in Starbucks down the street. He walked back into the café and said, "A truck or a van with listening devices should be here soon. Like I said, they play by the book. The guys that followed me are at Starbucks," as he pointed across the street. "Let's figure out a reason for us being here. In a few minutes it will be as if they are sitting at the table with us."

Matt started laughing, "I have it."

He looked at Gisele. "You just came to town to surprise us. You will love this. You and Frederic are getting engaged."

The table erupted. Frederic said, "I would be the luckiest guy in the world, but who would believe it? Real funny guys, come up with a better one," he said.

Gisele looked at him, "Frederic don't protest too much. You give yourself away. Don't forget, being engaged to me would come with great benefits," she said as she put her hand high on his inner leg to get a laugh from everyone.

They had their coffee and desserts and talked as if Frederic and Gisele were really getting married.

Matt thought to himself, "Who are we really talking to, those guys outside or Frederic?"

The next morning, even though they were assured that their home had not been bugged yet, they couldn't wait to leave and start their workouts. It seemed like BiBa was trying to get in better shape and redistribute her weight. Matt, on the other hand, seemed more preoccupied with trying to look younger and more athletic, even though he was in his forties. Their daily routine was such that Matt would walk BiBa to the YMCA for her running. He would venture down the street and get a banana and mango smoothie at Starbucks. Then he would get a New York Times and read for an hour. Then they would walk to the gym in the Chelsea market, which was six blocks away.

Around 12:00 pm, they were walking briskly along 14th Ave., and were confronted by three large Puerto Rican men. One man conspicuously wearing all black and a large gold chain around his neck grabbed for BiBa's athletic bag. If she were not so strong, he would have broken her arm. While clutching her bag with all her strength, one of the other men pulled out a small knife and cut the strap off her shoulder, took the bag and started running. Matt was busy with the third man whom he described to the police later as at least 6'2" tall and 240 pounds. In an instant, all three men fled down 14th St. and turned onto 5th Avenue. This was not a crime-ridden area of New York. To see three large Puerto Rican men, inappropriately dressed, running down the street in this upscale neighborhood was highly irregular. People, not wanting to get involved, just watched as a chase by Matt and BiBa ensued. In a predetermined and scripted fashion, the man carrying the bag ran under a stoop and handed the Nike bag to a fourth assailant, who was Caucasian. He replaced the sim card in BiBa's phone, pulled all of the money out of her wallet, put them back into the bag and gave it to the Puerto Rican, who continued to run down the street. This whole maneuver took less than twenty seconds. It all took place out of sight from Matt and BiBa as they rounded the corner forty to fifty seconds later. The man threw the bag into the street. As Matt and BiBa retrieved the bag, the three men ran into the crowd of people going into the Chelsea market. They vanished into the multitudes of shoppers and ran into a public restroom where a fifth assailant had a change of clothing for them. They each stripped off their gang clothing, put on jeans and short sleeve shirts, and blended into the thousands of people who frequented the upscale market.

Matt and BiBa stood looking at each other after they realized the assailants had disappeared into the crowd.

She said, "You may not believe this but I could have kicked his ass. While the whole thing was going down I realized that we might be set up." she whispered. "It had to be a set up. There are no Puerto Ricans up here in Chelsea," he whispered back.

"Believe it or not I felt like I had everything under control and there must've been a reason why he wanted my bag, so more or less I let him have it."

She opened the bag and realized that the only thing that was missing was money from her wallet. The phone had been replaced. "I only lost some money, they left everything else. I'm not kidding; I know I could've stopped that asshole."

Matt replied, "Me too, yeah me too. It would have been easy to stop those guys. I really didn't feel threatened, especially when I saw the guy's little knife. It looked like a Swiss Army knife. Everything seemed in slow motion and I knew you weren't in danger, so I kind of backed off just like you did. We both just let them go. Really strange we feel the same way."

They were talking loudly as if someone was listening. "Just lucky to be okay, but I never really sensed any danger. Strange." she said. "That's exactly how I feel. I think we better call the police."

She hugged Matt and said into his ear, "We have to talk to José about this. We will be at the gym in a few minutes. He'll have a better read on this than us."

Within ten minutes, they arrived at the gym "Hey guys, how are you?" José said.

They filled him in talking in very low voices, not to be heard.

"We're okay in here. They can't listen. Fill me in. You guys are indeed bad asses." he said.

Matt responded, "I think you will be happy and sure as hell proud of your number one student. I'm just talking, but she really handled herself well. Whoever these guys are they will kind of think that we are inept, but not totally helpless. What we did was pretty natural so it will play well. They will have no idea of what we are capable. I just hope we are never are put to the test again."

After describing what went on, Jose said, "It's all very predictable. If they wanted to hurt you, they could have. Let me look at your bag."

He checked the phone and it was evident that they had replaced the sim card, which would give them the ability to have one more channel to follow their every move.

“Now we have another way of giving them information," he whispered. "They must have a sense that we are just dumb rich people willing to part with money. I'm sure they think we are easy prey. If they thought we were anything else they would be much more sophisticated and not have hired some Puerto Rican gang kids to do their work."

BiBa was blown away by the cloak and dagger world she was living in now. José made the Puerto Ricans sound like school kids.

"They are harmless," he said. BiBa then did what her parents had always told her to do.

"I defer to the better and smarter, and in this case it's you," she said to Jose. She took the phone out of his hand.

"Do you want me to place the call to the police? That's exactly what they expect."

He smiled and said, "You are bad ass and smart. I will call Frederic and fill him in."

Chapter 17

Frederic called Matt a few hours after the incident. "I just talked to Jose. Are you guys okay? I didn't want to press, be overbearing and sound too protective so I waited to call. Are you all right? What's up with BiBa? How is she?"

Matt replied, "She is coming to grips with it, but she feels totally violated."

They knew they were being recorded so they played along with the cover of being innocent victims of a gang robbery.

"We figure it was some Puerto Rican guys who were out of their neighborhood looking for easy prey. Shit, I guess they figured it was us. To tell you the truth it didn't do a lot for my ego. I thought I looked like someone who could hold his own. Shit, it's embarrassing that they thought I looked like a punk. I'll get over it. BiBa will get over it. We're okay. That is enough about it, okay. What else is on your mind? I know you didn't call for some kind of update or some kind of pep talk. So, what's up?"

Frederic responded, "Did you get all the materials I sent you? By the way, the booster we put in your house works just great. It takes me 1/5 of the time to download materials and transmit them to you. I don't want to sound like an asshole, but are you remembering to turn the booster off when you're done? Like I said, it could cause unbelievable problems with your neighbor's electronic setups. We don't need them to be irritated with you."

Matt said, "Okay, okay. I got your papers on Capital Partner Solutions. They are pretty extensive. I'm almost finished. They look like a good place to warehouse our money. And yes, we turn off the transmitter whenever we are not using it and as far as I can see so does the maid."

The conversation between Matt and Frederic was generic, no specifics. At the restaurant a couple of nights earlier a verbal script was created as a baseline for all their communications so that the people who were surveilling them would be satisfied they were not threats to their operations. They wanted to make sure the Kenyan Alliance viewed their relationship and the interplay between them and the Alliance as normal. They did not want to be perceived as a menace. In fact, they wanted Martin Asrp Moi to view them as easy pickings. Moi's security team responsible for their surveillance and transmission of

Intel was almost done with its due diligence. Matt, Frederick, Alvarez, Gisele, and BiBa would be subjected to four or five more days of scrutiny. Up to this point all, their financial and personal histories were satisfactory and cleared the preliminary intelligence hurdles of Moi's associates. A few more days' ground surveillance would detect any anomalies in their daily routines if they existed. If not, the Kenyan Alliance's investigation of Matt Papaz and his co-horts would be over. The acceptance of his money and his role in the organization would be complete.

"Matt, come by my office later this afternoon with BiBa and Jose. We can finish up on the Capital Partnership Solutions perspective. It won't take more than 20-minutes. Then the five of us can go out to dinner. I just need you to sign some documents. I want to give this Alliance thing our full attention. So let's make a decision on Capital. I am hoping to hear from Moi pretty soon. If he likes us we can define our role in his charity."

They both knew every word of their conversation was being overheard so they didn't want to appear too theatrical or unnatural in their conversation. They just wanted to relay their interest to Moi. They wanted to play on Matt's excitement about a new partnership taking him and BiBa to Kenya. It was important they sound exuberant, almost giddy, about their impending partnership with the Alliance.

Upon arriving at the office, Frederic motioned to Matt to look at a note that he had placed in Partners Capital Solutions' file on his desk. Matt picked up the folder and read the note.

It said, "The office next door has been cleaned by our technicians and electronic surveillance is impossible."

Pulling out the next page in the folder, Matt signed it and handed it to Frederic.

"I have all the other documents in the next office so why don't we go over there."

"Okay," Matt said, following Frederic's lead.

After his office had been compromised by the Alliance, Frederic had his men sweep the room for bugging devices and planted prerecorded audio and visual computer-generated tapes that would be provided to Alliance's team as to the goings-on in the office. The technology of cloning and re-creating live situations in combinations of one, two, three, four, or all of them in any business or personal interplay looked authentic and could not be separated from real life interaction. Virtual interplay of Matt and his associates in any combination would be served up to Moi deflecting their real intentions and convincing him of their authenticity and desire to align with his charity. Frederic's technology allowed him to use the other office free of any threats of surveillance. It also acted as an information feeder to proactively controlling his relationship with Moi. His office allowed him to leak information to his adversary and control the playing field in an atmosphere free from scrutiny.

Once in the room with the door closed the electronics were activated, Gisele started to speak.

"We have completed an investigation of the Alliance and Moi. It is exactly as we thought. The charity's involvement with the Mungiki gang and Kenyatta is no more than a conduit for foreign exchange, albeit an important one. Moi's operation generates a sizable amount of money itself, almost $15 million a year, but its account activities, mostly in Swiss and Bahamian banks, are almost $400,000,000. The accounting differences are coming from two major sources other than the Alliance: the Chinese and money from conflict diamonds from Zimbabwe. Let me talk about the blood diamond trade in the Marange range first. It is in Eastern Zimbabwe. Robert Mugabe's military arm of the ZANU-PF and his political cronies ex-appropriated thousands of mining rights acres in the Zimbabwe central highland region by force and brutality. They killed almost 2,000 individual miners and small cooperative workers. They use the typical East African military tactics of torture, severing appendages, rape of family members, and the whole gamut. As far as we can tell, almost 5,000 people are held in camps as slave laborers by the army. You know the usual, young children, women, and even the elderly. Global Witness, a Canadian NGO, says the mines are outside the Kimberly Process. They don't comply with any international standards for their labor conditions or their financial reporting. They estimate more than one billion carats of uncut high quality diamonds are flowing into the world market from this one region alone. Our intelligence shows Matieu Yamba, Zimbabwe's finance minister has all by himself diverted as much as $350 million to Mugabe's inner circle. Mugabe and his cronies are pulling out more than $900 million a year and a large portion of that is going directly into Kenya. The political stability in Zimbabwe is tenuous and ZANU-PF considers the heavy investment in Kenya a safety valve. Mugabe is close with Kenyatta because of the relationship he had with his father. The United Nations is trying to put sanctions on the Zimbabwean government because of the brutal manner in which the land was obtained and the unacceptable labor conditions in Marange but any sanction proposals making it to the Security Council have been vetoed by China. Further investigation shows that the Chinese government's investment arm, Chinese Worldwide Holdings Inc, is the largest partner in the largest mine in Marange. This mine produces over 450 million carats a year. With large levels of Chinese investment and technology in the diamond mines in Marange there is a possibility of merging activities in Zimbabwe with future investments in Kenya. Some type of mining synergisms, as far as we can tell. There is reason to believe there are very large potential mining opportunities for diamonds in central Kenya. The geology is there. The Chinese feel they just have to do some exploratory mining and create an infrastructure. They think the potential for high quality diamonds in Kenya is greater than their new investments in mines in Canada and India. There is another point to their strategy. In the Rift Valley region, they have found large deposits of rare earth and heavy earth metals. The Chinese are trying to control and dominate the world's supply of these metals primarily used in manufacturing. The US Geological Survey has satellite images showing potential deposits of cobalt and magnesium and suggests there are huge deposits of molybdenum. They also feel the area has large enough concentrations of zinc, copper, and mercury to make mining for them profitable. There are also gold and silver deposits. As I had mentioned earlier, this is part of the Chinese strategy to control the world's rare earth and heavy metal production. There are also military advantages for them to have a presence in East Africa."

"In a nutshell it sounds like a two prong attack in Kenya." Matt said. "The Chinese and Zimbabweans are putting billions of dollars into Kenya and at the same time they are willing to de-stabilize the country politically by letting the Mungiki run wild. It looks like the Kikuyus are creating, or at least not attending to, deep poverty to promote tribal hatreds and an anti-colonial atmosphere that will allow them carte blanche to plunder Kenya's natural resource base. It is no more than simple imperialism. This time it's Asian not European. Wow, my problem is, I don't know what role we should play in this. Even if we place $20 million in some kind of business ventures, we will still be small players. I just know, and it is in my guts, that we should do something. I don't know what. At the extreme we have the potential to place hundreds of millions, if not billions of dollars into Kenya and East Africa through our agreements with the Tijuana Cartel."

BiBa did not know to what he was referring. She listened intently.

He looked at José, "You know Ricardo better than anybody. If he knew his investments in Kenya would be legal and would generate very high ROI's, would he back us on this?"

Jose said, "I am sure he would if Guzman gave him the okay."

"Ricardo Vargas was an associate indirectly involved in the Leopard Directive." Matt continued, "I can't speak for Guzman, but I think he will be all in on anything we want to do."

Jose Guzman, an associate involved in the South African affair, was another player BiBa had never heard mentioned.

"There is something really unsettling about all of this stuff in Kenya," Matt continued. "I guess corruption and tribal rule is all over East Africa. Maybe I should make the loop bigger to include all of Africa. I just feel I should do something about it. I am really lost on this, but I can't sit here and do nothing. I'm getting all of you involved and I know how selfish that is. I will understand if any of you want to back out. For some reason it is imperative for me to do something. Maybe it is the injustice of all this, I don't know. I have been sitting on my hands since Johannesburg and now I have to do something. What makes me surer than anything else is what the Alliance is doing and we only have $100,000 in this."

Chapter 18

"It's evident there's more to this than meets the eye, who would have guessed?" Frederic said. "The amount of Chinese investment shows the importance of this to them. Our analysis points to their trying to corner the metals market as well as uncut diamonds. The ZANU-PF partnership says to me they are comfortable challenging the South Africans for world dominance in the diamond markets. They are betting heavily on their ability to inject conflict stones into the major houses of Antwerp and London. I know a billions dollars is small change to them, but it is a considerable investment in such an unstable region of the world. They have to feel confidence in their abilities to control the Kikuyu's and the Mungiki gang. We also put them behind the political unrest in

Liberia and the Ivory Coast. At this point, we can't prove anything but substantial amounts of uncut diamonds are being sent out of West Africa and we think it is the Chinese who are responsible. They don't mind the political unrest in any of these countries. It's to their advantage. They must know something we don't about their ability to have long run control and who all the players are. Okay, let's accept the fact that the Chinese are pulling the strings. If we use that as a starting point maybe we can define our mission in Kenya."

Dialogue between the five concluded that being on the ground in Nairobi and throwing a lot of money around would be the most efficient way of getting answers.

José said, "Our problem is knowing the right questions to ask before we commit ourselves to this project."

Gisele summed it up, "We can't predetermine anything until we get there. That means our involvement, the amount of financial resources, personnel, our security, or any of it. Let's just say it's dynamic and that we have to be on their soil to get a handle on what we have to do. I don't want to sound contrary, but after we get there, we might not even have a mission. There's an old French saying, if you lose big on the first bet, then only a fool continues. Maybe $100,000 and our cost of the trip should be viewed as an exploratory cost. If we don't get a satisfactory response from Moi or his Kenyan counterparts, then it's over. There's one other thing. Before we embark on this trip, we have to develop financial ties that make us as valuable as benefactors to the Alliance or any other Kenyan organization that if we enter into a partnership with them they will guarantee our security. We want to be more valuable to them alive than dead. The premise being, they take our money and provide absolute protection while we are there. They will act as security for us because we are a greater asset in partnership with them than kidnapping us for ransom or letting somebody else get their hands on us. I know it sounds counterintuitive, but we are potentially more valuable to them as a client than as hostages. Our value as a partner will guarantee our safety. There's so much kidnapping and killing of foreigners in Kenya I don't think we have the ability to adequately protect ourselves. We will engage Moi and his associates to do it for us. They will protect their golden egg. Moi, or whoever else we will deal with, can't afford to kidnap and then ransom us for only a few million if in the long run a partnership can get him ten times that amount. I'll use your American phrase, trust me. That's right, trust me on this, they will protect us. I don't see them having any other alternative if we present ourselves as easy prey. As far as we can figure, the Chinese are calling all of the shots and the Kenyans and Zimbabweans are just following suit. The Chinese view things as long term. So if we play this out right, we will be safe. They will not let anything happen to us."

Matt responded, "Okay. I think we all agree. We have to figure out what it is we exactly want to do once we get there. I think we play it like rich extravagant Americans and tie business with pleasure.

We should set it up that we visit some national parks in Kenya and then go to Rwanda and see the silverback gorillas. We ask Moi to arrange for all of the flights, land transportation, hotels, and guides, whatever we need. We'll tell him we are very apprehensive about doing this ourselves because we've heard so much about highwaymen and kidnappers. We’ll tell him we know we’re a little skittish or even over-the-top frightened about potential terrorist plots and violence. We’ll say we heard so much about how it is not safe that we would feel much better if we left our safety in his hands. Frederic, you tell him no price is too much for our peace of mind. Tell him that we have talked to the representatives at Abercrombie and Kent's and are not very comfortable or satisfied with their proposed security for the trip. We just have to make Moi feel he has our complete trust. We have to flip him to make him feel we're weak, or stupid, or frightened. Anything to give us the advantage by being under estimated. We'll leave everything up to him. Let him do the scheduling, the whole ball of wax. We want him to salivate. Infer that if everything goes well, that means our recreation as well as our desire to engage in a partnership, that it's not unreasonable for us to pledge as much as 10 million the first year. Tell him we understand we are not the Gates Foundation, but we are flush with cash. It is only a matter of Mr. Papaz wanting to get involved. Tell him, he has your total support; he just has to get mine. Let him know it's really important I feel comfortable on a personal level. That’s why we are asking him to shepherd our activities while in Kenya. Give him a hook. Tell him if everything works out, we want to hire him on a personal service retainer of $250,000 a year. Tell him it cannot appear as a conflict of interest with his people in Kenya. Tell him we don't want to put him in any jeopardy, if he accepts our offer. Make him understand he has to be transparent in all our transactions. Tell him we are very flexible in any sensitive matters as long as we have prior knowledge. Make it ambiguous, the more he reads into it, the greedier he will be. Make him understand we will accept graft as long as our money makes a difference helping the poor in the Central Valley and the Nairobi slums. Tell him we feel the cause always comes first and how we obtain results can be tailored to how things are done in Kenya. Frederic, you're good at this stuff. You will know how to deal with him."

Matt found himself taking the lead. He sensed everyone not only agreed with this plan but deferred to it because of his passion.

Chapter 19

BiBa asked Frederic, "Are we taking too long on this? We've been in here for over 45 minutes. How much longer will we have a cover from their surveillance?"

He replied, "We're fine. Our electronics give us the ability to generate infinite amounts of dialogue. As I explained before, there are thousands of combinations of the five of us talking on thousands of different topics. We are totally insulated from the outside. But just to play it safe, we should tie everything up in the next couple of minutes. Let's get out of here and go for a walk on the High Rail Park. Then we will go over to Chelsea and have something to eat. I'm comfortable with what we have done so let's give it ten more minutes, max. Gisele and I will have a summary of all this for you tomorrow. You all have clean phones, so I will send you text by 10:00 am tomorrow morning. As per our normal protocol, when you're done reading the text, discard the phone. I will send you an itinerary about our travel plans I want to present to Moi."

Looking at Matt and BiBa he said, "The picture-taking safari and all of the national parks make a lot of sense for our cover. Maybe all that shopping in Beverly Hills wasn't such a bad idea. I'll let Moi determine if we vacation before or after we visit with his people. We will let him know that our generosity is incumbent upon us having a hands-on look at some of their outreach programs. I will prepare a list of people and organizations we want to have access with to an unannounced basis. I will specifically tailor our visits to organizations assisting people in the Central Valley and some of the inner-city slums. Getting back to the safari and animal parks, we will ask Moi to help us in outfitting ourselves and hiring some professional photographers to bring along with us. The more dependent he thinks we are on him the bigger edge we have."

They finished their discussions and went back into the other office. The electronic feed to their adversary's audio and visual tracking equipment spliced them back into the office as if they had never left it. Leaving the office, they ventured towards the High Rail Park walking path. They would walk its two-mile path and openly discuss their vacation in East Africa knowing their conversations would be overheard. Gisele felt that showing exuberance for an upcoming safari was normal and therefore should be a major topic on a walk.

By 6:00 pm, Matt and BiBa were back in their home on 15th St. they were standing in the kitchen on the second floor looking through the bay window. BiBa was working over the sink when she noticed two men across the street. She gestured Matt to come over and she gave him a hug.

Outwardly, she said, "Thanks for the great day sweetie." She kissed him on the side of the neck and whispered into his ear. "I've seen those guys before."

"Yeah," he said, "so have I." He started laughing and whispered, "Let's put on a show for them and whoever is listening or watching inside the house."

She immediately leaned forward, projecting her buttocks into his groin and tightened her cheeks. His response was to slowly thrust his penis into her and tightly place his arms around her waist. She grabbed his right hand pulled it up to her breasts and pulled his left hand down placing it on her throbbing vagina. He kissed her on the neck and whispered, "Let's go upstairs."

As they were walking up the stairwell, he said to her, "It's a little chilly. Do you mind if I turn on the heater? I'm sure we can find a way to keep warm."

As he kissed her while walking up the steps he whispered, "They are going to see us no matter what, so be as natural as you can when you get undressed but once we are under the covers let's not let those sons of bitches see anything. Let's drive them fucking crazy."

Chapter 20

In less than two weeks, an express courier arrived at Frederic's office with a preliminary itinerary for the group's African excursion. They would arrive in Nairobi on Thursday the 8th and be taken by limousine to the estate of Finance Minister William Nakruru, a prominent member on the Kenyan National Legislature. Business meetings would be scheduled starting on the ninth. Three activities were planned for the first day. At 12:00 pm, the group would go to a grammar school in the heart of Kibera, the largest slum in Nairobi. The visitation would include interviews with the school's administrators, classroom activities with the children, and a celebratory lunch. The third Precinct School, with a student population of 400 impoverished children of

Kikuyu origin, was partially funded by UNICEF and the William and Flora Packard Foundation. It was held to be the most successful project in Kenya. At 5:00 p.m. an early dinner and reception was scheduled with the Kenyan Youth Alliance at the old Norfork Hotel and Convention Center, which had played a prominent role in British colonial rule. The night would be capped off with drinks at the Hilton Hotel in the central business district of Nairobi. The gathering's guest list included prominent business and political members of Kenya's new professional class.

Matt commented to Frederic, "All the movers and shakers are no doubt Kikuyu and all they want is our money."

Matt only cared about organizational access to penetrate the Mungiki gang and get a read on its activities. The scheduling of events for the first day was a template for the next 5 days in Nairobi. After reading the scheduling of events and meetings, Frederic viewed the itinerary's safari arrangements. Air transportation would be arranged to fly from Nairobi to the famous Governor's Camp on a vintage 1942 DC 3, chartered from Air Kenya. It was the oldest commercial passenger plane in service in the world. The 90 passenger World War II transport would be taken out of commercial service from Air Kenya's fleet and be at the disposal of the Papaz party for the duration of their safari. They would stay in Governor's Camp in luxury tents with a gourmet chef from the Cordon Bleu. Arrangements included private safari guides who acted as security and had total run of the 200,000-acre reserve. Moi's materials suggested if the accommodations were too primitive and did not meet their standard of comfort, they could stay in the main lodge or its attendant villas. That would be determined upon arrival. From there they would travel to Samburu and stay at the reserve's five-star hotel with private guides and a security team for four nights. They would then travel to the Ambosile Reserve at the foot of Mt. Killaminjaro for two more days. Their final destination would be Kilgali in Rwanda to view the mountain gorillas. At the end of the 6-page itinerary were hand-written footnotes written in the margin: "We have a professional security team of 22 people at our disposal, but this is Kenya and I honestly think your concerns about highwaymen and terrorists are valid. We have special concerns about some Somalian terrorists groups. Even with a large security contingent, we suggest we confine your travel arrangements to tourist destinations have the army's support and protection. It is prudent to be conservative and prepared for the worst. Terrorist activities have been on the increase in Kenya for the last six months."

It was clear to Frederic that Moi was chomping at the bit for Papaz's charitable involvement.

Frederic called Moi. "I think Matt will like the effort and intentions of what you have done, but knowing him this will be a starting point. He is more directed by spontaneity and intuition. So much so, that he may think these activities are too structured. He will want to visit and see schools, clinics, cultural projects, whatever makes sense. First-hand knowledge of any project is important to him. He's extremely hands on. But, he thinks more along the lines of surprise visits. He does not want anything prearranged or orchestrated. I am speaking directly for him and say; give us a list of 20 to 30 organizations that you feel are prime targets for our money. We will study them and upon arrival in Kenya, we will ask you to set up visitations. This way there will be no prior communication with the organizations and we will know the exact extent of their activities. This is how Matt conducts business. He calls it, managing by walking around. He has a phrase that he uses in connection with his due diligence. Nothing prearranged except possibilities. That is the cornerstone of his charitable contributions."

Moi was silent. "That's fine Frederic," he said. "It is his way and his money. We will never get his support if I take him to places he does not want to see or take him to meet people he holds as suspicious. That is totally understandable. I will change the business part of the itinerary. I will arrange for you to see organizations, schools, clinics and medical facilities, cultural projects, micro-banks, and religious organizations with only a few hours notice. I don't have total faith in all of the organizations in Nairobi and the Central Valley but where I send you to I stand behind them. If you have organizations, you might want to view, we will be happy to express our opinions on their activities. Now, as far as the safari is concerned Mr. Papaz will have little or no leeway in both Kenya and Rwanda. No matter what I would like him to see or do, security comes first. We have contacts with the army and they will monitor all of the reserves and national parks for us. If there are any dangers, we will change the itinerary. As far as Rwanda is concerned, we will have to send a security force with you, but only at the consent of their military. Frederic, I want to show you my lead on this. I will be coming to Kenya to assist you in any possible way. With me in Kenya, I will feel more confident that everything will go smoothly. It's very obvious we want your support and I will do everything possible to show you that our organization is worthy. I want Mr. Matt to feel comfortable in letting us represent his interests."

It was always interesting to Frederic when people presented themselves as important and indispensable.

Chapter 21

Preparation for Kenya took two weeks. Matt and BiBa were at their physical peaks. Frederick and Gisele orchestrated financial relationships with Kenyan banks and deposited $20 million to show that the Papaz Group was real. José arranged with Malique to have a small security force ready in Kenya upon their arrival.

The group would fly together on British Airways from New York's Kennedy airport to London's Heathrow and stay at the old Savoy Hotel on the strand. A 5-day stopover in London would be a working trip. They would be seen conspicuously at diplomatic charitable functions and upscale haunts on Belgravia Road in the city's West End. From London, they would fly to Milan and stay at Hotel The Gray, which was walking distance to the famous Via Montenapoleone shopping area of Il Quadrilatero della Moda, so they could be seen in the higher end fashion boutiques looking for safari clothes and equipment. For the last leg of their trip, they would charter a Gulfstream 5 and fly directly into Nairobi.

Frederic had planned the trip not only to position the Matt party in civic organizations doing charitable work in Nairobi, but as a precursor to their arrival, he wanted to display their wealth and opulent lifestyle. He knew his Kenyan friends would have continual surveillance on them as they moved from New York to East Africa.

Malique would arrive in Nairobi two days before the group, with some Arab and Turkish mercenaries he had worked with in the shadowy operations in South Africa the year before.

At his estate thirty miles outside the city Kenya's finance minister, William Nakruru, would be entertaining and hosting Matt, BiBa, Frederic, Gisele, and José. Malique and his men would stay at the old Mount Kenya Safari club in Nairobi proper.

Posing as merchants on transit to Mombassa, Malique's contingency of himself and nine seasoned soldiers would have two days for surveillance and logistical preparation before the arrival of Matt's party. They would be at Nairobi's Jomo Kenyatta International Airport two hours before Matt's group to take control and command of the environments inside and outside of the terminal. They would set up a protective perimeter for their five associates from their point of disembarkation from the plane to the

Nakruru's estate. Electronic devices at five checkpoints, four miles apart will monitor the twenty plus mile route from the airport to the Minister's compound. Kenyan security forces hired by intermediaries of the Tijuana Cartel will oversee the security operation. Nothing will be left to chance.

As for the Papaz Group's protection while in Nairobi, Malique would dispatch his men to be stationed at meeting places that Moi had scheduled with the concurrence of Matt and Frederic. Every movement of the group would be foreknown to Malique and Jose.

Since he is unaware of the redundancy of Malique and his men, Moi will provide the Papaz Group with a force of four armed guards. The disposition of Moi's forces and their loyalties were unknown.

Gisele's strategy of alive and free, versus death and kidnapping would create a greater long-run value for Matt. His future value would be the major factor for Moi's protecting his American asset. Collecting a few million dollars for Matt in the short run would pale in comparison to millions of dollars of investments Moi and his associates could bleed out of a partnership in the long run. Malique and his men would be in place with the proper military hardware and wait for the eagle to land.

The chartered 20-passenger jet landed at a private terminal in the international airport. Nakruru and a team of customs officers were waiting on the tarmac. Two uniformed agents boarded the plane and asked the crew and Matt's party for their passports and visa documents. Within slightly more than 2-minutes they had finished their business and welcomed the five to Nairobi. It was a long-standing practice in Kenya for high-ranking politicians or powerful businesspeople to show their sway by getting people through customs. It was as if to say we can cut through any formalities. You are special guests in our home. As Matt and BiBa, and Frederic and Gisele, and then lastly José disembarked the plane, Nakruru met them warmly. He was in his early 40's, 5'7" tall, and weighed 240 pounds. His skin tone was deep black, his eyes were yellowish and bloodshot, and he smelled as if he had not bathed in weeks. His wife, Sony, was light-skinned, elegantly tall and had features that were pronouncedly Ethiopian. She wore a traditional African long flowing colorful loose fitting gown with a headscarf to match. He was wearing a black suit that was befitting a man of a sleek stature and his fat body flowed over his belt line. To make him look even worse, his jacket was at least two sizes too small. The suit had concentric rings of white salt under each arm from his body's perspiration. He and his wife were standing next to a security compliment of fifteen men. Three black Cadillac Escalades retrofitted with armor plate were waiting for the party in front of the private terminal.

Matt and BiBa were escorted to the first SUV to ride with Nakruru and his wife. The second SUV took Frederic, Gisele, and José. The third caravan vehicle took Moi and his associates. Accompanying them outside the airport onto the main highway, the three vehicles were flanked by two military jeeps and four motorcyclists. The military security stopping and directing traffic so the Minister and his guests in the SUV's could take the fastest, most expedient manner to the estate.

Chapter 22

Once inside of the SUV, Nakruru spoke in a British accent, "I hope your trip was pleasant. We have many activities planned for you and your friends over the next few days. Of course, we have business, but we have scheduled many other activities as well. My wife and I are most happy you will stay with us on our compound. It is much more pleasant than Nairobi. Our home is a working farm as well as an animal rescue center. I am blessed to have a wife who is a veterinarian. She has used this quite a lot to our advantage setting up programs to protect Kenyan wildlife. My family was very fortunate that after independence we were able to buy this property from the Thompson's estate. My father had worked for them as an overseer of their livestock. It is a complicated story but we were very lucky to have had a white family who was so good to us. My brothers and I were sent to England for our education, and as things progressed during the Mau Mau revolution, the Thompson's set up the transfer of property to my father. This was rather unusual and to this day, it can cause problems for us being seen as too close to the Europeans. Kenya can still be tribal and anti-western, but we're making progress. Enough of our family history. Suffice it to say, we are very fortunate. We will have to talk politics in much more detail later. You must know about our political currents if you are going to be involved in some of our community efforts."

Sony entered the conversation and it became quite obvious she was the consummate politician's wife. "We are most happy you will stay with us. I think you will find my country and fellow countrymen to your liking."

Matt thought to himself, "This must be the most Western family in all of Kenya for her to have a platform of equality."

Their Kenyan counterparts were saying all the right things. It was evident they had hosted many foreigners and played to their vanities.

The drive was uneventful, giving a false sense of security. The caravan of SUVs, flanked by Jeeps and motorcycles, drove north on the main highway for fifteen minutes before turning off on a frontage road that led to the estate. Once the Cadillac trucks left the highway and were on the dirt road the night blackened. The shrubbery and the overhanging trees became denser and covered any light from the moon.

Sony said, "You must forgive us. It is just the end of the rainy season and many of the roads have been washed out, or in our case have many potholes. So please hold on. We will be at the main house of the compound in five minutes."

As they approached, the compound Matt and BiBa noticed how isolated and dark it was and began to feel a little uneasy. They wondered if José, Frederic, and Gisele in the other SUV felt the same way. They pondered the question of where Malique and his men were.

Sony continued to speak, "We are very fortunate to live in such a beautiful place. We are two kilometers from our closest neighbors. Because of some of our animals, the isolation is necessary. It is a very peaceful and quiet life and we are only one half hour from Nairobi."

The caravan pulled off the dirt road onto a two-lane driveway encircling the main living quarters. The ranch style architecture with a veranda going from front to back punctuated with large bay windows and four chimneys for the master suite fireplaces and the three accompanying junior suites. There were also four guesthouses on the property, two barns, and an animal clinic.

Nakruru said, "We can make arrangements for you to stay in the main house or you can stay in the guest houses," pointing to the other SUV with José, Matt, and Giselle, "They can make up their own minds unless you want to make the decision for them."

Still sitting in the vehicle readying to get out, it was evident how elegant the property was. Its grounds were lush with vegetation and beautiful trees surrounding the house.

The driver of the last vehicle, carrying Moi and his associates, opened the door of his Escalade after the security guard who had been sitting shotgun was already outside and signaled that everything was in order and the passengers could exit. The passengers would leave their vehicles from last to first car for security purposes. The Nakruru's had developed a system with the house staff and internal security that their home's front door would not be opened and the security system would not be disarmed until visual identification had been verified. Standing on the driveway, the three parties were now outside the SUVs and were circled by the army ranger squad and the four motorcyclists. The assembled security detail with semi automatic rifles in hand waited for an all clear signal from the house. The protocol was that the door would open after an alarm system rang down from 10 to 1 with lights affixed to the veranda roof, turning on after the signal had gone down to 0. The large double door opened automatically and the security forces shouldered their weapons to escort Nakruru and his guests into the house. That is when all hell broke out.

Gunmen with sniper rifles sitting in the large Mueri trees that hovered over the house opened fire, killing all of the Army unit's task force. The four motorcycle escorts were killed by the drivers of the first SUV with a semi-automatic 9 millimeter they fired just after the first bullet from the trees ripped through the skull of the squad's commander. The driver that had driven the SUV carrying the Nakrurus, Matt and BiBa shouted orders into the house. The lights went on and three more hostage-takers came out to escort the group into the living room. Six snipers, two drivers, and three servants who had worked for the Nakrurus and turned to kidnapping for money had total control of the Matt party, the Nakrurus and Moi and his associates.

The first driver established himself as the ringleader by shooting Moi's three associates in the head without any provocation. In less than a minute, the result was clear. Dead bodies were facedown in pools of blood in the driveway with the kidnappers walking over them tying up their captives to be held in the great house's main room as its limestone fireplace flickered with the devil's light.

Malique and his men were two to three minutes behind, having lost any tactical leverage as soon as the kidnappers and their hostages were inside the house.

Chapter 23

The house was a killing field. Three long time Nakruru servants went rogue and aligned themselves with the kidnappers. Their payment was a small stash of street drugs and a few Kenyan shillings. They collected all of the other members of the compound's staff and killed them in a murderous rage. All three were disoriented and in a violent panic after smoking shabu, a methamphetamine stimulant. The brutal assassination of the other 12 members of the staff took them more than two hours and culminated in a savage act of cannibalism when one of assassins cut out the heart of an elderly groundskeeper and ate it in front of the last four remaining victims. The house servants had worked with their three kidnapper/killers for more than five years. They never saw their betrayal coming.

What made their murders even more hideous was the fact they were killed with machetes and axes in a slow methodical way as if to strike terror in them before they were dismembered and decapitated. The common thread to the murders was that the killers were Masai and the victims were Kikuyu. The living room of the house where the murders took place looked like a scene from a horror movie. The great fireplace with its yellow and blue flames backlit the dismembered body parts lying in pools of blood on the dark hardwood floors. Furniture was broken and thrown throughout the room. The walls were splattered with blood and human excretion from the horrified victims filling the room with stench. Mobike, the lead driver of the first SUV, ordered his men to tie up Matt and the other captives. They all had their hands bound behind their backs and ropes were placed around their necks that acted like a dog's leash. The eight were pushed up the stairs and onto the veranda. As they were, being pulled into the house the sight of the dismembered bodies lying in their own blood looked like a recreation of hell on earth. José began to scream for his life in an attempt to buy time until Malique and his men would arrive. As he screamed and whimpered like a coward, Mobike hit him in the face with the butt end of his semi automatic weapon. Jose went down on one knee and Mobike continued his vicious attack by kicking him in the ribs. When Jose finally rolled over on his back in agony and gasping for air Mobike hovered over him. The large black African released the belt of his trousers and pulled his immense penis out of his pants. He used his left hand and directed his enormous organ at his victim. He urinated upon Jose's face and when he was done, he spat upon him to show his total dominance. With a gun in his right hand, his penis in his left hand and his pants hovering around his ankles, he yelled orders in Masai ordering placement of all men prisoners along the wall and have women brought to him.

BiBa was the closest female hostage. He grabbed her by the rope affixed to her neck and pulled her down into a chair. He again yelling orders in Masai and two men tied her hands to the back of the chair and pulled the rope around her neck into a position that forced her to look straight up to the ceiling.

BiBa was screaming expletives at them; "Fuck you, fuck you, you fucking animals!"

Mobike ripped off her blouse and bra and placed his flaccid 9 inch penis directly into her face and shouted to his men

"After I fuck this white bitch she is yours. Then I will fuck the other white bitch," as he pointed to Gisele. "You can have her too. They will both be yours but don't let them die. These white whores will be useless if they're dead."

He looked at Sony and said, "She is yours if you want to fuck a Kikuyu dog. Kill her when you're done."

He lifted BiBa and the chair she was sitting in into the air and heaved her three feet toward the corner of the room. He pulled her up by the rope around her neck with his right hand and held her as tightly as he could with his left and untied her from the chair.

Standing her up, he pulled off the rest of her clothes and leaned her over a half-broken table.

Jose was screaming, trying to divert Mobike's attention towards him, hopefully creating more time for Malique and his men to intervene.

Frederic and Matt took his cue and began yelling and flailing in an attempt to free themselves and creating more chaos. The yellow and blue fire flickered in the background as Mobike stood over BiBa and tried to penetrate her with his erect penis. She lunged forward and frantically moved her body with such force that she and the table collapsed on the floor, saving herself from Mobike's violation. As he picked her up, flash bombs exploded and within seconds, Malique's men were in the room. In less than a minute, the trained mercenaries had either killed or subdued all their African counterparts. Their interaction prevented any more harm to BiBa and José. They came late to the killing party but were there early enough to prevent any more injury and suffering to their charges.

Three kidnappers were killed and the rest were severely wounded or rendered harmless. Mobike shot in the shoulder collapsed onto the floor. He was lying in his blood, half-naked on the floor, in front of the fireplace and screaming for help.

BiBa was cut loose and her reaction to her freedom was pure rage. Screaming, she picked herself up from the mahogany wood floor and wrapped what was left of her clothes around her body. She ran over to one of Malique's men and pulled his 9-inch military knife from his belt and calmly walked over to Mobike and stood over him. She struck at his penis with the knife and castrated him before anyone could intervene. It happened so fast and there was so much blood shooting up from the groin area of his body no one really knew what happened.

BiBa walked over to the fireplace and put a spade leaning next to the mantle into the fire. In little more than a minute, the metal spade had heated to a deep reddish color and became an instrument of death in her hand. She walked over to the bloody African, wailing in pain, and jammed the spade deep into his loin to cauterize his severed penis. The smell of burning flesh and blood filled the air. She stood over him, looked into his eyes and said, "Fuck you. You black piece of shit."

Jose stepped in, "Don't kill him. We need the bastard. Killing him would be too easy."

Chapter 24

It all happened so fast and unexpectedly that BiBa had free range to fulfill her revenge. Matt's hands were now untied. He ran across the room and grabbed her.

"Are you okay? Are you okay?"

She looked at him and said, "Fuck that asshole!"

The adrenaline level in the room was slowly dissipating and a collective calm started to prevail. José's ribs were broken, his face was battered but his act of faked cowardliness, and the subsequent punishment he took from Mobike created a long enough window for Malique and his men to breach the compound's security. Without the extra two minutes caused by his diversion, the situation would have escalated, rape and mayhem upon the Papaz Group.

BiBa was now in Matt's arms and was coming down from her burst of fury.

José said, "Are you okay?" Shaking his head and smiling he continued, "Maybe a little bit more than you were trained for." He put his arm around her. "There is not one of us who would not have done the exact same thing. You did good! Listen up everybody; we have a few more things to do before we leave the house."

He pulled the blood drenched Mobike up from the floor and placed him into a chair. He then called over to one of his men and whispered an order into his ear. The men ran outside and grabbed a medical kit from one of their vehicles parked in the driveway. José opened the black leather case, pulled out a set of syringes and injected Mobike in the neck. It was a coagulant. He waited 30 seconds after the injection and cut deep into his upper arm with a scalpel he had taken out of the bag. He put the metal blade back into the kit and fumbled around looking for a plastic bag filled with strange looking electronic chips. He pulled something out of the bag and placed it between his thumb and forefinger. Looking like a one-dimensional spider, it was an electronic device the size of a fingernail. He placed the device into the incision in Mobike's upper right shoulder. He closed the hole and placed a large butterfly bandage over it. There was quiet in the room as he finished his task.

He looked up and said, "It's a GPS tracking chip and an explosive device."

The whole time one of his men was videoing the operation.

Malique spoke up before Jose could say another word, "I will explain after we get out of here. We don't have much time. There is a safe house no more than 20 minutes from here. We secured it yesterday."

In an orderly manner, Malique and his men escorted the prisoners out to the driveway and placed them in one of the SUVs. Matt and the rest of the group followed, stepping over dead bodies to get into their waiting vehicles.

After a quick reconnaissance of the compound, the SUVs were ready to go. Matt and his group were placed in one of the Cadillac Escalades that had taken them from the airport to the house. Moi and the Nakrurus were placed in a second Escalade with two of the Arab mercenaries. In the third vehicle were two more mercenaries and the prisoners. A fourth vehicle with two more mercenaries who were explosive experts were left to set up ordinances to level the house. As the first three vehicle drove down the driveway the two explosives experts were seen carrying boxes of plastic C4 into the main house of the compound. It was placed in a configuration that would implode the house and its contents.

Kenyan police and their forensic scientists were not up to modern standards so it would be beyond their capabilities to determine accurately what took place.

While the caravan proceeded to the safe house, Malique placed a call on his cell to José Guzmán.

He only spoke three words, "It is done." He put his arm out of the window of his vehicle to stop the other SUVs. Once all three had come to a complete stop he walked over and gave the phone to Matt.

"Someone wants to talk to you." The conversation lasted three to four minutes and Matt concluded by saying, "You've been involved the whole time, haven't you? Thank you my friend. I will always be indebted to you."

Chapter 25

The three SUV's drove under the partially cloud covered skies until they arrived at the main highway. They waited fifteen minutes under radio silence for the remaining SUV that was being used in the demolition of the Nakruru's compound. Preparing the house and setting all the explosive devices would take seven minutes. Detonation of the C4 and travel time to the rendezvous point was another six to seven minutes.

When the skies lit up in a yellowish thunderous flash the group knew the other SUV would be there momentarily and it would be no more than a few minutes before they would be back on the main highway driving to the safe house. The fourth SUV, traveling at 20 miles an hour, flashed its bright lights at the three-parked vehicles and proceeded on to the asphalt highway; it would lead the caravan to the abandoned farm. For the next twenty minutes, all the vehicles ran silent. Their destination was a farmhouse on an abandoned dairy that had been out of operation for more than ten years. Three members of Malique's squad had been left on the property the day before to secure and retrofit the main house with communication equipment and secure a defendable perimeter. Just before the SUVs arrived at the farmhouse, Moi broke his silence.

He spoke to Nakruru in Kikuyu. "This is not an accident that we've been segregated from the others. They must think we are part of the kidnapping plan. After that remark by Matt's girlfriend, about you black bastard, all I think about is their hatred for us and that they think we set them up."

Nakruru nodded his head in affirmation. "There is nothing we can do. They have all the guns, they have all the men, and we saw what they did inside of the house. They could have captured those people. They did not have to kill them. We are their hostages and I don't know where we go from here. I am the Minister of Finance, and they kidnapped me? Who are these people? I thought you and the Alliance had a handle on them. What have you done to me? I would not have been involved in this unless I thought they would be benefactors to the poor. They are killers and you implicated us in this. You are responsible and I will not forget that. When we get out of here you will pay with your life."

Moi reacted, "Don't make threats my friend. I am not involved in this. Hold your tongue or I will kill you before the Americans do. If they wanted us dead, we would be. We need to stay strong. Acting like a coward and looking in the wrong direction only makes me question your role in all of this. They put us together for a reason and it looks like if they were looking for a weak link, they found it. Now shut up."

All of the passengers in the SUVs had exited and were standing in front of the dilapidated farmhouse.

Nakruru started screaming, "You can't do this to me. Who do you think you are? I demand to talk to General Olanga. Give me your cell."

Jose walked over to him and said, "You are in no position to make demands."

Malique gave a hand signal. Three mercenaries moved encircling Moi, Nakruru, and his wife. "Take them to the barn, gag them and tie them up. You have two options."

Moi started screaming, "We had nothing to do with this! Can't you see we had nothing to do with this? What are you going to do? It wasn't us!"

José watched for a moment and said, "My orders are to place a chip in each one of your arms. Malique says that he gave you two options, I will speak for him. That means the easy way or my way."

He walked into the barn to find a place to bring the three prisoners. He ordered the guards to bring them in one by one. Moi was first.

With a look of pure disgust and hate in his eyes, Jose said, "Give me your arm."

Moi acquiesced not wanting to be hurt and lifted up his right arm. In a matter of 4-minutes, Jose injected him with a local anesthetic and implanted the device.

The Nakruru's were next. Looking at the three after finishing the procedure José said, "My orders were to place the spiders in your arms. If and when, we see you are not involved in this, I will take them out. If we find you're behind any of this, I will use them. We gave you two choices, the hard way or the easy way. We are going to find out what your involvement is. It is just a matter of time. How we do, it is up to you. If you are not part of this then it will be the easy way."

He looked deep into Nakruru's eyes, "We will rebuild your house and oversee a security detail that will protect you. If you are part of this, then you are a dead man. That goes for the two of you too." he added as he looked at Nakruru's wife and Moi.

Upon a signal from Jose, Malique had his men bring Mobike into the barn and placed him on a stool that stood almost at the midpoint of the room. He placed a large plastic bag over the top part of his body but allowed his head to be free. It covered him from his neck down to the middle of his waist. Malique slapped him in the face and then threw water upon him to get his attention. He was going in and out of consciousness and for the last moment of his life Malique wanted him to realize his fate. José ordered one of the mercenaries to video what was to take place.

Jose took control of the interrogation, looked at Mobike, and said, "I'm going to ask you once. Do you hear me?"

Mobike ever so slightly nodded his head.

"Like I said, I am going to ask you once. Who paid you and how much, you miserable fuck?"

The video was on. José said, "You have ten seconds to determine your fate."

Without hesitation the cowardly Mobike blurted out, "It was the Alliance. It was the Alliance. They gave me 50,000 shillings."

Moi yelled, "You liar! There is no truth in that. They would never do this to me. Who put you up to this?"

Before another word was spoken, José pulled out his cell phone, dialed four numbers, and then hit pound. The explosives in Mobike's arm detonated and his body burst into pieces in the plastic bag as his head toppled from his fragmented trunk. Moi buckled at the knees and shit himself.

The prisoners screamed at the horror they witnessed. Malique and José could not speak Kikuyu or Masai. They had to calm down Moi and the Nakruru so one of them could be used as a translator.

"Listen up," José said, pointing to Moi. "Tell them that I will kill them slowly and that Mobike was lucky to be blown to shit compared to what I will do to them if they don't follow my orders. Don't fuck with me. Just do what the fuck I say. Tell them that only two of them will live and that I don't care who dies. Only two of them will survive. They don't have to know why. They don't have to know squat."

Moi spoke rapidly in a loud deep voice to the four with his arms flailing in the air. Their physical statures started to shrink as he told them of their plight. The expression on the prisoner's faces was proof enough for Jose to know he translated every word to the letter and the prisoners knew their fates were sealed. They knew they would all die. José wanted them to suffer as much as possible. The Masai gangsters weren't stupid in the ways of the streets where life was almost valueless. They weren't the kind of people who you could turn into assets and they had already chosen sides. Their loyalties had been established when they signed up with Mobike and were part of the plot to kidnap and torture the Papaz Group. A torturous death leading to a final bullet was their destiny. Creating a situation where their humanity would be stripped and unimaginable pain would be inflicted before their deaths seemed reasonable to Jose. The Masai tried to do the exact same thing to them when they were in control just an hour earlier.

José and Malique would brief everyone before they left the safe house. Matt and Frederic were completely comfortable in leaving everything in Jose's hands. They deferred to their colleague.

Malique initiated the first move by walking over to Moi and the Nakrurus and handing each one of them a stainless steel Rolex watch.

"Give me your watches," he said to both men. Turning to Sony he continued, "Your watch and your bracelet."

Now, pointing to the Rolexes he continued "Put these on. They will be our eyes and our ears. They have sophisticated electronics embedded in them. A camera and a microphone will monitor your every move. If you try to disable them or take them off, the spider in your arm will detonate. You will sleep in them, bathe in them, and take a shit in them. You will do everything in them. If anything disrupts their signal or the contact with your wrist, you will die. If you try to take the watch off, you're dead. When I find out which one of you set us up I will kill you. It doesn't matter where you are or what you are doing; you can't find a safe place in the world. The second that contact is broken, you are dead. If you cut off your arm, the contact will register a stoppage of the blood supply and you are dead. The watches have a 30-day battery life for the camera and the microphone. When the battery dies, the spider detonates. That means you have a minimum of 27 days and a max of 33 days for us to find out who's behind this. If we are no further along in finding out who set us up, then, when the batteries die, you die. Maybe that will be an incentive for you to help us find the fuck who is behind the kidnapping. One way or another we will find out who hired you and why and who your associates are. If you are alive or dead it is up to you."

Malique continued, "We will stay here until tomorrow morning." He grabbed Nakruru, "Then you're going to call the president and tell exactly what I tell you to tell him. You're going to have him get the Army out here. Outside of Nairobi there are no functioning police departments so for all intents and purposes, it's the Army. You're the Finance Minister, you're his friend, and he will send the Army. When you talk to him let him know that you got away, but tell him how afraid you still are and that we are with you. Implore him to get his men out here as soon as possible. Tell them that we are in bad shape. Tell him that we all escaped from the kidnapper. Mention Mobike's name so they can start looking for him as soon as possible. Tell him that you will give his men all the details, everything they need, but the sooner they get here the better the chance to catch Mobike. Tell him that your house was destroyed and we were brought here. You have to convince him that we were spared and Mobike turned on his own people for more money. Tell him that Matt gave Mobike $1 million and safe passage to Tanzania for our freedom. It will be simple. Mobike kidnapped us acting under someone's orders. You do not know who orchestrated this but we have to find out who is behind this because he implied that even the president isn't safe. Tell him maybe he's next. You just don't know how far this goes. Before we make the call, we will have Matt's plane leave Kenyatta international Airport with three African passengers. One will look like Mobike. Airport officials won't check the plane, it's leaving. A flight plan will be submitted for Arusha. Tanzania has no extradition treaties with Kenya so it will make sense that Mobike would take haven there. We will have it all worked out by tomorrow morning. You're not going to say it specifically but you are going to infer that the kidnappers targeted you, not us. That will make the president buy into the fact that he is open to major damage from somebody. Tell them the five of us were roughed up but we are okay, thanks to you buying Mobike off, even though it was Matt's money. After you make the phone call, the Special Forces will be here in no more than 30 minutes. That will give us time to kill these miserable Masai and make it look like Mobike did it just before he left. The only reason he brought us to this farm, as far as you can tell, is that there was supposed to be some type of prisoner exchange with whoever hired Mobike. You saved us all by making us more valuable to him by accepting Matt's offer over whoever hired him. You will tell the Special Forces that Mobike killed all of his men he brought with him from the compound. When we leave here, the Army will find six corpses in the driveway. Make it sound like two other men came, picked him up, and took him to the airport. Matt will tell the President's men he placed $1 million in the Swiss bank account under Mobike's name and provided all of the transactional information they require. Suggest they immediately contact Interpol. When Matt is interrogated, he will say he's willing to place a $1 million reward for Mobike and whoever's behind this. We will work all this out between now and tomorrow morning. It's your life; you have ten hours to get it right. I want you to listen very carefully. Me and my men will be here on the farm when the military get here. Understand me, make no mistake about it, we have the manpower and the assets for command-and-control in any situation. We know tactically what the Special Forces will do when they get here. The US army wrote the book for the

Kenyan military on how to deal with kidnapping so we know every move they will make. If something goes wrong, you will not make it out of here alive. There's nothing you can do but follow my orders. Tomorrow morning will come soon enough. You have work to do.

The next morning at 8 o'clock, Malique handed Nakruru a cell phone and told him to look at the screen. It was a picture of his mother and his children. They all had butterfly bandages on their arms. Sony screamed. Malique took the phone from the trembling Nakruru, pushed the power button, and gave it to Moi. It was a picture of his twin boys with butterfly bandages. Each one had a beige color bandage on the upper part of his right arm. He looked at both men and said, "You know what we are capable of. Don't fuck with us."

Malique walked up to Jose and put his arms around his shoulders.

"We are out of here." He looked at Matt and Frederic and said, "We'll talk soon. José has everything under control. We will be in the background until the Army leaves. Don't worry. It is what it is."

Looking at Gisele, he smiled. "I will always be at your back. There's no time to be sentimental but it's a pleasure to be in the same operation with you."

He looked at all of them and said, "I have a feeling this is just the beginning. We will be seeing a lot of each other."

Just before he got to the door, he looked at BiBa. "Sorry you had such a close call. This is not the way it's supposed to happen. This close call stuff is supposed to be for the movies. I know you've been through hell. Me telling you that I have your back isn't very reassuring after what that animal tried to do to you, but I do have your back. I'm sorry we failed you and that animal got as far as he did. No one should have gone through what happened to you. I know this doesn't make it any better but this stuff is not an exact science. All we can do is react and we were two minutes behind. That will never happen again. Knowing what you went through and how you handled yourself, I am proud to stand by you. You are awesome."

Malique and his mercenaries gathered the Masai and headed out the door. As soon as they exited the farmhouse and were in the driveway, Matt and the others heard four gunshots. In less than a minute, they saw flashing lights coming through the front windows and heard two thunderous explosions. Within two minutes of the blasts, the sound of truck tires passing from a concrete driveway to road, dissipated into silence. The death of four men, two explosions obliterating two Cadillac Escalades and ten of Malique's men hiding in the dense foliage of an abandoned dairy were the precursors to Nakruru telling his story to the Kenyan Special Forces.

Chapter 26

José gave Nakruru the phone. He immediately placed a call to William Kabiba, the Kenyan president, a close friend and political ally. Within 30-minutes, two squads of elite Special Forces arrived at the farmhouse. Malique had described their protocol perfectly. The search of the house, the interrogations, and the forensic discoveries, all played out.

As per script, Nakruru detailed the kidnapping, execution of Mobike's Masai gangsters and Mobike's payment acceptance for their freedom. He laid out how Matt's money and corporate jet trumped what Mobike was going to be compensated for by his employer's but he would not divulge any names. It was a simple business decision. He received twice the money from Matt and a guarantee of safe passage to

Tanzania. His disloyalty and greed were the key to everyone's freedom. The interrogation of Matt and his associates followed. At times, they were interrogated individually, there were group interrogations, but they all held to the same story. There was no breaking in the ranks. After two hours, a call was placed to Kabiba. Plans were put into motion to escort all the captives back to Nairobi. They would stay at the Hilton Hotel in Nairobi Center where international dignitaries have been housed and protected for years. Security procedures were already in place at the hotel. The federal government had standing orders for the total usage of the 11th floor.

Two large military vehicles and Special Forces escorts drove through the still of the morning from the desolate farm region to the city. It took 45 minutes to reach the hotel. Once inside of the lobby, Jose gestured to Moi and the Nakrurus that his eyes were on them at all times. He pointed to his watch. He intentionally addressed them in a loud voice, so he would be overheard by front desk people and their military escort. He thanked the Nakrurus for their bravery and for saving his life. They were escorted to the 11th floor on private elevators. Once inside of their suites, security teams were stationed in the hallway in front of each door. An army detail was placed in the lobby at the elevator bank as well as two men stationed at the elevator door on the 11th floor. All exits, dumbwaiters, fire escapes, and any entrances to the higher floors of the hotel were secured by the military. The hotel was on the highest alert.

Inside of the suite, Matt hugged BiBa and asked, "Are you all right? I'm so sorry! Look, I don't know what to say. I am really sorry I brought you into all of this."

She squeezed him and pulled back. "Don't worry, I only have one regret," she said softly.

He was stunned as she continued, because she displayed no signs of emotion. "Yeah, only one regret. I should have been the one with the cell phone in my hand. I wish I had pushed on those fucking keys and killed that black bastard myself!"

Matt let her continue, "Who are these people? They're like animals. He wanted to violate everything I stood for and rape me. He and his men wanted to kill innocent people and be praised like Gods for attacking white people. How could they think they had the right? I am sure what makes it so bad is how self-righteous that piece of shit was, and he thought it was his right to do that to me. Yeah, I'll be okay. Just dreaming about getting the rest of these guys and whoever set us up will get me through it. I didn't really understand what you went through in South Africa. I guess you felt pretty much like I feel now. The problem is I am also ashamed. I feel totally violated and anger doesn't describe how pissed I am. What makes it worse is that in some perverse way I kind of liked it. I mean it makes me feel powerful that I know I can get these bastards. I am sure I am not clear, but you understand. It is as if I lived the good life and somebody tried to take it from me. All this stuff is so unfamiliar to my world. Is it their hate, their jealousy, that fucking racism? You know how much they hate white people. It could even be their greed, I really don't understand. I didn't do anything to them. It is so personal to them and I did not do a thing. None of it makes sense to me. It's not part of my world. I am so pissed. I am so thankful for all I have and how hard I work for it. I've been taught to do the right thing and be humble and all those good things for other people. This guy wanted to violate me and did not even feel anything except self righteousness. He wanted to rape and dominate a white woman just because he feels he's entitled to it. Screw him. Screw them all. It is so perverse. I can't believe it. I want to say poor me because I'm a woman. Deep down inside me I feel he came after me because it is some kind of gender thing. I'm really fighting that. I didn't castrate him because he's black and I am white or because he is male and I am female. I think I did it because of who I am. It's not gender rage, it is my personality. If a woman had tried to violate me, I would've castrated her and hated her just as much. This is a lot for me to figure out. You know, we've never talked about it but I am sure this is what you went through. I don't think you're over it yet and it's been months. I'm okay for right now, just give me some space. I need my rage! Matt you know what I'm glad about? I am glad I am who I am and screw them. I am not ashamed about what I did. I just have some real mixed feelings of how I did it and why. But it felt good."

He listened with empathy. "I understand," he said. "I feel the exact same way. But I sure as hell could not have expressed it so clearly. My problem is that I need the bad guys to be in the game. I need them to feel alive. I think that is why I wanted to come to Kenya. Look at our lives. We have so much and most of these people have nothing. I hate when people take advantage of the weak. I need to hate these assholes to feel alive. I never talked about this stuff because I felt nobody would understand. It looks like you are at the same place I am. You did not push me when I came back from Cape Town. I had my ups and downs and still do, that's for sure. So if you want me to leave you alone, if you want me to hold your hand, anything you want me to do I am here. Believe me, I understand."

She looked at him and said, "There is no way I am going to let them win. There is no way those bastards will to change who I am. I love who I am and I love you."

She started to take her clothes off as she walked towards the master bedroom suite.

"Take a shower with me," she said. "I don't want to be alone for one second. Hold me and make love to me all night."

Chapter 27

Poolside on the fourth floor of the hotel Matt ordered breakfast for everyone, including Moi and the Nakrurus, for 10:30 am. It was summer. By the time everyone arrived, it was already uncomfortable. The humidity was high because of thunderclouds gathering overhead. It was 85°.

Frederic ordered drinks. They were very much like Tequila Sunrises. As the eight sat under a cabana overlooking the pool, Matt told everyone he had decided they would stay in Nairobi and pursue their goal of partnering up with an NGO or community active organization to help the poor.

"What happened last night shouldn't be a deterrent," he said. "We won't let the bad guys push us around."

He looked at Moi and the Nakrurus. "It's pretty clear what happened last night was because of you guys not us. So, I made up my mind we will stay here. You put us right in the middle of the whole thing. We will need help getting proper security from now on. I personally feel funny about having my own bodyguards, but I can't see any way around it. I think they are a necessity," looking directly at Nakruru.

Everyone at the table knew that the conversation was being listened to either by the government or by whoever was behind the kidnapping. Their surveillance was taken as a given.

Matt continued, "It is important that we act normal and don't change anything regarding how we do business. It would put us in a position of weakness and affect our abilities to get involved with the right organizations. I don't think whoever came after us last night will stop pursuing you guys," pointing across the table at the three Africans. "So we will do just what we planned on doing."

Speaking directly to Nakruru, he requested, "Please ask the president for help with our security. I feel more comfortable with a military escort than a private bodyguard. Hell, the more the better, I don't know what you are going to do, but I'm sure you're already working on it. As far as I am concerned, once we are done with our business here in Kenya, Rwanda is out. I don't mind visiting some reserves here if things cool down and the military can guarantee our safety. We will work on the park stuff later. My major concern right now is how we get on track and create relationships that will give us the ability to put our money to work and help these people. I'll let you guys, that includes Frederic, set all this stuff up. Let's just chill out today. We can get started tomorrow morning."

He finished up by saying, "There is something I would like to do and maybe some of you might want to come along. There is a national park right outside the city limits. I'd like to go and see the animals if we can work it out for this afternoon."

Frederic said, "William," referring to Nakruru by his first name, "I understand that there is a fine Italian restaurant called Tratoria Luigi, and it is only a couple blocks from here. Last night I took the liberty of having the front desk make reservations, so whatever you have planned for us put it on hold. I don't think Gisele and I are up for any entertainment after last night. I guess the restaurant is walking distance from the hotel. That is about as bold as I feel right now. Obviously, if you and your wife feel safe enough and would like to come with us, you are welcome. Martin of course you are invited. I think we should try to act as normal as possible. We should be seen outside the hotel as if nothing happened. I have no doubt, what took place last night is not a common occurrence. I have no clue on how hard it was on you and what the hell you're supposed to do about it. For us, we want to get back to normal as soon as possible. But as Matt said, we really would like help from the military for our security as long as we are here. If things change and we find out the kidnappers came after us and not you, then of course our position in partnering up with any of your organizations will change dramatically. If someone is trying to kill us, we sure as hell don't want to be here. I haven't talked to Matt about this and I shouldn't speak for José either, but I think whoever those guys were, they came after the three of you. I'm sure you and your wife and Moi will be conferring with the president's men, and the military. If I were you," looking at Nakruru, "I would be talking to the president himself. If there's anything we can add to the conversation and help, we certainly will. I went over what happened a million times in my head. I don't think I slept twenty minutes."

Still playing along with the surveillance, Frederic continued, "I want to thank the three of you because I know I wouldn't be alive if you hadn't negotiated with those people. I don't know if they're terrorists or if they are run of the mill kidnappers. All I know is you saved our lives by getting Mobike to accept our offer. I don't want to overstep my bounds and tell you something you already know, but if it weren't for our money, we would all be dead right now. I guess what I'm trying to say is that we are all in this together. I am not familiar with how things work here in Kenya. I'm sure that trying to kidnap a government Minister doesn't happen every day. There has to be a traitor among your people. The sooner you get to the bottom of this the better we will feel about our role around here. We have a stupid saying in America, the clock is ticking."

He looked directly at Nakruru's Rolex watch to make his point. "I've always been known for my candor. We don't have an infinite amount of time to deal with this situation. Not clearing this up endangers our participation in any charitable activities. It is obvious that we don't want to get killed over something that does not involve us. We all feel part of this situation because of what happened. No one wants any more senseless killings. None of us wants that. We want no part of this and will not be sucked into it. Understand that the clock is ticking. This has to be cleared up soon or we are out of here. We will just get on our plane and get the hell out of East Africa unless we have some immediate results. To facilitate a fact-finding about what actually went on our resources are at your disposal. I am telling you in no uncertain terms that you had better have some answers. I know that what you went through last night was just as bad for you as it was for us. It's gotta seem more important to you. They came directly after you in your own house. I can't imagine what you are going through right now. Your lives are in jeopardy. That clock is ticking. You live in this place. We are ancillary to all of this, but that doesn't mean they didn't try to kill us. Hell, we can leave any time we want. If we stay, we should at least have some say in what we do from this point. Like I said, they tried to kill us too."

Whoever was listening to the conversation was getting a working picture. They would conclude that the Papaz Group would continue their efforts to help community-based organizations and what they had been through was not enough deterrent to send them packing. They would also conclude that the Papaz Group had bought into the notion that the kidnapping attempt was not perpetrated upon them but it was directed at Moi or the Nakrurus or all three. This picture plus the military security they requested would hide their intentions and give them leverage to move about Nairobi. The ball was now in the court of their adversaries. The Papaz Group had not yet taken its best shot. Now it was time to go on the offensive.

Chapter 28

Moi left the table first. As soon as he arose, an army escort greeted him.

Sony was sitting there having trouble holding it together. A picture of her children shown to her by Malique was haunting her. He pointed to the picture and his watch. Her anger was at a fever pitch and she was ready to explode.

She started to say something and her husband grabbed her as he stood up and said, "We must be going my dear. Nothing you can say can make things any better. We just have to work through this and prove our resolve to God. You have had no sleep. Would you like to go back to the room for a while before I go over to my office?"

She had to hold her tongue. Her maternal instincts only allowed her to focus on her children and they were in jeopardy. She could only think about how the Americans had violated her. "Who were these people who had placed a bomb in her and her children's arms and threatened to kill her babies," she said to herself.

Almost blinded by her rage, she had to keep it together. If not her, whole world would be gone in an instant. The image of Mobike would haunt her but she was outraged by aftermath of the kidnappings.

As they were leaving, Nakruru said to her so everyone could hear, "The sooner we clear up this matter the sooner we will get back our lives."

He looked at the others at the table. "It is hard not knowing why someone is doing this to us. I have to get all this cleared up. I hope you trust me when I say your being in jeopardy is not because of anything my wife and I have done. I am but a mere government Minister. There must be some mistake. Why would someone want to kidnap, not only my wife and I, but all of you as well. It doesn't make any sense. You are foreigners and this is Kenya. It is a hard place to understand and its ways can be harsh. Sometimes we revert to old tribal hatreds and the ways of the past but this does not make sense to me. I am not sure how or why this happened, but this will be resolved."

He tried to obfuscate his every word and plead his case not to take the lives of his family.

Looking directly at José, Frederic, and Matt Nakruru said, “Gentlemen, we are all being threatened by someone. If it takes my last breath I will find out who."

Frederic responded, "We know the dangers that confront you. We saw them last night. We saw the arbitrary killings. We saw what they did to your house. They are animals and none of us will ever forget it. We will do the best we can in finding the truth of who is behind this. Kenya obviously is not our home so we are limited. We know our money can be of great benefit, not just, because it saved our own lives, but it can help your country. You bought our freedom with it. It was your idea to place a $1 million reward for any information and the arrest of those responsible. It was our money that you put out there and that is fine. We will let our money work for you. We personally will work with you and whoever your president has overseeing this affair, but we need to see results. In the United States, people we have relationships with are treated very generously. If people are not with us or viewed as threats then we do everything in our power to eliminate them. This is just business, good guys, bad guys. We saw how you reacted and protected us last night. We saw how you addressed the common threat to all of us and this will not be forgotten. Always I have been known to be upfront, but I have a problem. So I will express it. We know that you are with us. If people that are close to you are not, then what do we do?"

Nakruru wondered if he was referring to Moi. Whoever is behind the treachery will come to the light sooner rather than later.

"We are committed to helping you find the truth. We have resources beyond your imagination to get the truth about these people. The first thing we deal with is safety. Like I said, I am always up front. Our safety comes first. I don't want our safety and that of your family's to be mutually exclusive. We want to help Kenya and need you with us. I hope I haven't been too frank but it's better for me to be honest. We will be at your side as long as we know you or no one near you is involved. We will be the best friend you have ever had or your worst enemy."

Whoever was listening heard the words of an angry man who wanted to stay in Africa if possible. The Nakrurus got up from the table. Sony was composed as best a woman could be with her children's lives in jeopardy.

William said, "I understand completely. If we got you in this position, I hope you understand it wasn't intentional. You are innocent bystanders and I wish I had control over the situation, but obviously I don't."

He started to stand up for himself, "And to be frank, my family comes first to me. It is clear someone is after my wife and me and maybe even our children. Whatever I have to do to correct this, I will. I appreciate your offer of help and if needed will lean on your resources in dealing with this situation. Gentlemen, you can see what this has done to my wife. We must leave now. You're right about tonight. My wife needs rest and to be honest I've lost everything I have. Going out tonight and for the foreseeable future is out of the question until we find out who is behind this. There is nothing my wife and I can do until this is cleared up. I just want to protect my wife and children. I will get to the bottom of this. I'll call tomorrow. My staff will set up some meetings for you. Right now I have to attend to protecting my family."

A detail of four uniformed guards met the Nakrurus at the elevator and escorted William across the street from the Hilton Hotel complex to his office while his wife went back to their room. She would try to compose herself and deal with the ominous threat to her children.

Chapter 29

Gisele leaned across the table to talk to BiBa. "Everything happened so fast," she said, "We got rushed to our rooms yesterday and Frederic suggested I talk to you in the morning. I left a message and when you didn't get back to me, I thought I had better give you some privacy. I didn't get a chance to talk you. How are you doing?"

She was conscious about the fact they were being listened to by the kidnappers or some government agents. "Both Frederic and I are worried.

He said you looked like you were in good hands with Matt.

"Talk to her tomorrow morning was his way of saying keep out of it. Sorry I waited so long. Really, how are you doing?"

The conversation had to go around the fact she was almost raped. Knowing they were being listened to limited the scope of what could be said. BiBa understood.

"I'm fine. Thanks for the call but I wasn't up for it. Asking about how I am doing makes me feel better. It's all right. I think we would all like to forget what we went through, but shit happens. How are you doing?" BiBa said.

Gisele responded, "Oh, I will be all right. Thanks for the thought. It's weird, we were all in the same situation and none of us is any worse for the wear physically, but I feel like I was emotionally high jacked. I've got Frederic and you've got Matt, we can't ask for more, but it is hard to understand those poor Nakrurus. They lost everything. Moi just got roughed up a little. Considering everything we went through, we're lucky. Let me change the subject for a minute. We wouldn't mind going out later. How about you guys?"

BiBa tried to make a wise crack. "There's not much shopping here in Nairobi, so if you are talking about going to the animal park it doesn't sound bad at all. I want to do it later in the afternoon."

She looked across the table at Matt, "Well, are you up to it?"

Frederic felt the vibration of his iPhone in his pocket. He pulled it out and looked at the LCD screen. He had received an e-mail on his phone. The way the electronics had been reconfigured, the phone was clean (no outside ability to eavesdrop on the conversation). He hit the envelope icon and an e-mail appeared in his Gmail account.

The e-mail subject box said, "Chinese satellite surveillance stopped: 11:45 am."

He excused himself and said he would be back in a minute. Walking over to the pool deck on the other side of the patio overlooking the city and pool, he pulled up a lounge chair and sat under an umbrella. It took a few minutes to read the e-mail. He walked back to the table.

"We're clear; there is no surveillance out here. The Chinese satellites stopped tracking us and there appears to be no more electronic eaves dropping here at the hotel. Our Intel shows we might be followed, but for whatever reasons, whoever was behind yesterday is backing off electronically. As we speak there seems to be a modest Chinese interest in us. We don't know why. They can be paying a middleman for somebody to collect intelligence on us or following us for some unknown reason. We don't have a clue. There are people trying to follow us but Malique has our backs. There is lots of chatter out there about us and the Chinese. The rooms upstairs were just scanned and they are clean. We can talk here or go up there."

Everyone decided they should stay poolside.

"Whoever is behind this is probably backing off because they think we are real in terms of being philanthropists. It's our best estimate that they have no clue to our objectives. There is a real important second point to the e-mail. Moi is our guy. Later today, they will send me all the Intel but he is the person behind all this. The trail leads from New York all the way here. It is conclusive and irrefutable. We have to determine when we take him out. It is probably not my position to ask this," as he looked directly across the table. "BiBa, I would have no problem if you want to do-it-yourself. Do you want any part of this?"

Everyone at the table was quiet waiting for her response.

Intuitively she said, "Nah, after calming down last night with a little help from my shrink, the acclaimed Dr. Matt Papaz, I ratcheted down enough to understand that is not what I do. I don't have to kill the son of a bitch. But I will not lose one second of sleep when he's dead. I am sure there will be other situations you guys get me into where I can display my rage and anger. I have a feeling that getting into trouble is just part of the game. Like I said, I don't have to kill him. I just want him dead. Cutting off someone's dick and shoving a red-hot spade into his crotch is enough for me right now." She laughed, "It wouldn't be so funny if it didn't actually happen."

Everyone felt relieved. BiBa acting out her rage verbally because of the personal violation was part of a healing process. Knowing when to stop and not pushing herself to a point, she would regret showed how solid she was emotionally. Anger was a secondary stage of grief but it was absolutely necessary to move on to stages of acceptance. Hopefully, she could get by this tragedy without too much emotional damage. Dr. Matt Papaz, the armchair psychologist, had to throw his opinion into the conversation.

"BiBa, you're much more well-balanced than any of us. Certainly more well balanced than me. I am still not over the stuff that happened to me in South Africa and it has been months. You're like a rock and that's good, but you don't have to be. What we're trying to do here can put all of us in harm's way. Bad shit can happen again and probably will. That's just part of the deal. BiBa I am so proud of you."

Frederic cut in to finish talking about the rest of the e-mail. "After taking care of Moi, we are going to heavily invest here in Kenya. The Chinese and their partners from Zimbabwe are putting a lot of money into mining. Maybe they think our presence here threatens them somehow. I don't know. Our intel pretty much followed what you guys had developed," looking at Matt and BiBa. "Your analysis is spot on about heavy metals, rare earth metals, and diamonds, so I think they are behind this and we should compete with them. We're going to buy as much undeveloped property and farms in the Central Valley as possible. Our intelligence suggests the geologic makeup of the area is consistent with large minerals deposits. I've talked to our Mexican friends and they've committed $500 million to this project. After getting them onboard, it was easy to get Kasogi and his associates to commit to another $1,500,000,000. As per our way of doing business, I committed us to $400 million to make sure we have skin in the game. If we need more contributions in the future, it will not be a problem. I want us to go after the Chinese. Everyone agreed without a question or an objection. The first thing we have to do is smooth things over with Nakruru. We have to bring him onboard. We will tell him as soon as possible. He has direct access to Kabiba and his cronies. They are all corrupt as hell but I think they would rather do business with us than the Chinese. José, we have to give Nakruru a bone. Now that BiBa doesn't want to kill Moi, I want you to ask Nakruru if he would like to do it, if you think it would not bother him too much. Then maybe even ask his wife if she wants to kill the son of a bitch. She thinks we put her kids in jeopardy. We have to straighten this up and go through them for help with our charitable giving. We have to figure out a way to make them understand we had no alternatives but to suspect them as well as Moi. Does anyone else have a different take on this?"

Gisele said, "This is a lot to digest. Are you sure one e-mail said all of that or did you editorialize a bit? Just kidding. I think, at least for me I need a little more time. Let's take the rest of the day off and go to the reserve Matt mentioned earlier. When we get back later this afternoon, we can figure out what to do. Tomorrow morning if you want, I will have no problem talking to Nakruru's wife. That should give her some time to cool. I will explain we had no choice in what we did. Whoever set this up had to have been either Moi or her and her husband. I'll explain that the chips in her children's arms were not lethal. They were just GPS systems like the ones for cats and dogs. I will tell her that what we placed under her skin was not the same device we put into Mobike. We put the devices in her arm with the least possible amount of pain and it was not an explosive device. We would not kill women and children. I will tell her we know this doesn't make up for the terror her kids were put through and the unimaginable pain as a mother she must have gone through. I'll let her know the kids were always safe, even if we thought she and her husband were responsible for our kidnapping."

Jose shook his head and said, "Yah, they would have just been parentless. I am glad I am not the one talking to her."

Gisele continued, "I'll try to convey that we're not animals. We had to do something to protect ourselves, even if that meant putting them in a position of threatening them and their kids."

Everyone looked at her as if to say Gisele, there's got to be a better way to express this to a woman who would probably cut your heart out with a dull knife.

Chapter 30

The next morning Gisele reached out to Sony. She placed a call at 8 am to the Nakruru's suite. "Sony, this is Gisele Lapiner. Can we meet for breakfast in the restaurant upstairs? I know you're uncomfortable and it is the last thing you want to do, but it's important."

Sony curtly said, "In 15-minutes. I'll be there in 15-minutes. I have no time for this. We have to get our lives in order, so you have to make it quick." In a sarcastic tone, "I'm sure you are aware that we have no house and I have not seen my children for almost two days. I have to leave the hotel by 10 o'clock. I really have no time for this."

Sony was still under the assumption their conversation was being overheard. When Giselle got upstairs to the restaurant's front desk, Sony was already sitting at a table overlooking the skyline of Nairobi. No pleasantries were exchanged. Gisele sat down. Sony was biting her tongue as it were, holding back her anger that in normal circumstances would have put Gisele's life in jeopardy.

"Speak; I don't have much time for this. My children need me. I have to explain to my two boys what happened to their home and everything they have ever held dear. They are at their grandparent's house. That is where we left them two nights ago to entertain our American guests."

With exasperation in her tone, Gisele said, "Calm down, calm down. It is over. It was Moi. We have every reason to believe he is behind this. You and your children are safe. William is safe. There is no more electronic surveillance on any of us as far as we can tell. I am here to talk to you personally. William doesn't even know as we speak that it was Moi. You can call him and then we can talk. Or you can call him after we talk. I won't take much of your time. I just found out about Moi right before I called you. This is not a head game or plot to make things worse for you. It is over."

She called the waiter over and asked him to bring the house phone. "Call William. Tell him, and then we will talk. I know you don't trust me. You have your own cell, use it." Putting her hand in her purse, "You can use mine. The conversation will not be bugged."

Sony responded with cold steel eyes that were piercing with hate. "Finish what you came here for. Then I will call my husband."

"Okay, there's nothing I can say or do to lessen what you've gone through. Listen for one minute." She spelled out the scenario that the group had developed the day before.

"Look, Sony we had no choice. You don't have to believe me but your kids were always safe. I can't change anything. I wouldn't change anything. If you and William were in our shoes, you would have done the exact same thing. You would have put as much pressure as possible on anyone you thought was behind this. William said this was Kenyan way. You know and I know we would have been dead if it were you not us in this situation. Don't be sanctimonious about what we did to you. Under the circumstances, we both are still as whole as possible. BiBa will never be the same. Maybe I won't be able to forget this, but I sure as hell will not let it cripple me. I understand what this did to you and you will never forgive whoever is behind it. You have to know, it wasn't us. You would have killed us if you thought we were behind it. That is plain and simple. You're still alive and beat death because of us. I'm here to make some personal guarantees to you. You and your family will always be safe. We will do whatever we can to protect you. We will care for you and your children if something happens to William. We might not have the power to protect him wherever he goes. We do have the resources to develop intelligence that will make him more bulletproof and less susceptible to kidnapping or other personal threats. We will do our best. Here is what I am trying to say. If something happens, we will take care of all your finances and we will provide for any or all of you to leave the country. We have a place for you in Paris."

Sony stared deeply into Gisele's eyes. "We don't need your charity." she said. "You can't buy me after what you have done. This conversation is over."

"Let me finish," Gisele said, "We did not cause this problem, but our being here may have fueled your kidnapping. I feel, and so do the others, on a personal level we are partially to blame. We didn't do our homework well enough before we left New York. We underestimated the dangers here and maybe it had something to do with us all being so vulnerable. That might have caused whoever is behind this to think we were easy marks. I have no guilt but for some reason I feel somewhat responsible and have a sense of obligation to make this right. Pure and simple, no strings. If you don't want anything from us that's fine. I will withdraw my offer. There's a second part to this. The truth of the matter is that Matt wants to be here in Kenya. We want to place a lot of money in charitable causes and maybe even do business here in the future. We want you and William to help us. We will be better off with your participation because like it or not, you are like us. You two are not Kenyan. You both are worldlier and more educated. We can't change anything that's happened but we can make a better and safer future for Kenya and its people. Like I said no apologies. You don't have to like this but you know I'm right."

"I'm going to leave now, maybe you should call William. After you talk to your husband, Frederic will talk to him representing all of us. After the look I saw on your face last night when everything was going down, I felt I at least owed you something for what you went through. As for the matter of Moi, he will be dealt with as soon as we find out who is behind this. William will be given the choice of pulling the trigger. If he doesn't want to then we will offer him up to you. One way or another we will kill him. Moi is the villain here. He will pay with his life, but only after, we get every bit of information from him about his associates. We don't know how long it will take. We feel that if we put the blame on you and William maybe we can make Moi feel so comfortable he'll screw up. Then we'll get what we need and kill him."

Chapter 31

Sony replied in a subdued manner. She measured her words carefully. "I will never forgive you for any of this. If it is Moi, then death is not enough. Torturing him will not be enough. A slow death in the most painful way might not be enough for me. Put him in a box and bury him near a termite hill and let me see the pictures of him being eaten and that may satisfy my anger, but offering me money is offensive. How dare you talk to me after this? Why are you doing this to me? If you had children, you know what you put me through. Only a white childless bitch like you could do this to me. How could any woman have done this to my children?"

"You are right," Gisele said, "If the shoe was on the other foot, I would've killed you in an instant."

"You are French, you should've known better. You could've done better by me and my children. Don't ever turn your back on me, because in the future, if I get a chance I will kill all of you for what you have done. Is that clear? Is my honesty too much? What you have done to me is as great as Mobike's disloyalty. Do you think that because your friend cut off his penis and killed him cleans the slate? Well it doesn't. Do you think that having William kill Moi will make me forget all of this? Well it will not. Am I clear? This is between you and me, my white sister. The stench of this will always be with me. I know you did this to me because I'm black. The smell of this will never leave my nose. You asked for a business union with my husband and me. That is up to him and I will honor his wishes. I am a good wife but if it comes to just you and me, don't ever turn your back. As for my children and that you will guarantee their futures, be damned with you. It is your white way of dealing with your own guilt. We don't need your money. My husband may say it differently. He is a businessman first, then a father. He might want to do business with you and I will follow, but only because he is my husband and that is the way of Kenya. If he wants to do business I will not try to stop him, but I will have nothing to do with it."

She looked at her watch. "When will you take this off? When can I have this, pointing to her shoulder, taken out of my body? When will you have someone take these damn things out of my children and my mother in law?"

Gisele said, "Right now if you want. José is downstairs and all he has to do is make a call. In 10-minutes, one of our men will be here. That's all it takes. I know you don't trust me. I know I make you sick. Realize we did what we had to and you would have done the same. The only difference is you are alive and so are your children. You would have killed us. There's nothing you can ever do to persuade me that you wouldn't have let BiBa be raped and me next. Sister, as you call me, your hate is so deep for white people it is embarrassing. I hope it is just in the heat of the moment, because if it's not, you sicken me. Yes, we come from a different culture, and when Frederic said, we would make our friends whole and kill our enemies he was right, that's what we live by. It is your choice to be with us or not."

As she turned to get out of her chair she continued, "José will be up in a minute. He will take you to his room and take that disgusting chip out of your shoulder. One more thing, don't be so sanctimonious! When you get over this, and you will only because of our intervention, I hope you will entertain the thought of our future relationship. We are not white devils. In fact, and you don't want to admit it, we are very similar. So get over yourself."

She stared directly into Sony's eyes, "Don't ever call me a white bitch. Don't ever make this racial. You lose your credibility as a woman."

Frederic waited till later that afternoon to call Nakruru. "Minister, I would like to speak with you privately. Is it possible that we meet at the hotel early this evening? I need a few minutes of your time."

He placed another call to Moi. "Martin, my friend," as if he were following protocol for a conversation that was being overheard, "How are you? How are you dealing with all of this? We are still trying to put everything that happened into proper perspective. We all need to put things together so we can get past this. Matt is starting to feel a little bit better and wants to talk to you about setting up some meetings and appointments, maybe the school in Kibera and the Alliance. He wants you to float around an idea of setting up small medical clinics in cooperation with the Red Cross. We need to brainstorm and to get this thing going. We have to find the underlying cause of this as quickly as possible. Our philanthropy depends on our safety and the sooner this is cleared up the sooner we can get involved in these projects. Why don't we meet at the Alliance office and figure out a schedule for the next couple of days? We need to see some progress on catching the kidnappers. Our main concern is this is a Kenyan problem and we don't want to be collateral damage. Being innocent bystanders is a cost of doing business that's a deal breaker." At their meeting later that afternoon with Moi, Frederic said, "I haven't told Nakruru yet, but we are putting into place a cooperative deal with Kababi's Special Forces. If it works, then we will bring our own security team into Kenya. I am confident we will be safe, but we are apprehensive about Nakruru's involvement in all of this. Some things don't make sense and it is better if we don't keep him in the loop on everything we do. We have been given some internal information; there is a Masai Rogue element he is tied to. They wanted to fake Nakruru's kidnapping to pressure the Kabiba government for their crackdown in fourth district Masai territories. That's why they went after all of us. We assume Kabiba has aligned himself with the Mungiki gang and this is the Masai reaction. It doesn't quite make sense to us, so until we feel more comfortable, we are going to stay some distance from Nakruru. Obviously, we can't be blatant about withdrawing our trust from him. We need your help my friend. I have said too much."

Frederic was trying to deflect their knowledge of Moi's being complicit. When he left the brief meeting, he felt he accomplished two things. One, create a situation where Moi would be more susceptible to making a mistake; and two, set up Nakruru as a fall guy.

Frederic was confident he had conned Moi by telling him he was no longer suspected of being involved and they would take the chip out of his arm. He apologized to Moi on a personal level. Frederic had played out a script. The group would do anything to rectify the wrong and cure the problem of being so forceful with Moi. He was sorry for subjecting him to the chip and threatening his life. Frederic asked him to be on their team and be the lead in Kenya. Creating a situation of giving him, confidence by telling him they no longer believed in his involvement was an olive leaf. Security first he had said, but they would extend their stay for as long as it would take to find out who was behind this.

"We suspect Nakruru, but this is Kenya, so we will wait until everything plays out."

He knew Moi would buy it because he was too ambitious. They would work with Nakruru and create a sting operation ultimately leading through Moi to the Chinese. Time and money were on their side. Frederic knew he could get Nakruru on board. After leaving Moi, he placed a call to Nakruru.

Chapter 32

Frederic met with Nakruru at 8:30 pm in the hotel bar. He extended his hand and was denied the cordiality of greeting.

Frigidly Nakruru said, "I am only here to have that chip taken out of my shoulder. I should have had you arrested and killed. Tell me why I won't? My wife talked to me. You are sadly mistaken if you think your financial gestures are going to protect you form me or the Kenyan authorities. You will pay the price one way or another for what you did to us. Today or tomorrow, it does not matter; you will pay for what you did to my wife and me."

Frederic responded, "I did not set up this meeting to tell you I'm sorry or to apologize. You would have done the same thing to me if you could. There's no doubt in my mind that none of us would be alive today if you were in my position and we were in yours. That's plain to me. I am not here to apologize, nor am I here because I feel guilty. I am here because I have a proposition for you. Hear me out. Sony called you and told you it was Moi. There is no reason for me to apologize. He is your Kenyan brother and you were close enough to him that when he asked for assistance in getting easy money for your people or for you, you came running. So no, my friend, I will not apologize. It should be the other way around. As for the devices in your arm, what would you have done to protect yourself from an enemy? I'm sure it would have been a bullet to my head, not a chip in my arm. There is nothing I can do to make things better on my part regarding, you and your wife. You were innocent bystanders in a difficult situation. The kidnapping was setup by your friend, not mine. More to the point, I think the word innocent is operative because you would have fleeced us for as much money as you could. It might be that your hate for whites makes you complicit, not innocent. We are the white devils that are easy pickings. You're not so innocent. So don't be so self-righteous. Your friend Moi would have thrown you to the wolves, just like he was doing to us, but you are not blameless in this whole affair. Don't plead innocent or naïve with me. I didn't come to argue my position. I came here to present you with a proposition, so hear me out."

As Nakruru listened, he started to ease up on his adversary. Kikuyu culture put a strong emphasis on honesty. Frederic was as frank and forthright as a person could be.

"I am always direct and to the point, so here it is. You and your wife are very much like us. You are Western, no matter what you think or want to believe. You're not Kenyans. You're more like us, people of the world. Both of you are well educated and not tribal. You're not primitive in your spiritual beliefs. You are Eurocentric and have a European education. The belief system that you hold knows what is right from what is wrong. Put all this together and you are a strong advocate for the modernization of Kenya. For our part, we have a perception that you are very much a capitalist. That is where my proposal comes in. Understand that if you do well, your country does well. We want to bring you into our endeavors here in Kenya. We want an overseer. There will be great personal opportunity for you and your wife, but more importantly, there will be great potential for your country. Our intelligence over the last couple of days has provided enough information to put total blame for the kidnapping on Moi. We had initially thought he was only working for Chinese interests and with the Alliance. To some extent that is true. We also found, he was a private operator and followed us ever since we met him in New York. He worked for the Chinese and he wanted to freelance. The kidnapping, surveillance, ransom and attempted rape was premeditated and orchestrated by Moi. His greed and brutality overtook his clarity of thought to such an extent he couldn't see a long-run relationship with us or even the Chinese would generate more money for him than his kidnapping and ransom plan. He is stupid and very shortsighted. Virtually from the second we walked into his office in New York he was in contact with a Chinese gangster, Lo Chang, an American gangster who helped him set up surveillance from New York to Nairobi. Chang placed us under Chinese satellite surveillance. He has some connection with the Chinese government but we are not sure exactly what. His connection with them is so iffy, we ruled the Chinese out at first. That was a mistake. We won't know their total involvement until later. Obviously, money was no object in setting up the kidnapping. This is where we got tripped up. We thought the Chinese government was following us because of Chang and the expense of satellite surveillance sounded prohibitive to us. We felt this operation was too big for anybody except a government. We were thrown off track. We didn't think the Alliance or anyone in Kenya was sophisticated enough or had enough resources to pull this off by themselves. We thought either you or Moi must have been working with the Chinese and that you set us up. Our intelligence pointed to the Mungiki gang acting as an agent to facilitate our kidnapping on your behalf. When we found out the captors were Masai we thought it was some type of gang warfare or tribal dispute or some type of treachery. We thought whoever was behind this used the Masai instead of the

Mungiki to turn the trail around from the actual perpetrators. We initially thought the Chinese staged the duplicity. Further information ruled out the Asians and directly pointed to Moi. Someone always breaks the rules. Always there is someone so monomaniacal or greedy or just plain stupid things lead back to him. In this case, it was Moi. We think he wanted a greater role in the Kikuyu power structure here in Nairobi. By eliminating you and kidnapping us, he felt he would have credibility with Kabiba. So, it wasn't the Chinese, it wasn't us, it was Moi. His arrogance lead him to think he would have standing here in Kenya if he abducted all of us. We found out about the Masai's involvement because of his stupidity. He has a cousin who married a Masai woman and her brother was more than willing to be involved in the kidnapping. He was rogue and ambitious to the point of giving you and your wife up for a few shillings. Small world isn't it. His name was Mobike. This whole thing was for money and power. We both were brought into this mess because of Moi's ambition. It started out that he worked for the Chinese but when he went on his own all hell broke loose. So let's make the best of a bad situation. Here is the long and short of it. You want to be rich and you can help your people. We want some things out of this too. We want to create an investment vehicle in Kenya. We are offering you a partnership. Our goal is to be big players in Kenya. Believe it or not, we want to help the poor. Our help will be directed by you through a nonprofit. This can only be done if there is law and order and right now the Chinese are playing everyone against each other to create chaos. The more instability, the cheaper it is to enter your market place. That is all the Chinese are trying to do, buy on the cheap. We want to change that. We want to set up a national system of medical care facilities, initially 110 of them. To do it right, the set up costs will be about $100,000 U.S. per unit, all together $11,000,000. That is doable only if there is stability. The facilities will provide two services, health clinics and real estate investment firms. All will be run autonomously. In a nutshell, the facilities for the Kikuyu will be run by Kikuyu and all profits from the real estate investment arm will go back into the clinic. It will be operated as a cooperative and there will be profit distributions not only to the employees but to the community -- the same for the Bantu, the same for the Masai, the same for the Lao, the same for all tribes. We will buy properties and build buildings for each clinic. Whatever profits they generate will go directly to that clinic. If there are any losses, they will be absorbed by the Papaz Group. Each clinic will function as a freestanding financial entity. Eventually each entity will be a real estate investment firm that will buy land and mineral resources in the Central Valley. Over time, these business ventures will be vertically integrated mining primarily, but in some cases prefabrication and distribution of product in East Africa. It will be simple. We will create a model for all 110 units that make them totally autonomous. In Masai regions, we only hire Masai. The Masai will run the businesses. They will only reinvest in Masai projects. But, and this is very important, they render a service to all people regardless of gender, tribe, and ethnicity. No one will be turned away and none will be treated as separate people. All profits will be reinvested in Kenya. We want you to oversee this project and make sure there will be no corruption, no cronyism and more importantly, that these entities will not use their profits against each other. No more tribalism. For this, you will be paid handsomely. We are in, you are rich, and the Chinese will be out."

"There is more. We feel that if the tribes become wealthier because of their cooperative's distributions, then in the long run, the clinics and mining operations will be an agent for change. The Papaz Group will displace the Chinese who are trying to destabilize Kenya by subsidizing the Mungiki. They have their eyes on Kenya's mineral resources, heavy metals and diamonds in particular. They are no more than colonialists, not white European colonialists, but colonialists. They will just continue the exploitation of the British and take your wealth while you see marginal or no gains at all in Kenya's living standard. The Kikuyu government will benefit by having ties to the Chinese, but as usual, all other tribes will be subjugated to lives of indignity and poverty. I expect you know this cannot be allowed to happen... With the Chinese and the corruption of your government, there will be no trickle down of wealth to the poor. With our plan, you will benefit and so will you people. We are interested in indigenous self-rule. All the Papaz Group wants is to act as board of governors and make a reasonable rate of our investment return. We want you to give up your ministry position and become the organization's CEO. You benefit, your own people with no distinction to tribe will benefit. You run our businesses as you see fit with some major distinction. The business must be transparent and open to public scrutiny and the Kenyan people will be the beneficiaries. There will be no corruption or cronyism. You will have our backing in dealing with the Mungiki and the Masai gangs and we will use our resources to keep the government away from this project. We have the power to make this successful. I will give you references and some particulars about us; enough for you to conclude we are real. You will become exceedingly rich. Not wealthy by exploiting your people, but wealthy because of what you have created for them. There is more and this is not a bad thing. Matt and I feel you are politically ambitious over and above your present Ministry position. We will help you run for the presidency on a reform platform of anti-colonialism, anti-corruption, anti-cronyism, do I need to say more? You will run on a platform predicated on all the good things for your people. I know this is a lot to absorb, but it doesn’t even break the surface of what we want to do. Matt and I are not going anywhere right now. It looks like some of the pressure is off us at least for a little while. You will have enough time to digest all of this. There still is the question of Moi. He is a short run problem. We will use him to find out who our enemies are. Once we have gotten everything out of him, he is a dead man. I've taken up too much of your time. Go see your wife and children. We will talk tomorrow."

Chapter 33

The five days following the kidnapping and attempted rape were the longest days of BiBa's life. She sheltered herself in her room at night while the rest of the group attempted to act with a modicum of normalcy by going out to dinner and trying to be social. Her day would started by going to the gym in the hotel before breakfast. The physicality of her workouts was a form of emotional therapy. She would then meet Matt, Gisele and Frederic at 8 o'clock a.m. in the restaurant for a morning buffet. On two different occasions, José made himself available to eat with them. They would planned their day and scheduled different tourist activities such as picture taking at local reserves or going to one of the numerous animal rescue centers near Nairobi. They were in phone contact with Moi. He was still in the process of setting up appointments with various groups, private clinics, community organizations, or anything of a philanthropic nature. On the sixth day, she was coming out of the business center after her morning workout where she picked up a fax and ran into Sony.

Being brought up properly she said, "Hello," as she and Sony both got into the elevator.

As soon as the door shut and they were out of ear shot from any of the other guests, Sony pointed her finger in BiBa's face and said, "Never talk to me you bitch. For what you did to me and my children, you deserve what happened to you, you evil bitch. That wasn't even enough for what you did to me and my children."

BiBa dug deep into silence and just listened as the elevator moved down towards the lobby level of the hotel. Before it came to a halt, BiBa pushed the stop button and held it to keep the door shut.

In a calm measured manner she spoke, "Don't you ever talk that way to me, you cowardly piece of garbage."

Her mind flashed into a thousand thoughts as she tried to carefully weigh her words and articulate a powerful response. She knew using expletives and raising her voice would only diminish her authority and put her in a position of weakness. Everything in the elevator started to slow down and a clear picture emerged.

She responded, "You were frozen with fear you coward. How dare you act so righteously. You would have let them kill you and not defend yourself. Don't threaten me with empty words. You don't have the backbone to aggress upon me. Nothing is more pathetic than someone who is all mouth. After showing the whole world, she has no guts. I am talking to you!"

Sony turned her head as BiBa continued, "You are no more than a third person to me. You call yourself a mother; you call yourself a woman, that offends me. You are everything that is wrong with females. To make it worse, you get in my face and think I will not react to it? You're not only an arrogant coward, you're stupid. I will only tell you this once. Never, I said never, get in my face again. Don't even think of looking at me that way again. I will smack the self-righteous look off your face. We might have to be in the same room or at the same function in the future. Don't put yourself in danger by talking to me or even looking at me. It is embarrassing seeing you acting like the victim here. Nothing happened to you. Now get over it. How dare you dump this on me!"

Sony tried to turn her head and stare at the door of the elevator, as if it would magically open. BiBa continued, "You're not getting out of here until I am finished. From the very first time we met, you've been condescending, as if you were some kind of African Queen. Well honey, your Ethiopian blood, or whatever makes you whiter than me, doesn't cut it. You are a hypocritical condescending want-a-be. If it were not for your husband, you would probably be selling this skinny little bony-ass body of yours on some corner in Addis Ababa or wherever you're from. You are nothing more than a five dollar an hour whore. The only difference is whores have more backbone than you will ever have." She took her finger off the button that had frozen the door shut and said, "Get out of here. You have been warned."

Within 30-minutes, Nakruru called Matt. He was incredulous but held his tongue. He knew BiBa was right, but had to defer to his wife's feelings and display outrage at how she had been treated. Deep down inside he was upset at his wife's actions at the farmhouse and her focusing on the Papaz Group and their handling what they considered a threat. He understood their questioning of both he and his wife and Moi. He knew the explosive devices in their arms were not an extraordinary tactical measure to find out who was behind the kidnapping. He even understood bringing their children and his mother into the picture, but he could not confide any of this to his wife. Frederic and Matt were correct in saying that he would have done worse. Deep down inside he knew he would have had the Papaz Group killed if he had thought they were responsible for the kidnapping and he had power over the situation. If the shoe were on the other foot, five Americans would have been added to the casualty list at the farm as far as he was concerned. He, just as BiBa had done when she was speaking to his wife, measured his words carefully before talking to Matt.

He spoke up, "I don't want to make it personal between you and me. All I will say is keep your wife in line if we are to do business together. Now we will talk about business. I want to let you know we will have a relationship, but only my participation is for sale. My wife will not be involved in any of our dealings. That means business or personal. She will not subject herself or lend her name to any project. She never wants to see any of you again or be in your presence under any circumstances. That goes especially for Ms. Lamanas after she threatened her."

"We can work out details of an agreement between you and me," Matt answered.

"I will only participate if Sony has no involvement whatsoever. I want a letter of intent about the particulars of our union so I can study it and then we can work out the specifics. Yes, in general everything that Frederic expressed to me I can live with. I want my people to prosper. I want to be rich and of course, I welcome the opportunity to be the president and bring Kenya into the 21st century. Not one black African nation has sustainable governance for its own people and I want Kenya to be first. Surely, South Africa is not sustainable and is the standard-bearer for all sub-Saharan governments. As was put to me the other day, no corruption and no cronyism, is the only way I will be part of this. Your model of autonomous investment and micro banks will work here in Kenya. Raising the standard of living for each ethnic group and eliminating tribalism can only take place if we are willing to forgo a democracy. Freedom and democratic rule will not work because our people are not educated enough to leave the past behind. Moving foreword is only doable if there are no outside interests like the Chinese who want to colonize us and pit our people against each other. There is much to do to overcome our past and none of it can be accomplished in a democratic society or one with outside interference. If you really think you can bring all our people together towards a common goal, then you are sadly mistaken. We will need the army, police, and maybe even international forces to deal with the Mungiki and Masai gangs because they are so entrenched in our culture. We will need to modernize Kenya. That is impossible to conceive, because our older people have fought each other for centuries. Our youths are out of control. In practical terms, it will take a military coup to oust the present government that benefits from all this chaos. It will take an army to confront the problems we face. We have to think this out very carefully."

Matt interrupted and said, "Much of this you can leave to us. We have done this before. I will bring you up to speed once we have settled on our intentions."

Nakruru said, "It is easy for you to say. You will be like all absentee landlords or owners; you will make decisions from afar. If you are wrong or indecisive, I will pay with my life. It is me who has his life on the line."

Matt responded, "When we decide on our roles and the exact nature of our organization I will show you how we're going to pull this off and modernize

Kenya. We have resources beyond your imagination. You want to know who, exactly what we are and what our capabilities are, and you will. You will know enough to understand you are safe. Our vision can bring Kenya into the 21st century. Neither I nor the rest of my group would promise something we can't deliver. We know what is at risk and you have seen how we react. We're not foolish and we are very risk averse. We will never put you in a position of danger again. If you were threatened, then it would endanger us. William, you're a businessperson. Have you ever heard the expression, skin in the game? Well, our involvement will be more than just our money. We will have personal skin in the game. We will show you what we have done in Mexico and in the Middle East. With our resources, the process of change won't take as long as you think. We will have men on the ground at all times to protect and support you."

Chapter 34

Matt continued, "As for the matter of Sony and BiBa, what we are doing is bigger than both of them. I cannot control BiBa's temper and anger over what has happened just as you can't control Sony's meltdown. The truth is not hard to see. It is sometimes hard to live with. Both women are out of control. Don't light any more fires by consoling Sony too much. She is trying to deflect all of this by putting the blame on us and it is understandable in the short run, but it certainly won't help her emotional state in the long run. More importantly, their conflict can harm us all. It will weaken our options in dealing with these terrorists. We think we have sent them a powerful message, but if they sense any, in fighting they will come after us because they think they can. If they smell blood, so to speak, they will think we are soft. Maybe in the long run that is good because they will underestimate us, but we don't want to take that chance. Today it is not in our best interest to appear weak. We are not at full strength and we are still vulnerable to attack. Jose and our man Malique are here getting things ready but we will not be fully constituted and operational for at least two weeks. We are just a defensive force. We have enough men on the ground for protection, but not enough to inflict our will on our enemies. I want to put all of my cards on the table, so don't be angry with me. Let me give you a metaphor. You find it tough getting up in the morning and doing dirty work when you wear silk pajamas. Sony is viewing the world as a wealthy entitled Minister's wife who is kept. This will not bode well for her future. She has lost all of her skills for survival. That was pretty clear at the farmhouse. She sat there, let the terrorists have their way with her, and didn't try to protect herself or us. She did nothing to protect you, her husband. She passively watched as they tried to rape BiBa, knowing what they would do to her next. Her cowardice was made worse by how she is handling the incident. As far as BiBa is concerned, her actions are no better. She is acting like a loose cannon and wants to inflict her will on anybody she perceives as weaker than her. Her actions have no bearing on reality. I think she figures, if she can kill somebody, she will feel better. She has enough anger in her to harm Sony, but that will never happen. I guarantee you your wife is safe. They both must come to grips with reality. It is totally understandable what they are both going through. It's easy for us to see that neither one is right and their actions can negatively affect all of us. Knowing all of this and dealing with it is another matter. For whatever reasons, we are both problem solvers. We both have to deal with this personal hurdle between our wives. It has infected us and it can endanger the group. We have to put a stop to it as soon as possible. You and I can do this. The women will ultimately soften their anger. It is just a matter of time and damage control. There is an American cliché -- time heals all wounds. We just have to live by the adage and make sure their actions don't disrupt our goals."

"Let's just get through the next couple of days," William said. "You're correct about both of our wives. Neither one is weak. Both of them were put in life-threatening situations and were not prepared to deal with them. It will take time and a lot of work on my part to placate my wife. I have never seen her so upset. No more has to be said. Things will change in my household. I appreciate your candor but there is no way to move my wife to be civil or even be in your company in the short run. Now let's discuss Moi and our mission here in Kenya. I would like the letter of intent in the next couple of days so I can analyze it and give you my input. I think we can put all this together in a short time period. As for Moi, I have the same concerns as you. You are right if we keep him close to us, we will find out who our enemies are. If he tries to get us to do business with any of his associates then we know they want to do us harm. We need him to get information on the Mungiki and Masai. The Chinese will be another issue. They are the last on my list because we have to deal with Moi right now, but they might be the most important issue in Kenya's future. Chinese investment is small compared to the British and the American's but they are laying the groundwork for huge plays in the next calendar year."

Chapter 35

"Moi is on the phone," BiBa said.

"Martin, how are we coming along with those appointments?"

Matt asked. "Where are we with the Alliance?"

Moi was calling to establish an agenda for the week and feel out Matt on his acceptance of his innocence in the kidnapping plot.

"Do you have everything lined-up for the next couple of days?"

Moi responded, "There are appointments running for three days straight. We will start at the end of the week. I thought that would give us enough time to get together. You could tell me exactly what you want. I have called the Alliance and the President himself. I have been assured their best people will represent us in all our discussions. I am assuming Nakruru will be with us but I'm not sure of my role and how you want me to approach our dealings with him. You confided in me about his treachery and I don't know how to proceed."

Moi was hedging his bet on placing all the blame for the kidnapping on Nakruru.

"Martin, we are comfortable with the Minister being on the negotiating table with us. Keep your enemies close, that's something you must learn. He has no inkling or knowledge of our feelings towards him. He thinks you are the prime suspect. Nothing has changed, we think you should act like you feel uncomfortable, that will be disarming to him. Maybe he will start to feel more at ease and make some mistakes. He will be our partner until we have no further need for him. We are starting to uncover a lot of his relationships and there is a clear money trail leading directly to the slums and gangs in Kerbia. We won't kill him until we get all of the information we need that leads to the people behind this. We also need to be creative enough to get everything we can on him and his wife. We are looking at her relationships in Ethiopia. We don't need her interfering once he is gone. Frederic has our people investigating his early involvement in the Alliance's youth program. We are trying to get information on almost everybody in the Kabiba administration. They all came up the political ladder together when they were young and radical. I will keep you posted. On your end, if anything comes to your attention, I don't have to remind you we need it immediately. I have another call. Be sure to send me an e-mail on all the appointments you have set up as soon as possible. We will go from there. By the way, Frederic has some ideas. I will have him call you."

Frederic called after they received an appointment calendar from Moi. "Martin, how are you? Everything you have set up looks good, but we have to have assurances of the Mungiki and the Masai before we move forward. I'm going to instruct you to set up a meeting with the two gangs. I know you can get it done. Do it before we have any meetings with the clinic's administrators, or any of the schools, or NGOs, or any of your community organizations. Do it before we talk to the Alliance. You're resourceful. Get it done. Whatever it takes set it up. I don't care how or where, but make sure there is plenty of security! We will leave everything up to you. Have your people coordinate with José. I'll have him call you tomorrow. Give him enough time to set things up on our side. Don't disappoint me. Matt has a lot of confidence in you. He thinks we would not be alive without you. He feels if we decide any partner organizations, we want you on the board of directors. He wants you in some decision capacity to protect our interest. Most importantly, he wants you directly involved in the micro-banks. We know most of President Kababi's cabinet is made up of family members and close friends. We think our investment will be a lot safer if you can get some of their involvement in our partnerships. We have to be very careful because of international auditing and banking requirements. We have to create some transparency as far as his cronies are concerned. If it is impossible to get his people involved because of their public stature or their proximity to the President himself then we will bring them in on the backend. We are willing to pay whatever it takes. We also have a matter of the Mungiki and the Masai. They will not have any participation in any of our medical clinics or the banks. They will have to stay out of our business. We will pay but it is up to negotiations. We will have you deal with them and present our offer. In real terms, the biggest split they will get is 15 points. 85-15, but as an incentive to you, anything you can get them to accept below 15 we will share 50-50 with you. If you get them down to 10-percent, we will divide the 5-percent into shares of 2-1/2% for you and 2 1/2% for us. If you can't get an 85–15 split, then you will lose, not us. It comes off your backend profit. This should be an incentive for you. This is our way for you to have some skin in the game. You are our man. We can't do this without you. We feel this is exceedingly fair. Nakruru will be told of an incentive program for any of his participation to keep him on a string until we get everything we need. Then we will get rid of him. Matt thinks there are a couple of options relative to killing him. You can be there when we kill him or we can have him killed and you can see his execution on a real-time video. It won't be pretty because we will make it long and painful but it will be our proof of death to you. It is important you know the Nakruru chapter is closed and we can move forward with our business here in Kenya. Matt feels this will make you more at ease. He also wants the bastard killed. His death should be a strong statement to whoever is behind this. They need to know who they are dealing with and how long our arms are. Set up the meetings with the Mungiki and the Masai."

In a stern voice, he finished saying, "Get back to me and we will go from there. Like I said, José will call later."

Moi placed a conference call to both Kamau Kingara of the Mungiki gang and Parasayip Koyati of the Masai. He told them of conversations with Matt and Frederic and proposed his own set of rules for the Matt investment. He presented them with a 95-5 arrangement and said he wasn't greedy. Their cut would increase with other jobs as contractors for him or Matt. Their fees would be negotiated in the future. He told them that Matt and Frederic were extremely dangerous, but could easily be contained because they were white people and weren't smart in the ways of Kenya. He painted a picture of them acting as lackeys for the white colonialists until the opportunity arose when they would take over the organization. He suggested he, as well as them, follow the general stereotype of being lazy, over-reactive and not attending to business.

"All you have to do is act like fools or slaves of the whites for a short period of time." he said.

He did not use the word deference, but he told the two men that they would have to back off from their instincts of being in control. He told them they should ask for 10% for their protection and safe passage for their operations in the slums.

"Ask for ten and accept five. That will bring them to the table."

He implored them to be patient because it would only be a matter of time until they could take over the whole operation and make millions and millions of US dollars. Moi said they would take control over the operation when it was seasoned and it had acquired vast land holdings in the Central Valley.

"Waiting for the plan to come to fruition and receiving only 5% was a sacrifice, but in time they would all be very rich men." He continued, "I don't have to show you how to negotiate with them, but be outwardly aggressive. Only talk to Nakruru and me directly. Let them know they are white and you will not follow their orders. Tell them you don't deal with white people. You will only deal with Nakruru and me. You are Kikuyu and Kikuyu don't talk to whites, they kill whites. Be as intimidating as possible, but don't put your hands on them. Have lots of security, many men with automatic weapons. Make sure there are women. Bring in a stable of prostitutes and make Matt and Frederic feel uncomfortable. Offer them drugs and insist they take them or you will be offended. Make the white devils know how powerful you are. Tell them what you are capable of, but don't touch them. You will know how hard to push. We can take millions if we play them right. Don't mess this up by being too aggressive, but put the fear of their god in them. I have their trust. Play to it. They will put more faith in me. The more they rely on me the more we can take from them. They think they are smarter than us. Let their arrogance cause their pockets to bleed. Make sure they know how violent and unpredictable you are. Lose your temper and inflict pain on one of your lieutenants. Beat him badly in front of the whites. Let Matt in particular walk away with the feeling you are animals. Make him feel he is smarter than you. I will do the rest. I will tell him I can control you. I will make him understand he has no worries under my control. We can control them because they are predictably white and arrogant."

Chapter 36

As prearranged, an armada of two minivans and three taxis flagged down and pulled over the Cadillac Escalade carrying Matt, Frederic and Nakruru. Part of the Mungiki's transportation fleet monopoly in Nairobi. The Escalade was escorted through the slums through streets closed-off by gang members as if it were a presidential motorcade.

Gang security in the heavily populated intercity was at its highest. The group's SUV would meander through one of the worst neighborhoods of Nairobi's west side on dirt roads for almost 20 minutes before it reached its final destination. José, Malique and their complement of mercenaries were dispersed along the SUV's route to provide security for the Papaz Group. Moi had been kept under surveillance from the time of the kidnapping. All his movements and communications packaged into an analysis provided pinpoint accuracy to the meeting destination. Malique's men were in constant visual contact with the caravan as it drove down the dirt roads through the crowded masses populating this hellhole. The stench and filth of the slum was almost overwhelming to the outsiders. The slow pace of the caravan and the hoards of people watching it as it went to its rendezvous almost made it an event. Looking out the window of the SUV Matt remarked that this was as poor as any place he had ever seen. He could not get over the overcrowded streets and lack of the simplest of living comforts.

Kibera had no open areas, dilapidated storefronts after storefronts, corrugated aluminum sided buildings with metal sheeting acted as roofs housing thousands of people. The poor residents of the slum were either standing or sitting in front of their homes because they lacked electricity and running water. The streets were garbage littered and smelled of human excrement. Matt said the slum was worse than Soweto in South Africa. Many of the people who gathered at corners were vendors selling grilled meats and vegetables. Cardboard boxes used as shelving or tables to hold sundries such as clothing, toiletries, small toys, used garments, anything that could be sold to generate an income. In some places the streets were lined two deep with retail kiosks. Children as well as adults were holding their goods for sale to make a living. Almost all the buildings in Kibera were no more than ramshackle temporary structures made from discarded materials. Electrical cables threading from one telephone pole to another were hanging overhead as if netting had been dropped over the city to keep its inhabitants in check.

In front of a market/restaurant, the lead taxi stopped and its driver waved the caravan to stop. Three men were standing in front of the doorway with AK-47's slung over their shoulders. It was apparent Kibera was lawless and the Papaz Group was in the middle of a Mungiki fiefdom. In this area, neither the local police nor federal army troops ventured. Law and order stopped at the gates of the slum. A bright yellow, red and green flag was hanging on the side of the restaurant's front wall. It was a statement of territorial assertion. Just like dogs marking their spots, the Mungikis were telling its enemies this was its main headquarters. No more than five blocks away was a white and light blue flag hanging from a liquor store in a similar neighborhood that pronounced its ownership was Masai. The door of the first taxi opened and a large man wearing army fatigues got out and started speaking in Kikuyu. The men in the other two taxis and the two minivans followed suit. Twelve men encircled the Escalade and the Papaz Group was ordered to come out. Matt, Frederic and Nakruru were standing in the middle of the street as a display for the onlookers in the neighborhood. The visual picture was clear, black supremacy over Kenya's white colonial pasts. The group was there for all to see. People walking on the crowded street stopped and stared. The Mungiki were displaying the Papaz Group as a trophy. In a little more than 2-minutes they were ushered into the restaurant by their handlers. Fifteen men in all were escorting the whites and one token black into the building.

Matt said, "I guess this is the beginning. We just have to play it out." as he walked next to Frederic. "Realize that the only thing they want is our money."

"I hope you are right!" Frederic shot back to Matt just as one of the guards told them to shut up in Kikuyu. They did not understand a word but they understood his intentions.

Moments before they were taken out of the SUV José sent Matt a text. It said, "Everything is in place and no matter how well armed the Mungiki and Masai seem; they are tactically inferior and outflanked." In capital letters the final line of the text said, "DON'T WORRY WE GOT YOUR BACKS."

As soon as they entered the dimly lit restaurant Moi's voice greeted them. "Follow me. They will frisk you to see if you have any weapons and check for microphones or wires. Give them your cell phones. This is how the Mungiki do business." He pointed to the other side of the kitchen and said, "Follow me."

As they pushed through the kitchen, Matt noticed a wood burning stove and a pre-revolutionary icebox that must have been there since British rule. There was a gas burning range using propane and cooking goods shelving made from plastic pipe. The floors were filthy and vermin deposits were noticeable under all the appliances and in corners of the long thin room.

"The conditions and poverty was worse than 19th century hell holes in England," Matt thought to himself.

Moi was ten feet in front of them and had already entered the makeshift office. Matt and Frederic entered the room first, and then Nakruru followed. The Mungiki bodyguards had not laid a hand on any of the group, but their sheer numbers and intimidating behavior were enough to herd them into the outer office of the restaurant. Kingara, the Mungiki leader, was sitting on a tattered sofa with two prostitutes engaging in oral sex upon him. Koyati, his Masai counterpart, was sitting directly across from him in a large black leather chair with a scantily clad woman on his lap. At the first sight of the group, Kingara pushed both women off him and displayed his large penis. Not saying a word, he placed a pillow over it as if nothing out of the ordinary had happened and in Kikuyu ordered the two women to gather their clothing and leave the room.

Matt looked around to get his bearings. He surmised the large room at the back of the restaurant had been a patio. Three sides of the room were floor-to-ceiling glass blacked-out with dark gray paint. The room itself was probably 25' x 25' as best he could calculate. It was large enough for all the people in it not to be in such close proximity they were on top of one another.

Matt, Frederic and Nakruru were in the center of the room facing Kingara and Koyati while their guards pressed back to the walls and corners of the structure. The Mungiki leader said something in Kikuyu and his men evenly separated themselves to create equal spacing on the perimeter of the room. Matt and Frederick were ordered to sit on the sofa next to the dirty perspiration soaked Mungiki leader whose body odor was the most oppressive either man had ever smelled, as per Moi's plan. Only Kingara spoke. Kotati sat in silence with his whore sitting on his lap.

The Mungiki leader only spoke to Moi in Kikuyu to put Matt at a disadvantage. He instructed Nakruru to act as an interpreter and gave him no input in the conversation relegating him to a person of little importance in the negotiations. Kingara made it clear he only interacted with Africans. Moi was confident his plan was working and the negotiations for the gang's protection and agreement not to interfere would be accepted without a hitch.

His mind was racing into the future where Nakruru would be killed and the Mungiki and Masai under his direction would financially bleed millions of dollars out of Matt's Kenyan operation. After almost 10-minutes, Moi finally said something directly to Nakruru as if he were a subordinate.

Nakruru walked over to the center of the room where Matt and Frederic were still sitting and said, "They have accepted the 10%. They will guarantee protection from the police as well as the army. Their own people know better than to come after you so your operation will have total protection. Part of the deal is all of your private contractor's work; kidnapping, protection and security, bribes, whatever has to be done for you to do business here in Nairobi. They also want a finder's fee if you do business in the Central Valley. Something else, he refuses to lower himself and personally talk to you or any other white. From this point on, all business will have to go through Moi."

Kingara got up off the sofa and started to walk away. Matt locked eyes onto him. He was very small in stature with a deep ebony color that was in contrast to the bright African short-sleeved shirt he was wearing. His face was full and he had yellowish misshapen teeth and bloodshot eyes. It was evident he had been doing drugs for many years. He was much shorter than Matt had anticipated.

Once he had passed Matt and Frederic, he turned around and said in English, "Don't ever try to contact me directly. I will have you killed and I will fuck your women. I will do this myself. To me you are nothing but white pigs."

Before he could utter another word, a smoke bomb exploded and Malique's forces entered the room by coming through shattering the floor to ceiling glass walls.

Five minutes before the operation had begun; Malique had seized total control of the Mungiki radio and communications systems that were used for the gang's transportation business and their illegal activities. Kingara was totally in the dark and separated from the majority of his forces before Matt,

Frederic and Nakruru had entered the headquarters. He did not realize, divided from his main security forces he was left bare to fend for himself. With skilled surgeon's team precision, Jose and Malique's men took control and command of the restaurant and its patio. Five men with automatic weapons and one man sitting on an army Jeep with a 50-caliber machine gun were stationed in front of the restaurant in an instant. Simultaneously five men were stationed in the back. This was not only a tactical maneuver but it was a show of force to the neighborhood. Each of the contiguous buildings to the east and to the west of the eatery were manned by four Bantu mercenaries who were commissioned earlier in the week in Nairobi. Nine of the Arab forces Malique brought with him on the operation jumped through the windows following the smoke bomb's explosion and killed all of the Mungiki guards without suffering any casualties. Without incident, Martin Moi, Kamau Kingara and Parasayip Koyati with his prostitute were taken and driven down onto the floor.

Matt looked across the room, the smoke had dispersed. Both Matt and Frederic understood that knowing something would be happening would be a lot different than actually going through the event. Staying on the couch as things unfolded was extremely difficult and courageous. They held a steady course as Malique's men butchered their adversaries' right in front of them.

Matt was frozen still on the sofa when José handed him a cell phone. From the beginning of the operation to the end, it took less than 60 seconds. It was over and Matt had a cell phone in his hand. Ten of the Mungiki and Masai guards were lying on the floor in pools of their own blood. Moi, Kingara, Koyati and a drugged out prostitute were facedown on the floor at his feet.

José said, "Guzman will call in a couple of seconds. I have some things to finish up," and he walked towards Malique.

One of the mercenaries handed Malique a medical bag with a scalpel, some syringes filled with powerful narcotics, and a plastic pouch filled with spider-like electronic devices. Within a few minutes, all four of the hostages were drugged and the explosive devices were put in their arms. Matt, standing there with phone in hand, looked at the aftermath of the mismatch between a professional army and two of Kenya's most notorious gangs. He looked at Moi on the ground and the scum he had brought into the plot.

He said to himself, "This sure as hell wasn't a fair fight but shit, these bastards deserved it."

He looked at Frederic and started to walk back towards the couch.

The phone rang. It was Guzman. "I saw everything in real time," he said. "Tell Malique and Jose, job well done. How are Frederic and your African? Are they okay?"

Before Matt responded, Guzman continued, "Everything went exactly as planned. There is no need to question Moi. We have all of the information we are going to get from him. Let me talk to Malique."

Matt handed him the phone. Malique shook his head with affirmation in response to what was being said on the other end.

"Yes sir, when we finish, I will have Matt get back to you. Like I said, everything is in place. Do you have any special orders? Then everything is a go." and he hung up.

Malique said something in Arabic to one of his mercenaries. Four wooden chairs brought in from the restaurant were lined-up in front of some of the dead bodies resting on the floor. All of the hostages including the prostitute were placed in the chairs, Moi on the left, the 2-gang members in the middle, and the woman on the far right. It was in order of descending value of the 4-captives. Cameras were set up with electronic feeds to a laptop computer. Moi and his associates had their hands and feet tied together and large plastic bags were placed over their bodies at the shoulders to free their heads. They had been forced into the chairs and strapped down with nylon ties and would be left there until the fog of their drugs wore off and they became conscious. The killings would take place one by one starting from the prostitute and finally to Moi. The spiders in their arms would take their lives. The horrific sight of bodies exploding and heads being severed from one's thorax would be the last thing Moi would see.

After the traitor Moi and his associates were killed, Matt called Guzman. "It is over. Jose says we are ready to move out."

Guzman replied, "You don't have to be in a hurry. No one will come to help them. Our men are still in front of the restaurant. You are safe. Clean everything up that can be traced back to you or the men. We can't be too careful. The Chinese will be in this soon enough. We know who is behind the Chinese investment in Kenya. Everything is on tape and it will be on UTube within the day. It will show our resolve, but first we have to e-mail the video directly to a Chinese government trading company run by Chin Mao, the vice-chairman's brother-in-law. He will receive the e-mail from an account emanating from the Minister of Defense's office in Beijing. It will show four masked men acting as executioners preparing Moi and his associates for their deaths. Then their bodies will explode as a message streams across the screen; you are next if you compete in Kenya for mineral resources. We have total control over the Chinese electronic communications and we'll send the e-mail via the Ministry's server. We will back channel the e-mail to a Japanese corporate executive to mask the electronic trail and make it harder for them to find the source. We want Chin to know we can get to him at any time. Frederic's people have worked all this out. He will fill you in. Good work my friend."

Chapter 37

They arrived back at the Hilton Hotel almost four hours after they had driven to Kibera. The day had been surreal. A neighborhood taken hostage by gunmen; a dozen gang members killed in their own headquarters, and not one sign of the police or the military. There was no mention of the incident on the internet or in the local media in Nairobi. It was as if nothing had happened.

The slums were a black hole. Life meant nothing in Kibera. The killing of gang leaders and the display of Malique's forces stationed outside the restaurant with standard military weapons did not stir any opposition or even excitement in the densely populated slum. The Cadillac Escalade with the Papaz Group and the other members pulled up to valet parking and they all exited the vehicle. Once inside the hotel lobby Matt suggested that they all clean up and come to his suite in an hour.

"We will order room service, not that I'm hungry after everything that's happened, but we probably should eat something. We need to discuss what we to do from here."

He looked at Nakruru and continued, "Of course your wife is invited even though she will emphatically reject our offer. Over time, she will react differently. I want you to tell her we asked for her participation."

They all got into the elevator and total quiet overcame them as it ascended to the eleventh floor. It was noticeable that the government's security detail was no longer in force. There were no men placed in front of the suites. After what they had gone through, Frederic thought an hour to clean up was unreasonable. He felt everyone probably felt the same way but no one wanted to assert themselves.

He couldn't help himself and sarcastically said, "Yeah, it shouldn't take more than 30 minutes to wash off all the blood and shit. All we did was kill four people in plastic bags and watched their heads roll off. Shit, who needs time to reflect on that. I will run right into the shower, wash off and get dressed. Okay sure. You know, and then we can start to plan, for what, I don't know, to buy the country or kill off half its population. Sure," looking at Matt, "I will be ready in an hour."

Matt said, "I know we all feel the same way but we have to get on with it. It's never the same and it is never easy. Don't get me wrong, I feel like shit too. A couple nights ago, stuff happened because we were not as prepared as we should have been. Today we had it under control, but none of it is easy. Since we have been here, we have had to fight for our lives at the farm then we had to take advantage of a situation with Moi before he came after us again. I know we got into this because of me. I don't blame you for being pissed. No one does. Every one of us wants to be here, there is no question why we are here. We just screwed up the other night and today we had no choice but to strike first. It’s my fault we are here, but we all agreed Kenya was a cause worth sacrificing our lives, didn't we? We all want to do something about what's going on here. I’m sorry I seem a little more callous than you. Like I said, it never gets easier, it only gets more predictable and you lose less sleep over it. Sometimes it's easy to question our motives and our actions. Don't ever forget, we’re the good guys. We question our mistakes. We don't question ourselves. Guzman always says when you’re in someone else's house you play by their rules. Our problem is we do it much better than anyone else. God, I'm really sorry about what happened and all the killing, but in this game if you're not brutal and more violent than the other guy then you are dead. After we clean up and get a couple minutes of rest, believe it or not, we will both feel better. You’ve been to hell and it's really hard to digest. I'm not trying to be condescending but we have gone through this before. In an hour, we will all feel much better. It's either them or us. For all of our sakes whatever it takes it's going to be us."

Alone in their room, Matt approached BiBa and said, "I'm sorry. I did not think this through before I got any of us involved in this mess. I went off half-cocked after reading that article. I don't know, being back at home, I felt so empty and thought I needed a cause. Well, like I said, I didn't put as much thought into this as I should have. That is pretty fucking obvious. Coming over here was supposed to be exploratory and for sure, it was supposed to be safe. None of this killing stuff. Nothing was etched in stone about getting involved or doing business over here. I believe after what we've been through and this will sound absolutely crazy, we should invest money here. We should at least try to help in any way we can, even if it's from a distance. We can get someone else to run our operation. Nakruru can be our point man. The place needs help. Maybe we can't even put a dent in the corruption and poverty but I really want to give it a shot. With all that said, it will not be at your expense. I'm going to call this thing off when everyone gets together. I have enough money that putting $15 or $20 million in here won't be a problem. If we do this right, it might even make some financial sense. Sorry sweetheart, I brought you into this mess."

BiBa's response was not expected. "You can't possibly think I'm going to walk away on this, do you? After all the shit I've gone through, now it's personal. I came here with you because I honestly was jealous of what I thought you and your friends did. I told you all this before. The adventure of Africa, having some purpose, not just shopping and indulging myself everyday and most importantly sharing something with you, that's why I came here. But, now, it is real personal. Do you think I can really walk away after some son of a bitch tried to have me raped? Sure, we killed some of them but the rest of them are probably laughing or even worse, these animals probably don't give a shit. I want to make all of them pay a price. I want all of them to understand with whom they are dealing. They think they can mess with us with impunity. That is not going to happen. I am not going to leave this place on their terms. It is even more than revenge. Who do these people think they are? They kill each other off. There is no value for human life in this godforsaken place. Maybe we can't do much, but I'm not going anywhere until we can get back at these bastards. Whoever is behind Moi is my target. I think we should stay until we find out who it is and get the bastard!"

Matt understood her need for anger but could not comprehend its depth. They had different agendas for staying in Kenya and he was sure Frederic, Gisele, Jose and Malique were there for their own reasons. He felt responsible for bringing them there and he would make sure they would stay the course.

Matt let her continue to ramble. She was all over the place and now she was talking about the medical and investment projects.

"Maybe we can't do much. The problem is probably too vast, but your ideas of medical centers and purchasing land for the indigenous tribes make a lot of sense to me. What I'm really interested in is the micro-banks, and how they will empower women. These things mean enough to me that I'm willing to give up everything I have. This might sound crazy, and you probably think it's because of the attempted rape, but I think I'm even willing to give up my life for this cause."

He had never heard her vent like this.

"I am willing to give up anything, you know a big sacrifice. I always played it safe. This means a lot to me. And no, I don't have a death wish. I'm not some kind of emotional female who fell apart after some trauma. Don't look at me that way."

Matt had a blank look on his face because he did not know how to respond.

"I am trying to be honest with you. I heard Frederic's outburst in the hallway, he was sarcastic about all we have been through. Well I have been through a lot and I don't know any other way to deal with this either. You know me and how pissed I can get. That sure as hell is better than falling apart. I can handle this but don't try to take away my anger. No one has the right to tell me not to be angry and not to want to go after these bastards. I don't want to be late; we have to meet everybody in a couple of minutes. I need to get cleaned up. My day was not like yours, but I need a shower."

She dropped off her clothes in the middle of the room and walked towards the master bedroom. The door shut and Matt could hear her turn on the shower as he stood there in the living quarters of the large suite.

Unintentionally Frederic and Gisele meet Nakruru at the conference room door. Frederic looked at his watch and noticed it was exactly one hour since the declaration of the meeting. "I must be late. My father used to say, if you are on time, you are late."

Nakruru reacted, "In Kenya a man separates himself by being punctual. A man's word is very important and can be measured by his actions. If someone is late, it catches my attention and tells me to be skeptical. He is either lazy or arrogant. Neither one of us would accept that. You and I have much in common."

Frederic knocked on the mahogany door.

"Well, nothing changes. You're on time. Just like clockwork, Matt said. "We have a lot to talk about."

As he ushered the three into the room, BiBa was sitting on the sofa with a bottle of still water in her hand. "Can I get something for anyone?"

They all said no and proceeded to sit down.

Frederic said, "By the time we got back to our room there was a lot of intel waiting for us. Obviously, I didn't get a chance to go over it in detail and I haven't had a lot of time to digest it, but it's clear our Chinese friends are behind all this. They didn't say it directly, but they were pretty explicit in what they wanted the Kenyans to do about any interference from outsiders. Let me start by saying, Matt, when you and BiBa initially looked into this you talked about Chinese involvement and that was an understatement. It seems they want to totally destabilize not only Kenya, but the whole region. Kenya will be a starting point for them in minerals. They want to create a real estate bear market where there is essentially no foreign investment to bid up prices. A trading company of theirs wants to corner the international markets for rare earth metals, heavy metals, and diamonds. It is the exactly scenario you presented a couple of months ago. There is one caveat. It is much bigger and much more pervasive than we ever imagined. They are willing to put Kenya on the brink of revolution just as they are doing in Somalia. In Somalia, they are trying to monopolize the oil reserves and all attendant industries. They are in the process of building pipelines through Darfur. Look at the hundreds of thousands of casualties they accept as part of doing business. In Mogadishu, they have engineers and architects developing plans for petrochemical processing and refineries. They are willing to wait up to a decade before they start construction. We have seen some of their intelligence and they are throwing numbers around as high as one million deaths, as a tipping point before the international community will act on the behalf of the disenfranchised. They almost laugh at Western involvement. Our analysis shows the United Nations and any intra-African military presence will have a negligible affect on what they want to do.

Their thirst for resources is insatiable and as usual, they plan for the long run. Kenya is no different. They want to try to destabilize it. We know Chinese contractors back the Somali terrorists crossing the border and kidnapping French nationalists in Mombassa because of their Chinese weapons. That couldn't happen without the authorization of the Chinese military. Next, we looked at the World Court ruling on war crimes here in Kenya. Deputy Prime Minister Uhuru Kenyatta, Member of Parliament Eldoret North, Head of Civil Servants William Ruto, and journalist Francis Muthaurs, who were responsible for human rights violations in their civil war and were held guilty in absentia, were all Kikuyu working for Kenyatta. They all have financial ties to the Chinese. We have bank account numbers, electronic transfers, correspondence, and the whole ball of wax. Then we looked at the Mungiki and the Masai gangs and have evidence the Chinese are investing their monies. It even gets better. Guzman alerted us to a Chinese trading company doing business in Costa Rica he said was throwing around too much money. A name came up, Chin Mao, the guy Guzman mentioned earlier. The long and short of it is he’s a person of bad intentions. Not only does he want to corner the markets for resources in Costa Rica, but we are finding his fingerprints here in Kenya. He is the lead man for the Chinese government through its investment arm, CTC, the Chinese Trading Company. It has at least twenty subsidiaries doing business all over the world. They’re acquiring heavy metals and rare earth elements as well as being a major player in the commodity market. Pure and simple, they want to control these markets. Chin has the Chinese government's financial resources. He has an unlimited bank account. In another point of reference, the intelligence looks at the moral fiber of Chin himself. He personally is into human trafficking and the sex trade. It is substantiated and we have pictures of him with eight and ten year old children in Costa Rica. Also we found that in China he runs an illegal organ transplant industry. He is such a bad guy he has negotiated deals with provincial and federal prisons in China that sell him organs harvested from people on death row. He sells almost 15,000 organs a year. That is more than 60% of the transplants in China. There are more than 1,500,000 people on waiting lists for organs in the legalized markets so you can see the profit potential for illegal organs. Up to 15% of the organs are harvested while the prisoners are still alive. He has a fleet of medical ambulances that go directly to the prisons before execution and harvest the organs then are packed in ice and shipped all over China for transplants. He even has a fleet of planes able to deliver live organs anywhere in China in less than six hours. The operation is a little more complicated, but I think you get the idea. He also sells babies for adoption, primarily to the United States. He runs all the for profit abortion clinics in China. Obviously, the government has its own clinics but because of the stigma associated with an abortion, many people go to his clinics or have a midwife help them with the operation. There are about 3 million legal abortions per year in China and the estimates are his clinics perform another one million with the conditions of anonymity. Legal abortions are public information and sometimes names are published in local newspapers. His clinics perform both legal and illegal abortions, but in many of the cases, they kidnap young women and inventory them until their babies come to term. Then they put them up for adoption. He houses the women in dormitories that would make slum land lords in the United States look like they are renting Beverly Hills properties. The mortality rate for these women is higher than 50%. I can go on and on and present other activities he is involved with, but you have a more detailed analysis in the packets I will give you. I have come up with an axiom I regard as a path to dealing with the Chinese. I add together what is going on here in Kenya, to my Chinese business experiences in the U.S., and I have a deep sense of pessimism as to who they are and what they want. Don't ever expect them to have Western democratic values, no matter how they paint themselves. Nothing is below them in terms of power seeking or in the new reality of the world, seeking money. They totally understand how to disrupt democracy as evidenced by what they are doing in Kenya and Somalia. They are old hands at subterfuge and duplicity."

Gisele interrupted, "I have not had any more time than Frederic to look at these materials, but my analysis goes in a different direction. If we assume all of this is correct, and we have no reason to believe otherwise, then I have some pertinent questions. Let me be as direct as I can. Is all of this our problem? If so, that leads me to another question. What do we do about their relationship to our resources and can our commitment be great enough to have any impact? Can we essentially wage war against the Chinese government? That's what it looks like it will take to bring about any substantial change in their behavior. Frederic did not have time to discuss Chin's relation with the Chinese government. Let me tell you it is deep. He is the brother-in-law of the vice-chairman of the Communist Party. In France, we have a saying, only a fool fights a war he knows he cannot win. Valor is no substitute for life. Many people say it's why the French have historically surrendered to their enemies. There may be some truth in that, but if we can't win this war against the Chinese, should we proceed? I have asked myself on two separate occasions, since we have been in Kenya, what are we doing here? My life has been at risk. In the last week, I've seen things I only heard about from agents in the field and to be honest with you, I did not believe them. I have been in this business all my adult life, and have gone through more in this week than in my whole professional career. I ask myself, are we alive because we are good or because we are lucky? Luck will not allow us to prevail over the Chinese. Do I want to give up my life for this? Our friend Matt wanted us to come here on a fact-finding mission to see if we have the ability to do good. We have the facts now. My question is what do you want to do?"

Chapter 38

Emotions ran high for the first two hours of the meeting. BiBa vacillated from a position of pure retribution to the more tempered view; we do what we have to do to help these people.

Nakruru found himself in a troublesome flux of admiring white people and feeling Western civility was honorable versus the old primitive and tribal decision-making ways in Kenya that were unacceptable on every level. He knew if Kenya were to position itself in the 21st century, that political corruption and tribal violence had to cease.

Gisele was steady in her analytical approach to all the information gathered by her staff. Her analysis of thousands of pages of sophisticated data was always objective and clear minded. Her number crunching and inputting data into traditional game theory or input-output analysis was void of emotions.

Frederic was pragmatic and always took the lead. He accepted responsibility and thrived on decision-making.

Matt, for his part, was trying to deflect the guilt of putting his friends into a life-threatening situation. He was conciliatory to anyone's concerns and opinions. Because of the kidnapping of his friends he felt he had lost his right to, as he put it, call the shots on anything important.

Gisele felt her cell phone vibrate in the right pocket of her jeans as she sat on the sofa in the midst of debating the need to stay in Kenya. She lifted it out of her pants and excused herself. She walked into the other room and sat down to read the text. It was a communication from José. After reading it, she came back into the room.

“I have some news from José. It will make all of this back and forth a little easier.”

She read the 27-word text aloud.

"Have kidnapped Kababi’s oldest son and 2 daughters. Implanted the devices. Video will follow to the Pres. YOU ARE SAFE IN KENYA IF YOU WANT TO STAY."

Gisele said, "That is good news.”

They were at a loss for words. They would await further communication.

Gisele said, "I am getting a little tired and so much is happening, lets slow down. I will order up something to eat and some coffee and tea. I think we all need a break. I know I do."

They all agreed but it was hard for everyone to come down from such a serious place. After an hour that included going back to their rooms to freshen and take a bathroom break, they felt it was time to resume. Coming back, eating and lowering their tension levels by simple conversation was not easy.

Giselle said, "I guess it's time to get back to brainstorming."

She was the de facto secretary and Frederic was the team's leader in discussing their collective futures. During the break, he and Gisele had gone back to their room, found intelligence, and accompanying summaries about the Chinese involvement in Kenya in the printer's tray.

After a cursory look at the materials, Frederic asked Gisele if she would present it to the group. "It would go over better with BiBa if you do it," he said. "Look sweetheart, you have to do this. Coming from a man it would be much harder to accept. I'm not saying she's going to go off on me but why take the chance."

The gathered information showed cause to limit the roles of Gisele and BiBa in any future operations in China. Frederic thought anything problematical in interfacing with BiBa, after what she had gone through, was better suited for Gisele to deal with than any of the men in the group.

He said, "You know I'm not a sexist. I really think this is the right course. You have to talk to her. If you have any objections, say something now before we go back to their room."

They still had the text from Jose to discuss. At the meeting, Gisele passed out copies of the intelligence that had been e-mailed to her and Frederic's suite. With materials in hand, they resumed their discussions.

She looked at Frederic and said, "Do you mind if I start this off by briefing everyone on the intelligence?"

He said, "Sure, why don't you fill us in? Let me just say a couple of words to summarize what we discussed before we took our break. I am assuming we are continuing our efforts here in Nairobi. I think we all agree with that assessment, but we have to define our roles in any future operations. If we are to have a presence here, referring to Kenya, then Jose's text surely makes it easier. We don't know all the ramifications, but he says our safety is assured if we want to do business here. After reading the intelligence you will see he has done a lot more to guarantee our safety. With dispatch and discretion, he found one of Kababi's co-horts who had intentionally slipped away from his security team to be with a prostitute. It made him vulnerable and of course, José and his men used that to their advantage and kidnapped him. He was the journalist, Francis Muthaura, who was one of the four men indicted by the World Court during the civil insurrection. They placed an explosive device in his arm and drugged him. Then Jose paid one of the journalist's own men to drop him off at Kababi's house. That tells us how loyal these guys are. The President's security team and his aides recognized Muthaura and let him in as if he were there on personal business. As soon as Kabiba came downstairs to meet his friend in the library of the presidential mansion, José, from a remote position approximately three blocks away, detonated the device. Our electronic capabilities then gave us the ability to place a call on Kababi's personal cell phone. José told him there was no place he could hide from us. He told him Nakruru, his American associates in the Papaz Group were to have safe passage in Kenya, and if any harm came to them, his children were next. He told Kabiba he was personally responsible for Nakruru, Gisele's and BiBa's safety. The horror of Muthaura being blown to bits and the realization of Kababi's own mortality and that of his children's will guarantee safety for the Papaz Group. Okay, that's one theater of operation. The other issue is China."

There was a little uneasiness in the room as to José's methods, but everyone realized it was the only way to have safety in Kenya. Between Malique's mercenaries, who would be a permanent security detail for Nakruru ,and any of the Papaz Group that would do business in Kenya and the President's life being at stake if something happened to them, José felt their safety was guaranteed.

Gisele now addressed the issue of China. "Our intelligence strongly suggests that BiBa and I cannot be part of any operation in China itself. The cultural pressures of dealing with women would jeopardize any efforts we put forth to partner with them or have any type of dialogue. They are averse to allowing foreign women to have any decision-making authority. We can only cloud the operation if BiBa and I are involved. Whatever we do with Chin Mao has to be done without our involvement. His misogyny has no bounds. The sex slave traffic, his piquant for pedophilia and his illegal selling babies tells us of his sexual proclivities and his anti-feminine bias. There is no room in China for the two of us."

Gisele looked at BiBa, "You don't have to react now, but after you look at the intelligence, we can discuss this. I think you'll agree but there is always room for conversation and competing ideas."

To Gisele's surprise BiBa said, "If you think we should not be there, I am fine with that as long as I can have a future here in Kenya. José's text suggests I will be safe. I hope you and I will work in concert with William on our programs. I only need to know we will continue to go after anybody who was involved in trying to rape me. As long as I have a role here, you bet I'm okay with not going to China. I still would appreciate a voice on what we do there, but I don't need to be on Chinese soil. If that would be counterproductive, and it sounds as if it is the case, I don't need to be there."

Gisele said, "Is everybody in agreement that we proceed on two fronts?"

There was full agreement. Matt did not know what to say.

Gisele continued, "I think we are all getting a little tired, so let me sum all of this up before we call it a night. We all have agreed in principle to have two teams. Nakruru, BiBa, and I will represent our interests here in Kenya. Matt and Frederic will represent us in China. Jose and Malique will protect all of us by with specific security details to be ironed out later. José will be a floater. Wherever he is needed, he will physically be with that team. Our friend Guzman will be consulting on strategic guidance and we will look to our Arab partner, Kasogi, who had experience in China, to give us direction in dealing with Chin. I think we have accomplished a lot. Does anyone have anything further to add?"

They agreed they would meet for breakfast. Matt suggested 10:00AM.

Chapter 39

At breakfast, the meeting the night before went a collective unanimity well. Everyone was comfortable with its results and glad it was over. Matt was right for calling a late morning brunch. They were all emotionally exhausted. An extensive burst was the term for their collective mental state. The adrenaline rush caused by their kidnapping, execution of Moi and his gang member associates, and their brainstorming the night before, had taken its toll. Their tanks were on empty and they all needed some well-earned time off.

Nakruru was late to the restaurant because he had breakfast in his room with his wife.

She was still boycotting the group with proclamations of, "They are your associates not mine. Never, I said never, expect me to be in their presence. You made the decision to align yourself with them, knowing my feelings. I can deal with that, but don't expect me to ever be a part of whatever they are into."

"William," Frederic said, "You don't have to explain why you are a little late, because it's written all over your face. It was a war this morning wasn't it. She will learn to live with us and more importantly, over time she will come over to our side. It is actually better for her that she hates us if it will get her through all this. It is called paradoxical intention. That is when you loathe someone to feel better about yourself. It is like dressing up in bright colored clothing when you're depressed. It has a way of making you feel better and it is not emotionally very expensive. I am sure she will come out of this soon enough. Until then just, take it. Somebody has to be the recipient of her wrath. We know and she knows you didn't cause this. Deep down inside she knows we didn't cause this. It is the reality of Kenya. She will change her mind when she sees all the good things we have the ability to do for Kenya's people. Once she understands you have taken over our foundation and are responsible for bringing Kenya into the 21st century, her attitude will change. Now, there is something else I want to say, I am known for my forthrightness. We keep no secrets and everything is on the table. Whatever we do, however, we do, if it relates to our business then everything is fair game between us. That means you as well as us. If you are to be part of our team, then know the worst thing we can ever have is a surprise. No surprises, no secrets. That is our mantra within the group. We don't want to grow past our friends, in this case we mean business associates. What we really are saying is we collectively are always moving forward in an upward trajectory and if you are inert or static, you will fall by the wayside. Don't let our anticipations of your work and your visions be ahead of your product. We can only measure you by what you do, not by our anticipations or your proclamations. We would not ask you to be a partner with us if we expected any problems with you meeting our standards. You will have to be nimble and creative enough to follow through on our specific goals within a specific timetable. Once we have defined our goals, our objectives, and timetables, you will be given unlimited resources. We call it an unlimited expense account. You will be charged with putting everything together here in Kenya. The clinics, the banks, and land acquisition will all be under your supervision. Like I said earlier, it is important for me to be frank, don't disappoint us. There will be a simple process. You make all of the determinations of what should be done here on the ground. Pass your recommendations to BiBa and Gisele. The three of you will have an equal vote in decision-making. Once a consensus has been reached, your ideas get sent to Matt and me. If we need to, we will make changes or suggestions or accept the proposals on face. We then pass along everything to Guzman. He makes the final determination. No secrets, no surprises. We all pull our own weight on a common agenda. We would not want you in this process if we did not have complete confidence in you. There are no back room deals. There is no hidden agenda. There is only what is good for Kenya."

Matt interjected, "We will all do well together or we will all fail together. That is you, that is us and that is Kenya. We want your country and your people to come into the 21st century with you as its leader. There is an historical analogy in our thinking. Our organization functions like Alexander the Great at the height of Grecian antiquity. Outsiders assimilate into your society by ridding it of all that is evil and corrupt. I didn't say conquer, I said assimilate, that is very important. People, or institutions, or anything that gets in the way of the new order will be eliminated with draconian force. Examples will be made of what we do to people who do not comply to our new order. The population will be forced to understand the importance of change. All elements of the past that stifle change will be purged. No exceptions, not even for us. Let me change that, especially for us. We lead by example with the understanding that the common good is greater than any individual within society. Greece was the center of the world. Alexander's colonies in the Middle East and North Africa were no more than extensions of mother Greece. People were brought into a new better world and resistance was not tolerated if it held back the betterment of the whole. I'm sure it sounds very arrogant to you, but we look at Kenya as a colony of our new world order. Over time, you will learn much more about our model and its roots. We have deep investments in Latin and South America, the Middle East, and even one of your neighbors to the south. As Frederic says, we are the good guys. I'm sure you think we are narcissistic and that we think the world revolves around us. Well, we think we can make the world a better place and as you have seen, we are willing to put our lives at stake for the betterment of people who have no voice. You have observed only a fraction of our resolve and capabilities. We chose you for a reason. You are a beacon of light in Africa. With our vision and your leadership, we can make a difference. A lot rests on your shoulders don't disappoint us. Don't let us outgrow you."

BiBa said, "Okay guys, that's enough. William has been here five minutes. You just unleashed on him. That's not a good way to start the morning, first your wife, now our men. We all understand the importance of this and we are not going anywhere soon, so why don't you get something to eat or drink. Maybe we can discuss something more pleasant?"

William smiled for the first time in their presence. "We have a saying in Kenya, a lion's roar deafens even the best of ears but neither you nor my wife can make my life void of sound. I am honored to be a part of all this and as you say, in time she will be too."

They sat and talked of small things for the next thirty minutes while Nakruru drank his coffee.

Just as they were ready to leave Gisele said, "We have one more item of business."

Looking at Nakruru, "We need a list of everything you want to get this enterprise started. That means an office, staff support, supplies and communication equipment, everything and anything you need. If you need help, contract it out. Be sure to vet whoever you use. We will need names of all of your contractors, subcontractors, business consultants, anybody with whom you deal. Between your due diligence and ours, we will be safe. Nothing is 100%, but certainly two searches are better than one. In the next four weeks, we will need you to identify all the locations for our clinics throughout Kenya. We want to place the first two in Nairobi to use as templates. After we have worked out all the kinks and have these two locations functioning and somewhat mature, we will roll out medical clinics across the country. The first two will give us the information to know if we are on the right track. If they work in Nairobi that should be a good indication, they will be successful throughout Kenya. We want to get the clinics online in Nairobi within 90 days. Is that doable? Is that enough time?"

"It should be. I will try to get it done within three months," said Nakruru.

Gisele jumped in, "Don't try my friend. If you say you can do it, then you do it. If you need 120 days, then you will get 120 days. All of us are held to the same standard. When we are given a task where other people use our product or information, whatever we are charged with, move forward and never miss your deadlines. Neither you nor I or anyone else at this table has the right to slow down progression of our work by not being responsive to timetables. As was said earlier, no surprises. I will ask again, is 90 days enough time? Don't ever let us grow faster than you."

Nakruru thought for a second, "90 days is adequate."

He had never been in an environment where people were held responsible for their actions or where getting something done was more important than verbalizing one's intentions.

Frederic continued his discussion of the clinics, "All the clinics, regardless of their location, will have the same architectural design and the same staffing and the same equipment and medical supplies. The only differences between clinics will be that in Kikuyu territory, they will be run by Kikuyu, and in Masai territory, they will be run by Masai and so on. There will be no crossover of clinical staff and indigenous tribes. Initially, Kikuyus will not provide services to Masai or visa versa. That will come later. Nothing will be allowed on the premises of any clinics, if it differentiates it from any other clinic. I will call it the MacDonald's or the KFC model. Each and every location is identical. I'm sure you get the point. Differentiation will promote hatred. We need inclusion not exclusion. I think that's enough business for one day."

Matt said they would wrap it up in Nairobi in a few days. "We don't need any more formal meetings. What we agreed upon last night and we talked about this morning is a good road map. William, we as a group are as always in constant contact. There is always communication between us so there are no mistakes, or as we like to say, no surprises. If it is important, call or text 24 hours a day. We all have a twelve hour turn around on e-mails. You will be held to the same standard. We do things fast and we are expeditious with our time. That does not mean we do things just to get them done. Our objective is to bring about meaningful change. It is important to remember, we don't do things for our own sake but we do things for the betterment of all. We are never sedentary. It is better to act and make a mistake that can be rectified than be paralyzed by inaction. Our ways might be strange but they work. Welcome aboard my friend. What we have gone through in the last few days is the beginning of our journey. I know it is overwhelming, but anything meaningful has a price. We are a good fit. A good fit indeed."

Chapter 40

Back in New York, Matt and BiBa easily went back to their old habits. It only took two days for her to get back to the gym and start her training. This time it would be a little different because José had other responsibilities. He had hand picked a new trainer for her. His name was Richard Dixon and his specialties were weapons and striking techniques. She would train in one of the most aggressive martial arts styles. Both she and José figured she was competent enough and had a high enough skill level to learn to do more than just defend herself.

Matt decided he would change his training schedule by setting up a gym in their house and working his way through X90P.

Frederic resumed financial management of the Papaz Group, overseeing the vast holdings of the Tijuana Cartel and Guzman's assets.

Gisele would split her time between Paris and New York. Heading a network of information gathering was time intensive but did not call for her to be in France for more than two weeks a month. She could spend much of her time in New York with Frederic and have adequate time to be with BiBa and plan for their philanthropic ventures in Kenya. Nakruru was in transition from the post of Minister of Finance to the CEO of the Matt Papaz foundation. José and Malique were charged with security matters in United States and Kenya.

Approximately four weeks had passed when one afternoon Matt returned from a brisk two-mile run along the track on the High Rail Park; he saw Frederic and Gisele sitting on the stoop of his brownstone.

"What are you guys doing here? I guess BiBa isn't back from her workout yet?"

Frederic said, "We were in Washington Square and decided we would walk over and see if you were home. We just got here five minutes ago. I knocked on the door and unless BiBa is in the shower, she's not home."

"Come on in," Matt said, "I will run upstairs and see if she's here. I'll be back in just a minute, so make yourself comfortable. Why don't you go to the kitchen, there is food and stuff to drink in the refrigerator? I'll be right back."

In less than one minute, Matt yelled, "She's not here. I'm going to jump into the shower. I will be down in no more than a few minutes."

BiBa arrived shortly thereafter and greeted Gisele and Frederic. "God, I haven't seen you guys in so long. Let me run upstairs and cleanup. It's really good to see you. I'll be back in a second."

As she went up to shower, she ran into Matt as he was coming down the stairwell. "When did you guys get here?" she said.

"They were sitting on the stoop when I got done with my workout. That could not have been more than ten minutes ago. Go clean up. We will be in the kitchen."

After a couple glasses of Santa Margarita Pinot Noir, a California wine Matt found at the Chelsea Market, Frederic said, "May the truth be told. This is more than a social visit. We got an e-mail from José. Let me preface by saying, we are not in any imminent danger."

He said, "We are being followed by the Chinese gang Moi employed a few months ago. We have been under surveillance for almost two weeks. He said it could be longer. Our people are looking into it. We are having our connections in the NYPD go through some of their surveillance tapes to try to pin down exactly how long these guys have been tailing us. The Chinese have actually doubled down the last couple of weeks. They started with six people following us.

Now it's up to twelve. As far as we can tell, they have two teams alternating following you then us. They are not all Chinese. In fact, José is impressed by their professionalism. He actually said they're pretty good for gang kids. We have tapped into their communications and don't see them as a threat. As soon as we left Kenya, Chin hired them. We think he is doing this to cover his bases after his guy Moi was killed and he received our video. His people have come up with a timeline of us being in Kenya and all hell is breaking loose. They can't prove a direct correlation between us and Moi, other than we are persons of interest. The kidnapping and our close proximity to Moi make us look like we might be involved. We have overheard communications between Chin and James Mobontu Miles. He was the heir apparent to the Mungiki gang's leadership for all Kenya. He is only the de facto head of the gang's Kibera operations. Now that Kingara is dead, Miles is trying to consolidate his power base and take over all the Mungiki activities in Nairobi. Then he will move to the Central Valley. He thinks it is more than a coincidence his friends and Moi were killed after we entered the picture. We have thrown some false leads his way pointing to one of Moi's wife's cousins. We're trying to give Miles as many different pictures as possible. That should give Malique the needed time to establish proper security measures for Gisele and BiBa when they return to Nairobi. Miles knows something is up. He's trying to understand our relationship with Nakruru and how that corresponds to Moi's assassination. The information they have gathered portrays us as only probable suspects. They don't have much to work with, but they are watching us. It is more like, they want to watch us and wait for us to screw up. Jose sees this as a benefit. He thinks we are safer being under surveillance because they feel we have something they need. José's assessment is that Miles is so arrogant he thinks he can play us. He thinks in the long run it is better than killing us. You know, you don't kill the golden goose."

"Your friend Guzman is very intuitive," said Gisele.

"That video of the killings has gone viral. It had over 100 million hits since we've been back from Kenya. It is the most successful video in UTube history. It is even bigger than the 'Kony and the Lords Resistance Army' video of the Ugandan warlord a few years ago. Our intelligence tells us everyone in Kababi's inner circle is petrified. A directive has been given by the President to protect Nakruru. After Muthaura was killed in the President's house he is not quite as arrogant." José added, "Once Chin got our tape, all hell broke loose in China's Secret Service. The tape, sent from a computer in the regional Ministry of Defense office in Nanking, was sent from a Communist Party office in the lobby of the ministerial building. Everyone who goes in and out of the lobby had access to this computer. No one knows it emanated from our office here in New York through Japan. We have technological advantage when it comes to protecting the origin of our IP address. They will never know where this originated, unless we tell them ourselves. The video must be perceived as a direct threat to Chin. There is a lot about his personal life he can't tell his brother-in-law. The video put us a little under the radar. There is no way it can be traced back to us. Chin is under the belief that somehow we are involved, but doesn't know if we are coming after him. He's very paranoid and the tape is pushing him over the edge."

"BiBa and I are going to have to go back to Nairobi in a few weeks," Gisele said. "We will be safe. José uses the word bulletproof. He stressed that between the security team he and Malique will have in place and the paranoia Kabiba has about protecting us; no one will be foolish enough to come after us. I have been in contact with Nakruru. He wants us to come and see the progress he made. He wants our input before the project is completed. We all agreed it's easier to make changes now rather than later. He is convinced the completion dates of the two clinics will best the 90-day timetable by at least ten days. I don't know if he was being sarcastic or showing signs of stress, but he said, 'I don't want your anticipation to grow faster than what I can achieve. I not only want to deliver things on time, but if I'm early, I have a margin for error. It's important to me that I carry out my responsibilities. I want to be treated as a partner because of my accomplishments."

Giselle continued, "As far as his wife, Sony, is concerned, he thinks she's coming along. She has accepted him working with us but will not utter our names or mention anything about clinics. He laughed when he said she wanted to know about his work but held her tongue. At least that was an improvement over the pure hatred she displayed after the kidnapping."

Looking around the kitchen, BiBa said, "Do you know this is really the first time the four of us have been together and discussed any of this since we've been home? Not actually as bad as I thought it would be. Does this mean our vacation is over?"

Frederic said, "It ain't exactly over, but we do have a lot to do before Matt and I go to China. The way things look; it's about a year off. The clinics have to be set up and the investment arm has to be in place for buying properties and securing mineral rights. We need time not only to rollout the clinics but we have to make sure they work. This is a long process and we are on a knife's edge. If we move too fast, the whole project doesn't have time to come together. If we move too slowly, the Chinese will be in a position where we can't dislodge them from Kenya. If that happens, then they will be able to corner the markets for rare earth elements and heavy metals. The diamond market, because it is bigger, will be more problematical. On that front, we will have more time. Like I said, we are about a year away from going to China. You guys," as he looked at Gisele and BiBa, "will be fixtures in Nairobi before we ever get over there. By then the foundation and Nakruru will be part of the Kenyan landscape."

No one had anything else to add, so Frederic continued, "I don't want to sound rude," as he looked into the refrigerator, "the wine was great but there's nothing to eat. Why don't we get out of here and find some place for dinner. I'm hungry, how about you?" looking at Gisele.

Matt said, "All we have to do is activate the alarm system and we're ready. There are a few new restaurants in the village. Do you guys mind walking or should I call a cab?"

Chapter 41

Six months had elapsed since the last meeting at Matt and BiBa's house. The two women had been in Kenya on four occasions. Matt and Frederic were still in the throes of determining a strategy as to what had to be done in China.

Gisele was in Paris sitting in front of her desk when Frederic called. "Hi beautiful, how are you doing? Something has come up. I am setting up a telephone conference call on our computers in a few minutes. I wanted to talk to you first. I wish I had this information last week when you were here. I guess it always works that way. Nothing is ever easy. We just got some intelligence today. I want to follow our usual protocol and pass it by you and then the others. After your in-put, I will put everybody else online. We have just found that Nakruru's wife is trying to destabilize the clinics in the Central Valley. I want to talk about some specifics and determine the best way to present it to the group. Her involvement is bad. There's more, I want to ask you about what you want to do. This directly involves you and BiBa. Someone has to be killed. Before I get into the meat of this, I just want to know your feelings about you and BiBa going alone on whatever we have to do. Do you want to be out of the equation and have Malique handle it? You are going to have to go to Kenya early. Let me get started and tell you what we have uncovered."

"Frederic, you're starting to worry me. We always bounce ideas off each other, that's how we organized our intelligence gathering. As for Matt, BiBa, and José, they have never been, nor ever will be out of the loop. What is going on? I need to hear about us killing someone!"

Frederic responded, "We are going to have to kill Nakruru's wife. I just didn't want the burden to fall on you and BiBa because we voted or something like that. I wanted to give you a way out if need be."

"Okay," she said, "We will see what happens. I can't speak for BiBa, but whatever happens to that bitch Sony I am sure she is fine with it. I don't think she is up to killing her herself, but she sure as hell wants her dead."

"I will set the conference call and everyone will be online in no more than a couple minutes. I will be sending all of you copies of our intelligence gathered by Malique. We have everything in a document to substantiate her advances on the clinics."

"We are all here," Frederic said.

The group was sitting in front of their computers in different offices around the world. Gisele was in Paris, Frederic, Matt, José and BiBa were in New York, and Malique was in Nairobi.

"We have proof that Nakruru's computer in his home has been hacked. On two occasions, his wife has compromised his personal office computer with all his clinic files. After each breach, she had her people infiltrate some of the Central Valley clinics. We checked the time when the computer was on with Nakruru's schedule and he was not home. In both cases, we can substantiate his whereabouts. That led us to looking at our surveillance of his house and again in both cases we have her on tape sitting at his desk looking at his computer. We know when, which files she entered, and the information she copied was related to the clinics in the Central Valley. Our satellite surveillance shows only one person in the office. The rest of her staff were doing normal chores in other parts of the house. We had expected her curiosity would lead her to breaking into her husband's computer. What we did not know is what she would do with the information. We have proof she hired some family members in Lake Navash to infiltrate the clinics. They used her name to get access to jobs. It took a little more than a month for them to have oversight of medical supplies in each clinic. They tainted some antibiotics, mostly the broad-based antibiotic tetracycline and dispersed it to the Masai. In effect, they went on a killing spree. More than 80 Masai died in the Lake Navash region in a 2-week period. Their goal was to discredit the clinics and cause enough unrest to destroy all the goodwill and trust that had been created. She conspired with some of the Kikuyu mafia type leaders engaging in a rampage of ethnic cleansing. The goal was to get the Masai react to the deaths of their people by burning down the clinics and go on a killing spree of their own. Sony's men left enough evidence behind that pointed directly to the Kikuyu. Their involvement would lead to tribal warfare. She, as far as we can tell, is not only extremely ambitious but this is her form of retribution against her husband. We have tapes of her talking to some of her family members and Kikuyu gang members discussing the blood letting in the Central Valley. I will sum it up. This could be the beginning of a Civil War solidifying Kikuyu rule. There is no doubt about her role in all this. We think she might want a place in Kakiba's government in the future. She does not know we control him. She thinks this is her card to get a position in the Interior Ministry. Nakruru is not at all in any way shape or form involved. We need the two of you," referring to Gisele and BiBa, "to predict his actions. Can we trust him? What will his reaction be when we get rid of his wife? Finally, how do you want to play this?"

BiBa was the first to react. "How much time do we have?"

Frederic responded, "Two weeks max."

"Do we know all of the players?"

He replied, "Yes, We have a lid on this. Here is my suggestion. This is a generalization but I think it will hold true for Nakruru. Most Kikuyu men don't love their wives. At best, their marriages are marriages of convenience, many predetermined by tribal ritual or family ties. In Sony's case, I think she cost him 100-cows, 40-bulls and a number of goats. That is her family's herding background. I also think his family had to throw in some land in North Eastern Kenya close to the Somali border as part of the dowry. This was an arranged marriage. I don't know if love plays any part of it. I don't think he would kill her himself, but I really don't think he would react in any way that might jeopardize his ambition to be president. He wants to be president more than we know. The surveillance of his house shows how distant they have been since the kidnapping. I think her treachery would be the last straw for him. Gisele's take on Nakruru was very consistent with BiBa's position. She wants to get him out of the equation. I don't know if he will authorize her killing. I really did not see this coming. I guess we should have expected something because of her abhorrent behavior the last six months. Her anger towards us has been so excessive we should've figured it would lead to something like this. The sooner we deal with this the better. I think we have to set up her death in such a way as not to disturb any tribal or family relationships. Her family is very wealthy and has a lot of political ties in Kenya, even though they are

Ethiopian. We have to be very careful. I don't know some kind of accident."

"As far as I am concerned," BiBa said, "we will handle this."

Gisele continued, "BiBa, do you want to set up a meeting with Nakruru next week under some pretext of a new deal with that German pharmaceutical company? That way we can get to Kenya early and he won't be suspicious of why we moved up our schedule."

BiBa said she would contact him and set up the trip. There was no doubt Sony's death would make BiBa more whole.

Frederic took over the moderator's role on the conference call. "Gisele, BiBa, you let me know if you need anything. You can fill me in if there is anything out of the ordinary. I think this is about all in regards to Kenya, as far as I am concerned. Does anyone have anything else to add?" There were no responses.

"Okay, I have some things on the Chinese I would like to pass by you guys. All our information directly ties Chin into the kidnapping plot against us. He’s not hiding anything. It’s as if he’s saying I am here, I did it, what are you going to do about it? He is very open about cornering the metals markets worldwide. He didn't start out coming after us in particular. After we contacted Moi in the U.S., even though it was philanthropic in nature, our information says he figured the only reason we would be in Kenya was for purchasing land and metal extraction. Charity was a pretext to him. We don't know how he came to that conclusion, but he did. Our intelligence points to the kidnapping and assassination of three other potential investors. All of them were big in doing Kenyan charity work. They were all interested in mineral rights and land in the Central Valley as well. He had the Mungiki kill every one of them in Nairobi. An Argentine, Hotel by a housekeeper. The others were run over by taxis. All their deaths were signature Mungiki assassinations. Chin went after anybody he perceived as competing with him and locked on to philanthropy for some reason. We hacked into his company's mainframe. He is very transparent on financial matters. Standard accounting principles, but for some reason he set up accounts for bribery, payoffs and foreign political contributions. He is so compulsive that each expenditure has notes for the purpose of the transaction as if he had to report everything he did to some superior. Ledger entry #1125 was for 600,000 Yuan to Kingara with a Matt Papaz notation affixed to it. With China's trading companies behind him, he is a heavy hitter in the futures market. We figure he must report to them. We are still working on who he reports to. There is a connection there, but who he works for is still up in the air. The Chinese, through him, have invested in a lot of US hedge funds. That gives Chin a lot of leverage. The sheer amount of foreign currencies the Chinese accumulate each year because of foreign trade surpluses has to go somewhere and Chin has a lot of it at his access. Almost all of their manufacturing and industrial production is still held in government hands with not much privatization. The banking system is totally centralized. With their trade surpluses, they have to set up trading companies to find places for their money. It is as if there is no end in sight for their economic growth and impending world domination. That is where Chin comes in. He places their money and will do anything to corner a market. When they need speedy access into any country with untapped mineral resources, they use him. He can be described as Chinese Mafia, anything goes. Our analysis shows they cannot continue to grow at rates of 10 to 12% a year for much longer and we forecast an eminent decline in their GDP. We are in a small minority of forecasters but we are convinced they are headed for an economic turndown. All of our studies suggest a severe recession if not depression within the next five years. If that is the case, then we think their international investments, especially in highly leveraged commodities, will be a huge liability to them. These are all the investments they have Chin manage. To a great extent, we think, an economic collapse will cause political chaos and force them to sell off many of their foreign holdings. This will sound counterintuitive, but if we get Chin into a bidding war for minimal rights in Kenya early on, then we will be buying properties at much higher prices today. When their economy falters, then we can purchase the assets back in 5 years for pennies on the dollar. This will be a major sting operation on our part. Our people don't think it is a gamble. The market will collapse, it is just a matter of time, and we have time and money. We will wait them out. This will essentially guarantee our Kenyan friends a higher price on undervalued assets that in effect will subsidize their arrival into the 21st century. Every dollar we put in will leverage the Chinese money amount and therefore subsidize our Kenyan goals. We figured the leveraged to be as much as 15 to 1. If Chin can't kill us, he will do whatever it takes to out bid us. Muscle first, money next. It is simple. The Chinese economy can't continue to grow at 10% forever. We give it five years max. In the short run, Chinese world domination of the metals market is out of the question. With someone as aggressive as Chin running their major operations, it will fall apart sooner rather than later. If they have any downturn we make a financial killing and Kenya is the beneficiary."

Frederick continued, "Our model shows us that we can bid up prices of land in the Central Valley by as much as 900%. If we do it correctly, we can force the Chinese to buy these properties at extremely high prices. When the market crashes, we should be able to get them back and make a great profit. Obviously, when I say we, I am talking about the investment arms of our clinics. With our strategy of reinvesting any profits into infrastructure and education in Kenya, it should bring about remarkable economic growth and redistribution of wealth. We know we can influence the market to make the Chin venture in Kenya much more expensive than he anticipated. We can push him to invest billions more than he planned. Our analysis predicts there is a remarkable opportunity for Kenya. This should give you some insight into what we are trying to accomplish. My problem is it seems too easy. Maybe the Chinese have so much money they don't sense any moral hazard. For them to put trust in people like Chin shows how far they have gone off course. The faster we get our medical clinics online and start to invest, the faster we pull-in Chin. He might be playing us, but we can't see where or how he is doing it. We figure we have at least 10 to 12 months before he starts pursuing mineral rights in the Central Valley. We know a year goes by very quickly. We're lining up our financial backers. At this point, they have committed more than $1.2 billion. Guzman, Kasogi, and the Tijuana Cartel are all 100% behind us. They all feel the worst case is they end up with a good investment in Kenya. Guzman feels he can help. Some of the investments he has in Costa Rica are in partnerships with a US company. It's called C&A Investments. They are a large importer of Chinese raw materials and industrial supplies and are into products like mercury, nickel, and titanium. Most of these metals are used for manufactured goods. Guzman's trading partners in China have been there for over 30 years. C&A CEO, Allen Winters, will help deal with Chin and some of the other Chinese trading companies. Guzman feels that if we give him a small percentage in our Kenyan operation, C&A can act as middleman and open doors that would take years to open. Winters will give us a sense of how to deal with the Chinese. It is evident Chin has no loyalties to anyone other than the Chinese. The only thing he understands is money. Money gives him power and Guzman understands power better than any person I have ever met. So if he endorses Winter, then as far as I am concerned, it is a done deal. I am setting up a meeting with him. He will be in New York in three weeks."

Chapter 42

BiBa called Nakruru to reschedule their visit to Nairobi. His response was one of anticipation.

He concluded the call by saying, "Ms. BiBa," (that's what he called her); "I have much to discuss with you and Ms. Giselle. I need your council and guidance on a potential problem. There are some complications in the staffing of a few clinics in the north and the Lake Navash region. I welcome your early arrival."

BiBa found his apprehension on staffing interesting and coincidental. She asked herself if there could be any leaks in Frederic's Intel; a matter she would take up with him at the earliest opportunity. Doing business in Kenya was always a long and circuitous road. Serendipitously, she and Nakruru were on the same path. BiBa promised she would send him an itinerary and she and Gisele would be there within seven days. The week went by quickly for BiBa and Gisele. They had scripted six different versions of how they would approach Nakruru on his wife's duplicity. Gisele was even willing to show Nakruru the surveillance tapes in his house if necessary. BiBa thought that would be problematic for him because of the issue of trust. Knowing that someone was watching him in his own house would be an incredible violation.

"I couldn't get over something like that no matter how ambitious I was," BiBa said. "I don't think he will feel any different. The unintended consequences of our keeping tabs on him could blow the whole clinic and investment opportunity."

Gisele agreed to the point of using the tapes as a last resort. "We can tell him we were watching Sony and had no other way of doing it. Total surveillance of her movements had to include inside the house as well as out. We can make up something about our suspicions of her and that we did not want to confide in him early on because of the delicate nature of our suspicions."

"I'll tell him that we called and set up the meeting in Nairobi as soon as we confirmed the intelligence," said BiBa. "There is a two-month difference between her access to Nakruru's computer and our meeting with him next week. All the surveillance dates must be changed to make the timelines work. We will tell him we have only been spying in the house for a couple of weeks and did not want to bring him into this until we were quite sure."

Nakruru was waiting at the airport for his two associates. Coming off the airplane from their first-class cabin afforded them the opportunity of clearing customs in a few minutes. Nakruru and his limousine driver were at the baggage carousel with two skycaps as the women walked down the jet way. Upon seeing them, he extended his hands to both women and said he was relieved they got to Nairobi so soon.

"I have important matters to discuss," he said. "We can wait until you are at the hotel, but I would like to talk about them as soon as possible."

Gisele said, "We have a 30 to 40 minute ride, so why not talk on the way to the hotel? It is fine with us. It sounds important so let's start right now. You can brief us once we get to the car."

Nakruru started by saying, "Ms. BiBa, Ms. Gisele, everything we have done with the clinics up to this point has outpaced our projections. The only area I'm having a problem with is staffing. The tribalism is much more exaggerated than I anticipated. The Kikuyus are not willing to concede anything to the other tribes. They are even infiltrating the clinics to make sure they are not effective and sabotaging them to the extent that if people die is not beyond them. It doesn't matter who they go after. It could be the Luo, the Masai, or the Bantu. They will do anything as long as they inflict pain and suffering upon the other tribes. Their plan is to make the clinics unacceptable to the other tribes because they can't trust their lives in the hands of the staff. My problem is we can't detect any of the Kikuyu until it is too late. They misrepresent themselves as other tribe members doing work in the clinics. We don't find out they have done harm to the patients until after someone dies or is hurt. Some patients have died horrible deaths. Some have been gravely injured. It is impossible to catch the Kikuyus until they have literally done irreparable damage. In Lake Navash, we have clinics where three Kikuyu impersonated Masai and were employed as medical assistants. They performed female castration on two girls and intentionally left, them permanently disfigured with no prospect of ever bearing children. In another clinic in the Central Valley, five women were sedated and raped. By the time we understood what was happening and how grievously the Masai women were attacked, the perpetrators were gone. This is a coordinated attack on our clinics."

Gisele spoke first. Nakruru had been speaking to them while facing the two women as they were looking directly at him. His seat was facing the back of the car and the two women were looking at him facing the road ahead of them.

"I assume that the glass plate between you and the driver gives us total privacy."

He nodded his head, "I would not speak in such a manner if it didn't. We have no worries. The driver is forced to wear a headset that covers both ears and renders him deaf to outside communication. The earphones are controlled by the car following us and our driver can only hear whatever is provided to him. If he tries to disengage his earphones and tries to drop in on our conversation, we will know instantly. Our security team has been direct and emphatic in telling him that if we detect any attempt on his part to listen to our conversation that he will be killed. At random, intervals he is asked questions that can only be answered if his earphones are in place. Malique oversees my every move. He provides security for you as well, so I am sure you are familiar with how airtight his procedures are. So, as for the question of privacy, yes we are by ourselves and no one can hear."

BiBa interjected, "Obviously your staffing problems need to be looked into before we can proceed. What is Malique's take on all of this? Frederic has a whole host of surveillance tools at his disposal that might augment yours and Malique's. We want you to pass along all of your information and everything you told us directly to Frederic. He, you, and Malique will work closely to get to the bottom of this. We can hold off on the pharmaceutical matter until we clear this up. Infiltration of our clinics can derail the whole project. On first blush, excuse me that is an American saying. It means what are your gut reactions? What is your intuition on this? Sometimes people's intuitions are a good gauge of what actually is happening."

Nakruru said, “My reaction to all this is that I underestimated the Kikuyu. I think we have to purge every one of them from our clinics by a show of force. It has to be something for all of the tribes to see. If the Kikuyu have infiltrated our clinics, then the other tribes or clans are not far behind. I don't know how deep this is. That's why I'm so concerned. I feel we have to be bold and make a statement, a statement to all the tribes. We have to do it now. I have a list of over 200 people. They all are dangerous and would never show loyalty to me. These are people from different clans and tribes, and people in Kababi's inner circle. All 200 want to do us harm. What makes it so troubling is there are people who have been close to me. Some of my closest allies, both personally and politically. I have worked with and have been friends with many of them for years. I am willing to act and do whatever has to be done for Kenya."

BiBa said, "Have you ever heard that your first loss is your best loss? What it means is, do whatever you have to now because the price will be much greater later. I sense this is the case. I think you know once we set things in motion many people will die. Saying you know this is best for Kenya might be different than actually doing it. There might be a big problem to all of this. Do we have the resources to go after two hundred people?"

"This is Jose's and Malique's problem," he said. "I defer to them on these issues. They are our security experts. Do we have enough political capital to do this without causing a civil war?"

Gisele asked. "I think Kabiba is on a tight enough leash. We control him. He will not be a major problem. Our security has to be a given before we set a plan into motion to kill hundreds of people. Obviously this has to be taken to the highest degree of planning before we kill anyone."

She was looking directly into Nakruru's eyes, "Earlier you talked about the Kikuyu infiltration and the domino effect on the other tribes. I think you are correct in suggesting that if the Kikuyus are engaged, then we can surmise the other tribes are doing it as well. I have a delicate question to ask you. How would you react if we told you that your wife was involved in all of this? What would you say to the fact that Malique's and Frederic's intelligence have come to the same conclusion that Sony and her family were behind the plot in Lake Navash?"

Nakruru wasn't put off by the statement and said, "She is Ethiopian and she was very close to the Kikuyu through her uncle. He helped bring her up and he is traditional Kikuyu. She is like a reborn Christian when it comes to the Kikuyu traditions. She has strong ideas and is incapable of compromise. When we were married, I told you it was an arranged marriage. It was a traditional Kikuyu marriage. I even had to pay a dowry. She had to be educated in the Kikuyu traditions and learn the old ways of the tribe. Because of that, she has more loyalty to her uncle and his traditional Kikuyu ways than to me. Her uncle was instrumental in the last Civil War. His brother, her father, is weak minded and follows everything the uncle does. They were both responsible for killing many Masai in the Central Valley. They have ties to the Mungiki in Nairobi where hundreds of Masai were massacred. Neither was prosecuted by the World

Court, but are as guilty as any Kikuyu for war crimes. It would not surprise me if she were behind this. She is vengeful and vicious when it comes to protecting the Kikuyus. I would need proof before you condemn her to die, but this does not surprise me. We have a saying here in Kenya, you can't train a baboon to be a pet. It is only a matter of time before the beast turns on you. All you can do is be sure of their intentions and never give them an opportunity by turning your back. I know what Sony is. I have lived with her for many years. She is the mother of my children, and no, she means nothing else to me. It is important that if she is behind this, when we kill her it does not get back to my children. No, this does not surprise me."

Both Gisele and BiBa were taken aback by his cold response. "You see my friends, a new Kenya is much more important than an old defiant Kikuyu bitch who is the mother of my children. If Kenya is to move forward, we must westernize. People like Sony and her family are incapable of moving forward. People like her kill, just to live in the past."

They arrived at the hotel. It was evident Nakruru wanted to continue the conversation. "I know the flight was long. Do you need to clean-up and get something to eat or may we finish our discussion? We must deal with Sony and her family as soon as possible."

Chapter 43

Nakruru was not shocked about Sony's involvement in the killings in the Central Valley.

"I am dismayed at how open she must have been for you to detect her so easily," he said. "I never thought she would be so open about her activities after the World Court decisions to indict some of her cronies on crimes against humanity. I underestimated her hatred for me, and we've lived in the same house for over ten years. I will get back to her in a minute. I hope you understand how upsetting this is to me. Now I have some things I want to address."

He was very formal. This was his way of deflecting emotions. "I would like to discuss the clinics. That will be easier for me," he proceeded. "After all the kinks in the operations of the two Central Valley medical clinics are ironed out, I will be ready to roll out the clinics across Kenya. My original forecast had them at a break- even point in 8 months, and generating an operational profit by the 12 months. Then collectively the autonomous units will invest in local real estate for their own tribe. The totality of the 110 clinic's investments held in a limited liability corporation under the management of Nakruru Enterprises. The clinics will have a pro-rata participation predicated upon their profits. As the first choice of our investment, land and mineral rights will be purchased from foreign nationals or from the Kenyan National Trust. Tribes will not be allowed to purchase lands or mineral rights from other competing tribes. When there are any properties owned by the tribe's people running the clinic – Kikuyu clinic / Kikuyu existing landholder – then the investment committee will approach the landholder to negotiate a partnership. Cooperation within the tribe is our first priority. This would eliminate any conflict of interest and allow for greater amalgamation of wealth within the tribe itself. I, myself, will deal with inter-tribe purchases. As you said, all profits of the 110 clinics will be matched by Matt Papaz Foundation monies, dollar for dollar."

Nakruru's analysis of the real estate market in Kenya's Central Valley suggested that it could absorb small incremental increases in demand before the marketplace would adjust by seeing higher prices, thus giving them time before Chin was alerted to outside competition for heavy metals or rare earth metals properties or mineral rights. His estimate was that an injection of $300 million in small transactions of less than $100 thousand per parcel of land would not precipitously move the price structure of the market. Gradual price increases would go unnoticed for at least a year before a tipping point would signal a demand-pull inflationary pressure that would get Chin's attention. By the time, Chin found out Malique had taken over the Mungiki gangs and effectively squeezed him out of the marketplace, the clinics investment arms would be entrenched into real estate and mineral rights acquisitions. Nakruru would have a leg up on his Chinese counterpart in acquiring all the best properties in the Central Valley. He felt everything was in place and operative on the real estate front.

He took a deep breath, "Now I want to talk about Sony. She has to be dealt with. She and her father and uncle must be killed."

BiBa, Gisele, and Nakruru agreed the longer they waited, the more complicated the issue would become. Her activities and routines were now monitored on a daily basis; not only Malique but Nakruru would have his wife tailed. Nakruru knew his wife's whereabouts at all times. Malique infiltrated her staff and she was under constant electronic surveillance as they spoke. Her routines never changed. She would have breakfast with her children and then have them taken to school every morning at 7:30 a.m. by her own personal driver. She would attend to her office in the animal rescue center on their estate. It was still intact after the kidnapping and subsequent fire that demolished their home. Twice a week she would meet her uncle and her father for tea. She would seldom see Nakruru before 8 p.m. because of their conflicting schedules. She was very precise in her daily routines and never deviated from her patterns.

Nakruru said, "We have to develop a plan where her death will be covered up, as not to scar my children. They must never know anything about their mother's death."

His hatred for her was so overwhelming he wanted her to suffer great pain and humiliation. He also wanted her uncle and father killed at the same time. The two men were on the antagonist list that he had compiled. He devised a simple plan. It was important to Nakruru to be personally involved in his wife's death. He did not want to pull the trigger, but he wanted her killed.

"The three of them can be coaxed into a meeting at the office of the new leaders of the Mungiki gang," he said. "All we have to do is somehow offer them money and they will go to the heart of the Kibera district in downtown Nairobi. Upon entering the office, they will be apprehended, tortured and then killed. Their dead bodies will be placed in an SUV driven by one of my men who is disposable. The

SUV, with the four passengers, will be run into by a long-haul 18-wheel semi-truck and demolished beyond all recognition. Because of her prominence as the wife of an ex-government official, the accident would be played out in all of the newspapers and be seen on local television. The children will never learn the truth of their mother being killed over her treacherous disloyalty to me. It is obvious I have thought of my wife's death but I never thought I would have the opportunity to see it really happen. Let Malique put it together. My plan is sound."

Both BiBa and Gisele were shocked but understood.

Sitting in his office in Chongqing, the largest city in China, with a population of more than 33 million, Chin tried to determine how his adversaries had accomplished so much in such a short time. The news of Sony Nakruru's death acted as a warning to Chin. The killing of the Mungiki and Masai gang leaders and the e-mail that so vividly depicted their deaths was not so distant a memory. The three events created a critical mass of threatening information that got Chin's attention. It was Chin's custom when confronted with a problem to leave his office in Chongqing central business district and walk through the center's pedestrian only walkways to calm his nerves. His office was in the city's newly developed financial district that was composed of financial institutions and upscale retail malls. Encircled by 60 to 70 story high-rise buildings, the center's central plaza created a Rockefeller Center type skyline. High-end stores like Gucci, Rolex, Zygna, Paul and Shark,

Hugo Boss, and many others were dispersed between major upscale restaurants and western style coffee shops. The area, with its extremely wide walking corridors, was a car free zone. Chin would leave his office to smoke a cigarette and get lost in the mass of humanity that frantically walked from one establishment to another. The area had the vibrancy and ambiance of Hong Kong; its activity had a calming effect on Chin. Watching people milling around slowed down his mind and allowed him to focus and be a problem solver. It was counter intuitive but he functioned well in the midst of chaos. Being in the crowd was invigorating. He loved the tactile feel of the crowds pushing on him to get from one place to another. He loved the smell of the restaurants. He loved looking at all of the window displays of the world's most expensive stores. The environment of the central plaza was like eye candy to him. The high-pitched voices of women dressed in their tight fitting Western clothing was sexually arousing to him even though he had the proclivities of a pedophile. All the street action slowed down his overactive mind and allowed him to probe into problems confronting his future. Chaos and sensory stimulation were the drugs allowing him to focus. It was no different than someone with ADD given a drug like Ritalin to slow down their brain functions. Sitting at a small table in front of the China Construction Bank, with a cup of coffee and a cigarette, he could bring his pulse rate down to the low 40's just by looking at his surroundings. Seated at a table and taking a deep drag on his cigarette, he knew he had to accelerate his investments in Kenya.

The Papaz Group's message had struck a note of personal concern. The e-mail depicted the killing of Moi and the Mungiki gang leaders had emanated from General Lie Waungjian, office of defense's vice-minister, was a personal attack on him. It showed the capabilities of his adversaries. He felt the intense pressure of uncertainty. The new rich like Chin were psychopaths because of the short run nature of their existence. They were the Chinese risk-takers and were rewarded handsomely for it. He was only as safe as the people in power, in this case his brother-in-law. A new regime would extricate both of them from society. Many of the new rich life expectancies were predicated upon which faction in the Chinese Politburo was in power. He was very much like all young Chinese billionaires who had made their money fast and furiously by riding upon the shoulders of their Communist party sponsors. The uncertainty and brevity of his future made Chin a dangerous man. Long-run consequences of any of his activities were a moot point. All his decision-making was short term in nature and based on the great warrior, Sun Tsu, who articulated victory at any price, was acceptable. Brutality, loss of life, corruption, and amorality were the tools of Chin's trade. He was the ultimate Chinese warrior, fighting for China's world dominance. China had a group of young entrepreneurs, and Chin was one of many who made their money through back door agreements with the old communist guard members. Their relationship was predicated upon corruption and cronyism in their dealings with the party in selling off government infrastructure under the guise of privatization. Chin was in a group of the Chinese power elite who were necessary but expendable. Over the decades, since the fall of Mao, the names of the Chinese government's underworld movers and shakers were interchangeable, but their services were instrumental in China's economic miracle. They all had short-term lives of exaggerated wealth and power. Their decision-making was not rational or acceptable for the long-term goals of the government, but their methods to bring about change were imperative for China's future. By definition, they were a dying breed that was the byproduct of rampant capitalism. Chin knew of his eventual fate but Kenya dominated his thoughts.

Chin would have to make a play at Matt sooner rather than later. Sitting by himself and smoking his cigarette while contemplating how to proceed was an aphrodisiac for him. The people walking by and the sights and sounds of the financial center were the mental stimulus he needed to focus. Engaging in deep thought, despite foreseeable personal risks, was like an opiate for him. He lived for these moments. Preparing for battle was his existence. Planning was an elixir. The execution of putting an organization in place and buying property and mineral rights in Kenya would take him to war. The prospects of winning and the attendant spoils would only further his hedonistic lifestyle. He knew Kenya would be just one more step to his meteoric rise to power. He was manic, an offshoot of Asberger Disease, which meant he had the ability to focus for 30 to 40 straight hours without sleep or rest. He would self medicate by drinking coffee and smoking cigarettes. The caffeine and nicotine were a natural substitute for Adderall. The economic campaign victories in his short career had made him a billionaire, but more importantly, he needed the praise and adulation of the higher-ups in the Communist Party. Another economic victory, in this case Kenya, would lead to his acting out his sexual depravity. His life cycle was preparation, battle, and victory. His self-indulgence in the form of pedophilia and pure hedonism were the prizes for his efforts. The cycles of highs and lows were all too familiar to Chin. In preparation for war, he would get off his medicine to feel the power of his mania. Preparation, war, and finally the highest level of depravity, sex. This completed the upside of his cycle. Once he had achieved a new directive from his brother-in-law, he felt he had fulfilled his life's calling. Every war was his ultimate passion superseding anything he had ever done before. Meeting the task of war and ultimate success always led to severe depression. The perpetual, never-ending highs and lows could be mollified only by the civility and stability of his wife and children. His thirst forever-greater challenges would bring him to new higher ultimate stimulation that carried with them greater risks. It was as if he had to seek activities of greater danger to stay at the same emotional level. His highs were ever expanding which led to greater risks and personal vulnerability, but they fed his appetite for life. As he sat drinking a cup of coffee, the noise of the crowd created a symmetry that energized him for combat with the Papaz Group. It would not be long before he challenged his adversaries.

An hour and half after leaving his office, Chin calmly walked back to the World Trade Center and placed a call to his wife. He told her he would have to go to Shanghai on business and would be back in a couple of days. He talked to his brother-in-law and some other higher ranked members of the Communist Party to set up a meeting to present his plan for accumulating mineral rights and leases for diamond mines in Kenya. They would give him a blank check and a license to kill, or whatever was necessary, to ensure resources for China's economic miracle

The three-hour flight on a military plane was all business for Chin. He laid out his plans and strategies for cornering the nonferrous metal market and his plans for injecting $400 million into the fledgling diamond mining operations in Kenya. His analysis projected another $400 million from his Zimbabwean partners. He would find his plans inadequate because of the advent of Nakruru's and the Papaz Group's incremental investment. He was forced to jump into the marketplace as quickly as possible. Looking at surveys from the United States Geological Association, it became apparent Nakruru had already purchased large land tracts and leases for mineral rights in the most strategic areas of the Central Valley. Future land and leases purchases would be valueless to the Chinese because they would have no access to transportation hubs. The clinics, in some circumstances, had purchased large land tracks that made secondary investment worthless. Nakruru's preemptive purchases put Chin in a position of weakness. Walking off the plane, he was met by his brother-in-law, Li Xueming, and his assistant, Bo Xilai. These 3-men were similar in height but Chin was 15 years their junior and more muscled. All three were 5'7" tall, with jet-black hair and deep black eyes, with the southern Chinese characteristics of olive colored skin. China prided itself on ethnic diversity even though 90% of the people were Han. The 56 ethnic groups that cohabited mainland China were essentially Han and a scattering of other peoples. Everywhere in southern China, the features of the Han majority displayed the same DNA. They were all wiry with soft rounded shoulders. Their feet and hands were small even for their short stature. Most displayed poor oral hygiene as evidenced by bad teeth. Many had poor eyesight. The majority looked young for their age with flawless skin that held its elasticity well into their 60's. Chin was different. He was more westernized. He augmented his heavier set frame with weight training. His hair was shorter and less traditional than the average Chinese business person. His clothing was more stylish. He wore an Armani cut rather than the traditional Brooks Brothers suit of his contemporaries. His lips were fuller and his cheekbones were higher. All southern Chinese had similar bloodlines, even though China has a history of being invaded by outsiders. Conquering nations like the Mongols in northern China and the Vietnamese in southern China all assimilated into Chinese culture. After thousands of years, their DNA blended into the

Chinese gene pool, which made for a homogeneous population. Chin tried to differentiate his looks as a menacing warning for all to tread carefully. He was not deferential to equals or lesser. He treated incidentals, his phrase for people who offered him nothing, as no more than a beast of burden. He was harsh and condescending, but most of all he was brutal to people he felt superior to. He was not traditional in any sense of the word, but aggressive and assertive in his personal and professional dealings. His way of doing business was 21st-century cowboy laissez-faire. Through his relationships with his brother-in-law, he was given the most sensitive assignments to further China's economic hegemony. He was not a gangster like the Triads in Hong Kong. He did not act like a front man for China's large trading and holding companies. Chin was his own kind of brash. He was pathological and comfortable with it. He viewed himself as an expediter who could get things done, even if it meant the use of excessive force and society destabilization as evidenced by his work in Somalia and now Kenya. Chin was ready for war.

Chapter 44

Matt and Frederic flew Air Canada from New York to Hong Kong. The 16-hour flight over the polar route was arduous even for first-class passengers. Upon arrival at Hong Kong International Airport on Lantu Island, Syrial Lai and his wife Alice greeted them. Syrial an associate of Jose Guzman had business ties throughout Latin America. They invested together and successfully developed many hotel properties on the Costa Rican Pacific side. The 30-km drive from the airport to Hong Kong Island, where the

Lai's lived, took less than 45 minutes. In the Hong Kong's Victoria Peak District, their house was in one of the most exclusive neighborhoods in the world. The limousine pulled up to 87 Peak Road, the upper strata of living in the Chinese protectorate. The homes were owned by two types of Chinese, the old rich with inherited wealth and the new rich with political ties of cronyism to the Communist Party. The estates were on some of most beautiful property in all Asia. Syrial and Alice's house was an early 20th century colonial structure of 1,000m². It was modest by Peak standards but it would have a selling price of over $45 million if it were for sale. Matt and Frederic were mindful of their own substantial net worth, but their wealth paled in comparison to Syrial's and other Chinese business men living in the area.

Syrial was a slight man, 5 feet 3 inches tall weighing 120-pounds. He had a receding hairline and wore thick glasses since he was 11 years old. Despite being in his early 60, he looked ten years younger. As a young boy, he was sent to boarding school in England, where he attended the famous St. John Academy in the West End of London. In the mid 20th century, the great city considered gateway to the world. Because of his cultural environment, he considered himself a person of the world, not a Hong Kong Chinese. From high school, he went directly to the London School of Economics, where he received a degree in econometrics. From there he entered MIT and graduated with a Master's degree in business economics. At the age of 24, he moved with his younger brother to Toronto, Canada and took a job in the Bank of Montréal trading department. Leveraging family money, he began trading commodities on his own, and by the time he was 32 he had a net worth of over $750 million. He expanded his financial empire by purchasing real estate in Latin America. In his advanced years as a seasoned investor, he met Jose Guzman. They were principals that put together real estate syndications in Papagayo, Costa Rica, which was the first major development for foreigners in Costa Rica. Their projects included condominiums, golf courses, and a 5-star Four Seasons Hotel. Their total investment of more than $100 million was leveraged by the Construction Bank of China, which allowed them to purchase more than $500 million worth of beachfront property. Guzman, as per his general mode of operation, kept his personal anonymity through using an investment arm of one of the hedge funds. Jose's relationship with his Chinese friend was long standing. He felt comfortable asking his good friend Syrial to bring Matt and Frederic up to speed on China's internal politics. He would brief them on all the political and financial players. In the past, Syrial had financial dealings with Chin and had strong opinions Guzman felt his two associates should hear.

Their estate overlooked the Kowloon side of Hong Kong. Alice, the consummate businessperson's wife, welcomed Frederic and Matt to her home. "Please let me show you your rooms and you can freshen while I have one of our staff unpack your belongings. After you come down, we will have a little something to eat. Can I get a drink for you before you go up?"

Matt responded that he would like a Scotch on the rocks.

Frederick said, "The same for me."

Looking at Syrial before the two went up stairs Frederick uttered, "That is the most magnificent view I have ever seen," looking at the skyline across the Hong Kong channel.

The house sat directly across from Hong Kong's tallest building, the ICC Center, which housed the Ritz-Carlton Hotel.

Syrial said, "Before you go upstairs, please let Alice show you our home."

As they walked through the entryway of the house to the living room, the view was magnified by floor-to-ceiling windows overlooking the city. The main room was filled with Ming Dynasty antiques and Persian rugs Syrial had collected since his youth. Contiguous to the living room was his library and a collection of 16th century calligraphy tapestries. Alice's office was directly across from Syrial's book and art collection, but was more contemporary in its design. The remaining rooms on the first level of the Lai home were a dining room and an adjacent kitchen. The dining room table was a circular cherry wood antique that sat 18 people. As they climbed the circular staircase to the second floor, Alice pointed out their bedrooms that had the same magnificent view over looking the Star Ferry building on the Kowloon side of Hong Kong. She pointed to a double door carving of a Phoenix and a Dragon and said that was their master bedroom. The house was decorated with some of the most beautiful Chinese art and furniture Matt or Frederic had ever seen. The Lais had purchased most of the home's belongings in Europe because of the British proclivity to plunder their colonies. It was Matt's conjecture that the value of the collectibles in the house must be in the neighborhood of $15 million.

Before both men went to their rooms to clean up Syrial said, "This was my father's house. We treasure it and so do our children. We are very fortunate to have lived here for so many years and we are hopeful our son Nicholas will be able to say the same thing when he reaches our age. Family and homes are very important to the lives of people in Hong Kong."

After cleaning up and walking downstairs for another drink and some appetizers, the Lais and their guests walked outside to their waiting limousine. It took 15-minutes to cross under the channel and arrive at Hong Kong's most acclaimed restaurant, Hutong's, which was on the 28th floor of the One Peking Road Building. The decor was 18th century Chin Dynasty. The hostess escorted them to an area of the restaurant where they had to take off their shoes. This was usually a Japanese tradition and Frederic referenced it. They sat on benches with plush red cushions. On the wall behind them were antique tapestries. In front of them was a view of Hong Kong Island where the Lais lived. The buildings across from the Kowloon side where they were sitting consisted of some of the finest architecture in the world. The tallest and most important was the ICC 104-story counterpart to the Ritz-Carlton. There were at least 80 high-rise buildings of 70 stories or more. Most of the glass fascias of these immense buildings were of different color tinting. All of them had been developed with the aid of the ancient art of Feng Shui and were facing the tranquil waters of Hong Kong Island. At 9:00 pm, a laser show sent beams of green light into the sky and across the channel. Matt and Frederic were both sophisticated world travelers, but neither had ever seen a display of such beauty in so grand a setting. The juxtaposition of the ancient interior design of the restaurant, and the ultramodern skyline of Hong Kong, was a metaphor for the new China.

Alice said, "I hope you don't mind, but I have already ordered for us."

Over the next hour, a 15-course meal was placed on the lazy Susan in the center of the table. The feast consisted of pork, chicken, beef, jelly fish, small succulent sea water prawns, bear paws, white fish in peanut sauce, all accompanied by soy sauce and sweet-and-sour sauce. There were greens of all varieties; bamboo, succulent peas, pasta and dim sum filled with chicken and pork. The last course of the meal was a mango sherbet dessert. Syrial brought along three bottles of Chilean estate wines from his wine collection of over 5000 bottles. Absolutely charming Alice described the historical sites they would visit and professed her love for the city of Hong Kong. As Frederic said later, she should have been the mayor of Hong Kong. She discussed her childhood with such glowing emotion that Matt and Frederic felt the glory of the former British colony. Pointing at different places along the skyline, she discussed the dynamic nature of growth she had seen over a lifetime. She talked with great love and affection of her sisters and brothers and her lifelong friendships with her schoolmates in boarding school. It was evident the love of her life was her son Nicolas. Syrial talked about his family, how fortunate he was to be one of the early Jockey Club founders that generated many of his business relationships over the years. Both Lais held positions in social organizations and they were on boards of many civic and corporate entities in Hong Kong. Syrial was thankful for his inheritance from his family that allowed him to create wealth and prominence. His boarding school experience taught him to work hard and compete, forming relationships with the right people. He learned the importance of family. His equation for success was an amalgamation of his childhood experiences.

He made a statement that stuck with Matt, "I am fortunate to have inherited wealth, but to be able to compete in a great city like Hong Kong, which is the most competitive business environment in the world, you are not only successful by what you have been given, but you are successful by what you learn. It is a long road to success. Over the years, a road accumulating partnerships and relationships determining your fate. Our history here in China has given us the fundamentals to be successful. Without my parent's teachings, and my formal academic training, the values of our ancestors would be lost. Business is no more than a way to perpetuate society and it is been the calling of my family to do so."

Looking directly at Matt he continued, "I sense you feel it is a burden to be successful. It is not an obligation or burden, my friend. It's a blessing that has made China the most powerful country in the history of the world. Our wealth commands respect because it employs so many people. We, as yet, do not have labor laws, nor do we have a tax structure that redistributes wealth, but we have an emerging populist view of the future. Workers who come from the fields to the factories are wealthier than ever before. Companies like Foxcon, producing iPads and iPhones, brings millions of people into the new age of Chinese domination. Wages are low, less than a dollar an hour, but are 10-times higher than people were making in the old China twenty years ago. Labor laws and international oversight are creating better working conditions and better pay for millions of Chinese. Most of our people are now out of poverty. We call ourselves the old rich because we create jobs and products and render services. We were the forerunner to the new China. We call ourselves the millionaires of yesterday but we confront the young billionaires of today. All they do is trade paper, but they give the resources for growing China into the 21st century. They are solely money engineers, but I find them treacherous. They're like the locust. They accumulate wealth by stripping away the surface of our community. Men like Chin live above me on the Peak. Unimaginably, their houses are bigger, their bank accounts are filled with billions of dollars, and they have completely amoral political power. They live for their own short-run gain and have no regard for our beloved China and its people. For anyone, even me, to continue to do business in China, we must pay tax to these new rich. People like me, the old guard, who create jobs and allow China to advance to its rightful position of world leader, must learn to deal with the likes of Chin. He and people like him have been given franchises on all private financial matters from the Communist Party. Their influence in government circles can ensure success or failure in any business endeavor. To do business with them is to pay tribute by giving a percentage of ownership or direct money payments for the rest of our lives. They act as a Mafia. This type of corruption is very much what takes place in Russia or the Middle East. It is not efficient, it is not fair, but it is a price of cowboy capitalism. Their reckless investment and the huge amount of resources needed for large-scale projects, such as the massive skyscrapers, are the new China. The financial risks they take and the financial innovations they create are necessary for China to move into the 21st century, but it brings these people great power. They are vile masters who view people as their inferiors. At the same table, they will not sit with me, or anyone below me in the economic food chain. I feel their brashness and arrogance is only capable of producing a future that will crumble like many of the buildings they constructed in such short time periods. My China has five thousand years of history and monuments that will last forever, but these fellows are creating things that will last for 20 or 30 years, knowing that they can always produce more. They don't look at the human cost, they don't look at the social costs, and the new rich only want to make more and more money. When I was a young man at university and studied mathematics there was a term called a stochastic variable. Some mathematicians call it an extraneous root. It was a number generated by an equation and it didn't make sense. A number that is not necessary. It is, as if a family had a bastard child that was worthless. These new rich are bastard children that come from the very nature of our economic growth. If we are to grow because of laissez-faire cowboy capitalism, with limited government regulation, then the cost is the new rich. By bringing our people into the 21st-century, then we must face the consequences of the people like Chin. I have said to my wife Alice on many occasions, he is not smarter than me, he is no more important than me, and he surely doesn't add more to society than me, but he lives on the top of the hill and can buy and sell me in an instant. He lives for today and only for himself. He cares not about family or friends or the history of this great country, but men like him push us into the new world."

Syrial quickly changed the subject. Matt and Frederic could see the pain in his face.

"No more of this talk tonight. We are here to enjoy the food and the wonderful view. We will discuss Chin tomorrow."

When they finished dinner, Alice suggested they go for walk along the famous Nathan Road, but Syrial wanted to walk to the water's edge, to the observation platform in front of the art museum. As they approached the old Star Ferry building, they felt a gentle wind blowing off the channel. The air was crisp but invigorating. Walking past the art museum to the backend of the Intercontinental Hotel presented a view of Hong Kong Island that was totally different. In the clear night air, the lights glistened off the glass faces of large structures across from them. They felt the size and power of the architecture that lay before them. Matt questioned the amount of energy and resources needed to create such an artificial atmosphere. They were looking at the highest population density level in a major city in the world. Hong Kong had more than 120,000 people per square mile as a density ratio. What made it all the more impressive was how efficiently it worked. It was truly a miracle.

On the way back to the Hong Kong side, Syrial said they should sleep-in the next morning because they would need all their energy for his briefing on Chin and the new rich.

Matt woke up at approximately 8:30 a.m. to the smell of bacon. Alice and her cook were preparing a Western-style breakfast. It was a total surprise to both Matt and Frederic. By the time the two men had showered and come down, breakfast was presented in a continental fashion. It was as if they were eating a buffet in one of the leading restaurants in the city, with a spectacular view of Hong Kong laid out before them.

Alice was still the consummate host. She pointed out landmarks across the channel as if she were a tour guide. "Syrial and I have already discussed this and I feel you would get a better idea of China by traveling to the interior. It will help you make better judgments on our future and how to deal with Chin. There are people like him who will take us deep into the 21st century," she said. "You must know what they stand for, to engage with them. We have set up a two-week trip for you to review the inner-workings of our country. It should give you a better feeling for our diversity, our history, and our ability to amass hundreds of thousands of workers for projects all over China, creating our place of greatness in the world. To speak of China and not actually see it would be a mistake. You would misjudge our resolve and our abilities. Syrial and I have talked. It is unusual for a woman to speak of men's matters, but he thought it was appropriate for me to prepare you before his briefing on Chin. Syrial expects me to be the family historian. I will give you a little history of China you might feel is novel. Most Westerners' knowledge of China starts in the early 1900's, with the Boxer Rebellion, or if someone is a bit more sophisticated, maybe our history starts with the opium wars and British control. Many outsiders think of China in the 1930's and 40's and how the Japanese conquered us and enslaved our people. Some Westerners look at the 1940's and 50's thinking of Mao and the Cultural Revolution. Many look at China as a country of starvation, where millions of people died and others ravaged by great pandemics or national disasters. You may still look at China as a poor weak country, and do not understand we were the greatest civilization in the history of the world. We dominated the known world for more than 50 centuries. What is frightening to us Chinese is all that you understand about us is the period of weakness and decay from the last Emperor to 20 or 30 years ago. Today we are back on track to be the greatest country in the world once again. I maintain we have dominated others for thousands of years and we will do it again. You think your President and your country are the most powerful in the world, or at least you think you are the most important in the world. You have dominated the economic and political scene for only 50-years and during this period, you have become arrogant. We controlled the world 100-times longer and were never unaware of our responsibilities. I did not say we were ever democratic. That is another subject. What concerns me is you in the West have become blind to China's greatness and its rightful place as the most dominant power in the world. In the last 30 years, our growth rate has brought us from being one of the poorest countries in the world to one of the richest. The world has never seen this kind of growth. In 25 to 30 years, our per capita income will be higher than any industrial country. I want you to understand our ability to harness our labor and other resources with greater direction than any people in history. I want you to consider the greatness of China and its needs when you have to deal with Chin, and his quest for resources that will allow us to fulfill our destiny.

View our greatness with an open eye. Don't be fooled by your false pride in America and Europe. The world is no longer Eurocentric; it is centered in China. You will see it is our goal to retain our powers of the past and move our people into the future. Imagine the forces at work that can bring

1,300,000,000 people from death's door to the highest standard of living in your lifetime. Do you think the West can stop us? Do you think the resources we need for our growth, will be used better by the people in Africa or South America who have no direction and have no history? After you have seen our mighty country in an objective way, you will know it's impossible to stop our progress and more importantly, why would you want to? We will use the world's scarce resources more efficiently than the countries who possess the raw materials we seek. We will take those minerals and energy sources and fill the shelves of the world's stores with the best lowest cost products. We are not devils. We are the future. Gentlemen, I only ask of you to make sure your assessment of my country is not be prejudiced by your anger or you ignorance. China is to be reckoned with as a force headed toward world dominance. Chin is one of the many warriors bringing us back to that position. No matter how much we hate him, we need men with his skills. Think of all we have done in the last 50 years and understand the sheer number of people and resources needed to speed our entry into the 21st century. Think of the logistics and planning and ask yourself if any other people could do what we have done. It is impossible to stop our progress. I want you to see my country on the ground and be more objective about how to deal with us. Make sure you understand the role for China in today's world. Outsiders have never conquered my country for a long time period. No one has made my people assimilate into their culture. It has always been the other way around. For 5,000 years, anyone who came to China became Chinese. With new markets opening because of international trade, people are coming to our shores, and I guarantee you they will become Chinese. My friends, there is no other way. I apologize for my frankness and I apologize for my passion, but I know China. What I know most is China is the greatest country in the world because of its people. We will regain our history and we will do it in my lifetime. Gentlemen, I say this and I am old. There is no stopping us. You will learn the lessons of our greatness while you are here and you will become Chinese. This is the path people have taken for 5,000 years."

She turned around and started to walk towards the door and finished by saying, "I will leave you to my husband."

Matt and Frederic were speechless. She wasn't self-righteous. She was honest in her understanding of herself and her country. They had been in Hong Kong for less than one day and she had changed their thinking even before Syrial had begun to brief them.

Chapter 45

Syrial received a phone call from Guzman in the late morning that would be a game changer for his plans with Matt and Frederic. Chin had put a hit on both men in China. He also made contact with the Mungiki gang to kill BiBa and Gisele in Kenya. It was Al Qaeda-like in scope, multiple operations to eliminate an enemy or inflict as much damage as possible in one timeframe.

Syrial spoke to both men, "You are safe here in Hong Kong."

They didn't know what he was talking about but obviously, his bringing up their safety raised some questions.

"I just spoke with Guzman and he informed me that Chin is preparing to make a major move. Jose wants to talk to you as soon as possible but let me reassure you. While you are here in Hong Kong, you are safe. Mainland China treats Hong Kong and Macau as neutral zones from any type political killings. They are not like the Hong Kong Triad, but the communists will follow your movements while you are here. We have our problems here in Hong Kong but it won't come from Chin. The information from Guzman will not change our plans. He will fill you in on all of this. While you are here, I want you to know that Alice and I have very good security. I'm sure you did not know you were being followed by my security team. For your protection, all your movements were monitored. I have an 8-man detail that protects us. The limousine is bulletproof and we have the latest electronic security systems in my home. Guzman will call within the next 10-minutes. He will explain why you should still go to mainland China. He wants you to follow your itinerary to the letter, he will explain. You will be safe, but to venture to Beijing and to central China will not be as smooth as we would like."

At 10:00 am Hong Kong time, Matt's cell phone rang. "It has already started," Guzman said. "We have information Chin is planning to assassinate not only you two, but BiBa and Gisele as well. Our intelligence tells us they will come after the four of you but we don't know when or how. We have followed some transactions and money from Chin's personal accounts and from one of his investment subsidiaries identifying four assassins there in China. We think there are two more but we don't have their names. It's our goal to take out the 6-killers before they pose any threats. Chin knows you are in Hong Kong. We have good information he must honor your safety with the Lais. He is dangerous and crazy but he will not break the truce between the mainland and Hong Kong. He knows the connections of the Lais and does not want to embarrass his brother-in-law. As far as we can tell, he doesn't fully understand your relationship with Syrial. Once you are in mainland China, everything changes. José will be in Beijing when you get there. We have contacted some Chinese mercenaries to act as your bodyguards. I don't want you to change Syrial's plans. You will visit all of the different cities and keep all of the appointments he has set for you. Thinking you might be kidnapped, will make your travels extremely unpleasant but you have been through this before. You can't show your concern by changing anything. You are safe; we will protect you. There are some rules in China that even Chin must follow. His men are limited in how they can come after you. This does two things. It gives us the advantage and it guarantees your safety. Through back channels, we have guarantees the police, local officials and the Army will only interrogate you.

After a satisfactory time period, you will be released to one of our men showing Chin we have political connections greater than his. Your kidnapping and death will not be allowed to take place because of the international ramifications. We think this will push Chin over the edge and move him to disregard his brother-in-law. Like I said, we are on top of it and you are not in any physical danger. Once we're sure we have this contained, we will kill his assassins and send their severed heads to Chin. They will be delivered to his World Trade Center office during business hours so his staff can witness his humiliation. We have placed electronic listening devices and cameras in his office earlier this morning. When we kill his men, we will send the video to UTube to go viral. I want to drive that yellow dog crazy."

"As I said, he is going after BiBa and Gisele in Kenya. They are safe. He put a bounty on their head and presented it to the new leaders of the Mungiki gang. He has no way of knowing they are loyal to us. He contacted them three nights ago and paid for three of their soldiers to go after your women and Nakruru. Killing of you four is set up for the same day. This is to our advantage because when one of you is attacked, we will know it is just a short period of time before the other will be attacked. We have a backup plan for BiBa and Gisele. President Kababi has been alerted. He knows if anything happens to them or Nakruru, he is a dead man. They are all safe but we think Chin has a second plan for them. Because of that, Malique will be their driver and his men will always be close by. Let me repeat, they are safe. Their trip to Kenya might have to be changed some, but we have it under control. When we are sure of all the assets Chin has in place in Kenya, we will dispose of the threat and cut off the heads of the assassins. Of course, it will be videotaped and sent to UTube. We have a plane and men on standby that will pack the remains of their heads in ice and fly them directly to China. When we capture and kill the men coming after you, we can send all the assassin's heads to Chin at the same time. I will e-mail you all of the Intel as soon as possible. I want you to call BiBa and Gisele immediately. Let them know. It would be better if it comes from you than me. I want to scare the shit out of Chin and publicly humiliate him. No one puts a hit on us, let alone twice. I want to let him know he is not long for this world. We need to kill him but we need the permission of his brother-in-law to have credibility in the future. We want to show Li Xueming that the execution of his sister's husband is for his benefit. I want him to understand we are doing him a favor by killing this piece of shit. One of the many things the Chinese understand is favors."

BiBa and Gisele were in their respective rooms at the Hilton Hotel in Nairobi's central business district. Nakruru had a permanent hold on the 11th floor rooms. They were de facto timeshares that the clinic used for visiting guests. The rooms were taken out of the hotel's inventory when not occupied, which gave Nakruru a permanent base for visiting clinic management. For Gisele and BiBa it was a second residence while in Nairobi. Nakruru made reservations at the Black Parrot, a trendy new establishment which catered to a small growing professional class of East African business people.

The restaurant was close enough to the hotel for three to walk under escort. The contemporary decor and its African food with Indian accents made it the most popular meeting place in the city. The pre-ordered meal was ready upon their arrival. As per Nakruru's security regimen, he had ordered a fourth meal for a member of his security team so the food could be tested. Poisoning of food and tainting of the water was a historical way of killing one's enemy in East Africa. Sitting at one of the back tables in the highly stylized restaurant, the initial conversation was very awkward because of the death of Nakruru's wife. It seemed trite, but Gisele asked him how he was doing and how the kids were handling the situation. Could either she or BiBa do anything to help?

The conversation turned rapidly to business where Nakruru was much more comfortable. He presented them with an action plan for the next week. It was a compilation of visitations, meetings and hands-on work in some of the clinics for the two women to meet doctors and staff. Nakruru had also arranged meetings with real estate agents and lawyers to deal with land acquisition and leasing agreements for mineral rights. Social and political engagements would be the last obligation for the two women.

During Nakruru's overview of the clinics balance sheets, both Gisele and BiBa simultaneously received calls on their cell phones. The calls were from Frederic and Matt. They asked the women to set up a conference call so Nakruru would be on-line. Matt proceeded to tell them of the impending threat and made clear they were safe and that countermeasures were going into place as they spoke.

"Malique and his men will be with you 24-hours a day. You are safe, but we don't know when or where they will attack. Matt them Guzman was directing the whole operation. They should not change any part of their visitations or meetings. It's important, if there are any changes for any reasons, Malique know before hand. He will be one of your drivers so he will be with you constantly. Your safety is assured but we don't want you to do something out of the ordinary. Guzman wants to capture the assassins, not kill them. He wants to video their interrogation and torture. Then he will have their heads severed by one of their own men and then be executed. As usual, he wants to make a statement. He will send their heads to Chin and make a video that will go viral. He feels we must kill your assassins at the same time as we handle the situation here in China. The timing of the two events is extremely important. He wants to accumulate the human carnage of our victims and have them delivered to Chongqing at the exact same time."

Frederic interrupted, "I guess he forgot to tell you they have a hit on us too. The four of us are supposed to be killed the exact same day. This guy Chin is big into statements, so killing all of us at the same time is big. I remember reading somewhere that war and killing are a failed extension of diplomacy. Shit, with Chin there is no diplomacy or compromise. As long as it is not us, let the killing began. Guzman is right when he says we must initiate things first. The more brutal, the greater the statement. Neither one of you really had the pleasure of meeting Guzman, but believe me, we are lucky to have him on our side. No matter how formidable you think Chin is, he is no match for a person like Guzman. We have to get off the phone now, so go back to your dinners. We will send you all the information we have as soon as possible."

Frederic paused for a second and said, "Gisele be real careful. I wish I were there to help. Maybe it's not an appropriate time to say it, but I'm really sorry I got you into this mess. Love ya."

Matt got back on line, "BiBa take care. I promise that everything will be okay. When you said you wanted to be involved, I didn't expect anything like this. Sorry, I can't tell you how badly I feel. We will all get through it. As a friend of mine used to say, it's just one more barnacle on the old whale, it's just one more obstacle in the road. Love you, I'll call you later."

The three sitting in the restaurant looked at each other, started planning and treated this impending threat like business as usual. They all had expectations of Chin coming after them at some point. This was more specific and had to be played.

Nakruru said, "The next full week we will be all business. Then after seven days of performing our duties as members of the foundation board, I have a surprise for you."

He had set up a trip to the world-famous Amboseli Animal Reserve on the Serengeti Plain. Hopefully by then everything would be over. Hopefully, the two women's trip would allow them to temper their emotions. They would be viewing one of nature's greatest displays of beauty, East Africa's migration of the wildebeest.

Chapter 46

Malique picked up the two women at the Hilton Hotel complex. It was customary for him to meet them in the lobby while one of his men attended the parked SUV in the hotel driveway.

BiBa and Gisele sat in the Land Rover backseat while Malique drove and one of his men rode shotgun. Another vehicle always followed the SUV. The second vehicle changed daily giving any potential adversary more difficulty spotting backup. Predetermined routes were assigned and security forces were placed at strategic intersections along the way. Following United States presidential motorcade protocol, altogether 17 men were attached to Malique's security force while BiBa and Gisele were traveling inside Nairobi. There were an additional three security guards, making the total 20, for their trip to the Amboseli Game Reserve.

"Everything is in place," he told BiBa as she entered the vehicle.

"Preparation is something you can't overdo when it comes to your security," Malique told the two women.

"We are very fortunate," Malique said on the way to Nakruru's office.

"I don't know how Guzman did it, but I guess you noticed we have a new vehicle today. He somehow borrowed it. It is a virtual fortress on wheels. It came in this morning from Liberia. Some warlord or some government official will let us use this guy for a couple of weeks. It is bulletproof with military grade armor plating. It has an anti-landmine undercarriage, run flat tires, and a communication system tied directly into satellite surveillance. We'll be taking it to Amboseli tomorrow morning. We'll leave at 8 o'clock, if that is okay. I figure right after breakfast I will pick you up in the lobby. It looks like it is a six to seven hour trip if we don't push it. We will stop at Nakruru's office first for some business along the way we can stop for any conveniences or if you would like to get some food. Just in case it makes you feel safer, we don't have to leave the vehicle. I can also have the hotel prepare a lunch. If you can think of anything else you might want for the ride just let me know. I can't get over this vehicle. Whoever built it planned for every contingency. We will be safe, that's for sure. By the time, we get to the reserve we will have 16 men in place posing as park rangers, attendants at the hotel, maintenance staff members and even someone in the kitchen making sure your food hasn't been tainted."

"The two of us," pointing to the African mercenary sitting shotgun, "make our detail 18 men in the park. As we get closer to the reserve tomorrow, our men will peel off from our caravan. When we finally arrive, it will just be the four of us. We feel we have backups and redundancy and can handle any situation Chin throws at us. The staff at the hotel is primarily Masai so we are in contact with our person in Nairobi. As of an hour ago, he had not heard any chatter about us or anything about an assassination plot. Because of our relationship with him, it was his brother who we had killed with the leader of the Mungiki gang last year; he doesn't want to disappoint us. He says he has no control over some of the staff at the hotel. He says they will do anything for money and they are unpredictable because they are meth-heads. If he hears something, then we hear something. There are no rumblings. We are going to be in Amboseli for four full days. That is a short window for Chin's men to attack us. We think they will come after us at the beginning of your trip. Killing us early on will give them more time to coordinate their attacks on Matt and Frederic while they are in Shanghai. The two of them have pretty much finished up their trip in central China and will be in Shanghai later tonight."

The SUV reached Nakruru's office at 9:00 am. Malique escorted them into the building and waited for the secretary to come escort them to the Papaz Group's headquarters. Nakruru was waiting for them at the elevator.

"May I offer you some coffee or anything to drink?" he said with a smile on his face. Neither Gisele nor BiBa had seen him display such emotion or animation before. "I have great news, come in and please sit down."

As they entered the conference room, coffee was brought in by a secretary accompanied by two sets of materials in black leather folders.

He gave each woman a folder and began, "These are our monthlies. We have surpassed every benchmark we established. Every single one of the clinics is now making money, but more importantly, we are respected and beyond reproach. To date we have 110 operational clinics. We have 87 schools, first through 9th grade, fully operational. Another 23 will be opened within the next four months. Our problem is staffing, we have built out buildings for the new schools but we can't find the right ethnic mix of teachers. The average clinic has four doctors and eight staff members. We call them doctors but in reality, they are nurse practitioners. There is a shortage of doctors in East Africa. It is difficult to find a doctor with the proper tribal background. Our staff on average has a doctor/patient ratio of 12 per hour. That means in each clinic we see approximately 50 people per hour, the average clinic is open 10 hours a day, and like I said we have an average staff of four attending nurses. What this really means is we see more than 50,000 people per day. That is way beyond our best estimates. In the last 2 weeks, we have received a United Nation's designation as a dispenser of vaccinations, which gives us free access to serums and even mosquito netting. We are now looking at phase 2 of our operation. I intend to roll out another 150 clinics in the next 18-months. We have accomplished profitability 12 to 14 months ahead of schedule. The investment vehicles we established for clinics to purchase land and mineral rights is ahead of schedule. With Matt Foundation money, we are 20-months in front of our projections. We have effectively cancelled Chin's abilities to corner both rare earth and heavy metal leases markets and, of course, land purchase. We have done extremely well. On a personal note, I am embarrassed. I don't think I have thanked you for all your hard work and direction. I hope I have kept pace with your expectations. I know these clinics have exceeded my wildest dreams. I feel truly fortunate to be involved with you. I don't really have anything else to say. You have seen the operation and its results. I just want to thank you before you go to Amboseli."

He stood; the meeting had taken only 45 minutes. He extended his hand to both women and said, "I want to thank you, not only for me, but for Kenya."

The trip was uneventful. They arrived at the reserve's five-star hotel at 3 pm and were escorted to their rooms. Malique was not allowed to stay on the premises. The custom that drivers and tour operators were not allowed to eat or sleep with the guests was immutable. Outside the visitor's area, there was an adjacent building acting as a hotel for employees. The building was ramshackle. It was infested with flies and vermin. It had no running water, a communal area with bunk beds, and a bathroom with no European toilets. Food for the drivers and guides came from the hotel's dinner or lunch buffet leftovers. Malique had planned for this contingency of not being allowed on the hotel grounds after dropping Gisele and BiBa. Four of his Arab mercenaries had registered at the hotel and their rooms flanked the two women's cottage. It was set up beforehand that they would accidentally meet at the hotel registration desk and ask BiBa and Gisele if they wanted to share a dinner table. From that point, they would always be under constant protection. Combinations of four men and two women would be constant companions while in the resort's complex. Outside of the hotel's gates and on the savanna, they would be under the protection of Malique and his security team.

Malique registered the two women and their new Arab friends to leave the compound at first light the next morning. To venture outside the reserve's grounds, arrangements were made to open the gates at 5:30 am before dawn. It was the best time to view predators because most hunting was done late at night or early morning. Because of the poacher threat, guests had to register in and out of the hotel complex. While on the savanna, they had to check-in so guard-posts could track their whereabouts. All vehicles were required to have functioning cell phones because of the high crime rate perpetrated by bush highwaymen. On some occasions, poacher gangs attacked tourists and robbed them of their valuables. Amboseli had the highest crime incidence of any Kenya reserve. Malique was using this fact as a perfect cover for his operation. If Chin's assassins, because of their drug habits, were lacking in preparation or arrogant about their abilities, they would look at this job as nothing unusual. Malique hoped they would not be very vigilant. BiBa and Gisele's vehicle scheduled first to leave the compound, left with two additional vans carrying their Arab traveling companions. At first light, a three vehicles caravan headed north towards the foot of Mt. Kilimanjaro.

Their destination was the reserve's famous hippopotamus pools. A viewing room with Plexiglas sides and ceiling was constructed 6-feet below the waterline so guests could see hippopotamus in their natural environment. Many guests, in this case BiBa, Gisele and their Arab friends, wanted to be the first visitors to the pools for unobstructed viewing and picture taking. Malique's plan, of being the first on the open plain, would coax the assassins out into the vast Serengeti openness and create a tactical advantage of surprise and overwhelming firepower for his men. The assassins would have no indication BiBa and Gisele were being safeguarded by a security detail. Malique was sure they would not be aware of the trap he set for them.

The first half hour of the drive from the hotel complex to the hippo pool was uneventful. The alluvial plains of the savanna and the high dry grass made for unspectacular animal sightings. The 3-vehicle parade passed by small herds of antelope and zebra, through the reserve famous for large game, none was spotted. Midway through their drive Malique received a call from Guzman. Satellite reconnaissance showed 6-men coming from different directions and on their way to the underwater viewing center. Guzman told Malique to take the caravan directly to the pools. BiBa, Gisele and the Arab mercenaries were to walk down into the center and use it as a bunker. The rest of Malique's forces would outflank the assassins and take them hostage. As they approached the water suddenly flames engulfed them from a fire intentionally started by Chin's men,. The fire used the energy stored in the tall dry grass and brush to fuel its great rage. The tremendous heat generated by the fire would kill anybody in the visitor's center by either incineration or asphyxiation.

Guzman and Malique had not planned for this contingency. They had prepared for the party to be under direct assault from the assassins on the open savanna. Malique thought well on his feet and ordered everyone back into the Land Rover. He drove through dark sheets of gray smoke to find an opening of clear air. Great walls of flames encircled the vehicle. They were in the middle of what was now a 1-mile square wildfire. The armored Land Rover, which was chosen because of its abilities to deflect military ordinances and land mines, was now their savior. The armor plating acted as insulation from the heat and the run flat tires had the ability to navigate through the flames and the 500° temperature of the burning ground without blowing out. It took more than 15-minutes in the smoke-filled vehicle driving to a safety area. As soon as the vehicle stopped, everyone piled out to get into the open to get a breath of fresh air. Chin's killing spree was on, and by sheer luck, it was checked by Malique's quick thinking. As soon as they felt they were out of harm's way, a call was placed to Guzman who had witnessed the operation via satellite. He in turn made a call to Jose in Shanghai. It took over one hour for Malique's men to capture all six of the assassins who were separately on their way back to the hotel. Taken to a maintenance building five miles outside the hotel grounds and subjected to the worst kind of human torture, the terrorists were beheaded in front of a video camera. As per operational outcome, the video would arrive with the assassin's heads in Chongqing when needed.

Once the shoe had dropped in Kenya, Chin would come after Matt and Frederic. His men were captured and killed. Their heads and an accompanying video was delivered to Chin's office. The two packages delivered at the same time to make a clear statement.

The fires on the savanna would take more then 10-days to run their course and burnout. During that time, Chin would be under the false illusion that two of his four adversaries were dead. In his manic hyper-state, he would never second-guess his victories, and therefore would not follow-up on what happened in Kenya.

Malique set-up that his men would be in contact with Chin posing as African assassins and give him an all clear, meaning the hit was successful. Once he received the call, Chin was now ready to move on to Shanghai and finish his work. He had three days.

Chapter 47

Nakruru received a call from Malique minutes after Guzman hung up the phone.

"William, Chin's men came after us here in Amboseli, but everything is under control. We are all okay."

He didn't want to scare Nakruru by telling him any of the particulars, especially how they miscalculated at the point of attack.

"I want you to listen very carefully. My men in Nairobi have information about something coming down today. As far as we can tell, they will be coming after you sometime this afternoon. We are trying to change the attack timing. We want you to stay in your office until everything is in place. If you are still there, don't move. If you are out for some reason, get back as soon as possible."

Nakruru said he was still in his office waiting for a meeting with one of the managers of the Nairobi Westside clinic.

Malique told him, "Whatever you have to do, get rid of him and cancel the meeting, do it now. Under no circumstances let him come to the office. There is some chatter that some rogue Mungiki assassins are on their way and we can't take a chance that the person from the clinic has been turned. In any event, figure out a way to keep him outside the City Square area where your office is. We can contain him from there. It won't make a difference if he is with them or not if he is not at your headquarters. He won't be a danger if he is not in your office or the building. Even if he is an innocent bystander, if he is at your office, he limits our options on how we deal with Chin's men."

"As we speak we are sending three men to your office. I don't have much time right now because we are on our way to the airport. Let me briefly fill you in on what will be coming down. Once my men get to your office, they will escort you down the back stairwell. There is a waiting 2005 Toyota pickup truck in the alley. It shouldn't call attention to itself. After you are in the cabin of the truck put your head down until you hit the main street. Two cars will be waiting to escort the three of you to a safe house not far out of the city limits. The third man coming into your office will stay there, dress like you, and put on a mask we have created to match your face exactly. He will act as your double. Just before you leave to go downstairs you will call your secretary and tell her there has been a problem that needs your immediate attention. Tell her you have an emergency and you have to go to one of the clinics. Your double will pass by her desk in the lobby without saying a word on his way to the elevator. Once he gets downstairs he will enter your car, but the driver and the bodyguards will be our men. From there everything is lined up. By that time, you will have been taken directly to a safe house 15-minute from the old Norfork Hotel. You will be safe there. A more permanent security force, ten men from South Africa augmented our protection at the safe house. The car with your double will be on its way to Lusaka Road near the soccer stadium on the outskirts of Kikera. Chin's men will be right behind it like a magnet. We will set up an ambush. Our man's car will safely pass through an intersection followed by the assassin's car. Everyone in that car will be killed by automatic gunfire. The car rigged to explode. The real occupants of the car fired upon will be Chin's assassins and our men will be behind the AK-47s on the street. A fake police detail will come upon the scene minutes after the car catches fire and pull the dead bodies to the curbside. By the end of the day, they will be identified as you and two of your bodyguards. Our communication intercepts have shadowed Chin's men here in Nairobi and we will contact Chin directly in Chongqing, as if the hit was completed. The next morning everything will be in the Nairobi Times. As I said, you will be taken to a safe house. You have to be there three to four days without any contact to the outside world. That means no computer, cell phone, iPad, anything that's electrical. We don't want to give Chin a chance to track any communication that can lead to you. The safe house is self-contained and we have employed a full detail of men to guard you. The way we set this up, Chin will read about it in the paper as well as get a call. Our people have prepared news reports both from Nairobi and Amboseli that portray 6 people being burned to death on the savanna in one of Kenya's high-end resorts, and a for hire assassination of an ex-government official who refused to pay bribes to the Mungiki gang for access to real estate for his medical clinics. In the article relating to BiBa and Gisele, there will be reference to a wildfire, burnt out vehicles, and six bodies identified as them and some Arabs. In relationship to you, the article will have your name. This should be proof of death for Chin. Our analysis shows he will quickly change all his focus to Matt and Frederic. He will lock in on them and nothing else in the world will get his attention. We have everything in place to counter his attacks in Shanghai. All this should be over in a few days and you can get back to a normal life without ever looking over your shoulder again."

"I know I have thrown a lot at you, but trust me. This is the only way we can deal with Chin. We have put a lot of effort and planning into this and everything is in place. You have to accept this for what it is and that this ordeal will be over soon. When my men arrive, get the hell out of your office as soon as possible. By the time, you get to the safe house we will be half way to England via Cairo. I know this will end well, but with Chin, there is always blood and sacrifice. Very soon, this will be over."

"We will have effectively checked our Chinese counterpart. In a few days, you will be able to get back to your work at the clinics. Frederic wants you to put your run for the presidency into motion. He said you would have the next few days to think about it because you can't do much else. I know I am getting ahead of myself talking about political things, but he told me to tell you, 'all of our resources will be at your disposal'. We will help you push Kenya into the 21st century. As for right now, you are safe and everything is going according to plan. We will talk soon."

Nakruru thanked him and wished him, BiBa and Gisele a safe journey. Two minutes after he hung up three of Malique's associates walked into his office, telling his secretary they were expected.

Chapter 48

Sitting at the airport Matt said, "Man, I know this is the last leg of our trip, but it is unbelievable how much we have seen. I have been so engrossed in some of the things we've done, I haven't really thought much about that asshole Chin's threats. I guess that's how stupid I am. I have blocked out all that assassination shit because, I don't know, I guess I trust Guzman. That's stupid, isn't it?"

Frederic laughed. "I feel the same way. I think I have taken our safety for granted. We're both real stupid. I guess we don't have any alternatives but to trust Guzman and Lai. So far, we've had a good time in spite of all that is hanging over our heads. We made it safely up to here and we'll be in Shanghai in less than 2 hours, what more can we ask? When we get there, I'll have some time to rehash everything we've done from Hong Kong all the way here. We have done so much; I need some time for it to cope. I need to figure out why Syrial sent us to all these different places. It's been great but I am overloaded. From what José said, we're going to whole up in Shanghai until we can pull Chin's men out of whatever hole they are hiding. I think we are flying into Shanghai's new airport. It is supposed to be huge even though it is Shanghai's second airport. The city has 22 million people. It is absurd how many gigantic cities this country has. I know Shanghai is a financial hub, but to build a new airport along the lines of the newly constructed Beijing airport, built for the 2008 Summer Olympics, is unbelievable. I am sure we will be safe at the airport. Jose and Guzman planned for our protection. I know I am in good hands, but to be honest, I am scared shitless."

Matt responded, "We have the best chance to end all this stuff by letting Guzman handle it. I'm sure as hell more confident in him than anything I could come up with. Yeah, you're right, but I am more uneasy about this than anything in the last two weeks."

They arrived at Shanghai's new international airport completed 10-months earlier. Shanghai, one of China's fastest growing cities, needed a second transportation hub. The enormity of Shanghai's new airport was unimaginable. The newly constructed airport, built in less than three years, had a total cost of $32 billion dollars. The total labor force working on the project was 87,000 skilled/unskilled workers. It was the world's largest urban construction project and it was small fraction of China's new infrastructure booked for that time period. The sheer size of China's leap into modernity was exemplified by this project. To the world, it was a gigantic undertaking. To China, it was just another city needing an airport expansion. It was as if they had a template for airports and just rolled them out like Nakruru was rolling out clinics. Taking into consideration, all the new passenger and air cargo terminals built and commingled with the existing structures, it was now the second largest airport in the world.

Soon after their plane landed, a limousine was curbside as they passed through immigration. José and two of his men were waiting for them as they passed through the sliding glass exit doors of the terminal. They were whisked into the waiting vehicle and went directly to the Ritz-Carlton Hotel, in the heart of the city's financial district. Registration was accomplished with the men off-site. Upon entering the lobby, they walked through the main corridor to the elevators going to their suites on the 37th floor. The hotel was part of a real estate complex featuring some of the finest condominiums and commercial office space in the city. The hotel's ground floor was a retail shopping center rivaling some of the city's largest retail malls on Nanking Road, which was the famous transportation artery and frontage road to the hotel.

Upon exiting the limousine, the two men retired to their rooms where José said he would give them some time to clean up before he would brief them on the operation in Shanghai.

Their adjoining suites had a common boardroom. It was a usual practice of China's five-star hotels to effectively tie together sleeping quarters and office facilities. José was sitting at the conference table when Matt and Frederic entered the room from their separate suites. After they were seated, he asked if they would like anything.

He said, "There is a saying I heard somewhere. It stuck with me. I'm really not sure who said it but it goes something like this. 'After the whispers comes the shouting.' Well, all Chin has done so far is whisper. He thinks he has killed BiBa and Gisele through his African surrogates. When he is manic, like he is right now, all he hears is what he wants to hear. He thinks they are dead and it's time to come after you. In his mental state, we know he's crazy, but he's not dumb. We sure as hell know he is dangerous. He knows he has to distance himself from anything he does here in China because of his brother-in-law, but our Intel says he's going to come after us probably sometime today. He's coming no matter what. His signature is multiple hits. The only thing that killing someone in China means to him is that it can't be seen as anything political. He will use professionals from a different province than Shanghai and try to tie whatever goes on to some type of cause, like the Gulong Fong or accident or something. This is a country of strict law and order. The Communists have ruled here for more than 7 decades. For all intents and purposes, there is no opposition to the government. There is really no criminal element to speak of and for sure, there is no acceptable public dissent. That means Chin has to hire outsiders and our Intel tells us that's exactly what he has done. You guys have been safe your whole trip, but our surveillance discovered you were being followed by someone other than us. I am sure you didn't pick it up."

Jose handed them a picture, "These two young Chinese have been tailing you all the way from Beijing. They were at the airport in Xian and also on your plane from the Three Gorges to here."

He showed them eight other pictures of people he said were following them on different parts of the trip.

"They are all Chin's men," Jose continued. "They are outside guns he brought. We don't know how many more are here in Shanghai, but we do know they didn't come after you until now because they want to coordinate your killings with Africa. Like I said, Chin thinks the women are dead so he'll be coming after you as soon as possible. We think they will try to pull it off either before or during dinner tonight. Our plan is to keep you sequestered here at the hotel and call Chin's hand. We're going to set up reservations for dinner through the front desk. For sure, his men will pick it up. We have a place in mind not far from here. By 6 o'clock tonight, we'll have command and control and be able to take his men out. It is early so we have a lot of time to get everything in place before dinner. I will be with you. We are safe, don't worry. Ever since Chin found out that BiBa and Gisele were dead, there's been a lot of chatter, mostly by cell phone. He knows you are at the hotel so his men will do whatever they have to flush you out. The longer he waits the more jacked-up and hyperkinetic he will become. If we can keep his men on a string while he is in such an agitated state, he will become much riskier in his decision-making. It is all part of him being manic. He will think he is impervious to making mistakes because he feels the godlike power of his mania. We can't make him wait much longer than this afternoon because he will sense something is wrong. Right now, he doesn't have the cognitive abilities to realize he's being played. Like I said, he is so amped up he is coming out of his skin. We just have to play that. We're hoping the more pressure we put on him the more delusional he will become. Then he will make a mistake. Hopefully his intent to kill you here in Shanghai will become public and his brother-in-law will have to distance himself from Chin. If we push him hard enough, and he comes after you in the open, then this gets back to Li Xueming. Guzman can compromise him. From that point, we've got the two of them by the balls. Chin's mania has a way of leading to self-destruction. He's got a history of ups and downs. We are going to keep you guys in these suites as long as possible to squeeze him until he breaks."

Jose told the two men of his and Guzman's plan of delayed deployment. "With you guys staying here for 6 to 8 hours, it will push him over the top."

Frederic laughingly said, "Being locked up in here might push me over the top."

Jose added, "I know there is a lot of pressure on you guys, but really everything is all right. It is easy for me to say because I'm involved in all of the planning, but you are safe. I will be staying right here with you guys. I'm sure I don't have to tell you they'll be coming down on me as well as the two of you. Take the next few hours as time off and try to settle your nerves. You'll have time for yourselves, but all of us will be closely guarded. We have to provide for any contingency even here at the hotel. The longer he waits, the more manic he gets and the bolder his moves. We have put into place a security system called double redundancy while we are here. The lobby, the elevators, the hallway here on the 37th floor, and both rooms and conference center are all tied into a video system that is monitored constantly by two of my men. This video surveillance is only part of our security. The second part of our redundancy is we have men all the way from the front of the hotel to the front of each suite. You will never be left alone while you are here in the hotel. You won't even be able to go to the bathroom by yourselves. That bathroom reference is true; three men will be with you at all times. When you shower, shave; even take a crap you will be in unobstructed sight of our men."

"Guzman will make all of the calls from forward. We are in constant contact. There is a restaurant called the Bali Lagoon down the road, less then a mile from here. We are going to walk there. That's right," he said as he looked directly at both men. "We are going to walk there out in the open. It is a little bit outside the retail district on Nanking Road. It is an Indonesian restaurant in the middle of a park."

He pulled out a city map and placed it on the conference table in the middle of the room. "We will walk down six blocks, cross the street," he commented as he pointed to an intersection marked on the map. "Now, moving his finger to another spot on the map he said, "You can see in the middle of the 5 high-rise buildings. There is a 50 acre park that is a pedestrian area," he says as he points to a green area on the map. "Right next to the lake and the waterfalls is the restaurant. This is the newest part of Shanghai and none of the buildings has windows that open. So, unless one of their assassins is in one of the high-rises and breaks a window we are covered from the air. Again, we have double redundancy, we have 5-spotters on the ground looking upward and checking the rooftops as well. We have another 11-men in the park itself. We also have four men in the restaurant."

He showed them some pictures and after describing the Indonesian ambiance he said, "It is very similar to the restaurant Tavern on the Green in Central Park. Obviously, Central Park is much bigger, but the Bali Lagoon is a lot larger than the Green. The restaurant itself sits on the edge of the lagoon and looks like an Asian one room longhouse. It has bamboo walls and a thatched roof. When we get to the park we will walk along the side of the lagoon next to a cluster of waterfalls."

He pointed them out on the map. "The restaurant has a hostess station at the bottom of some steps. From the ground, the restaurant looks like a boathouse on stilts and rests about 3 feet above the lagoon. We will walk up through the hostess station into a long bar. The rest of the restaurant is one big room overlooking the 20-acre lagoon and some miniaturized longboats and statues depicting people in rice paddies. This place doesn't seem like it should be in the middle of one of the most urban areas in the world because it's so secluded and heavily landscaped with trees and shrubbery. It's a perfect place for them to come after us. The waterfalls, the koi ponds and the lagoon, they take up a lot of physical space. Our men will have swept the boats in the water just before we get there. The water itself is only one to two foot deep so there can't be anybody in the water. All this means is their men will be in the park. We will have the situation under control before we get there. I haven't said anything about the walk to the park, but it is covered. We have total command and control over the seven or eight blocks between here and there. We have a plan for every contingency. All we have to do now is waiting out this crazy son of a bitch and push him into doing something that will discredit him with his brother-in- law."

"Well guys, for a while it is rest and relaxation until Guzman calls. Do you have any questions?"

Neither man said a word for over 30 seconds.

Matt finally spoke up. "I know everything is in place. Hell, you're going to be with us so I know we will be safe, but what the hell am I going to do for eight hours?"

They all laughed, "Shit, you never change, do you?" José said. "Really, if you want food, everything is already up here. No one will be coming onto this floor from downstairs. You can't order anything up, but we have things in place just in case you need something. If you guys want a massage, we have a reflexologist in our crew. We got books and magazines. We got the whole shooting match, that was supposed to be a joke. You guys have to lighten up. I can't believe it," he said, looking directly at Matt, "I feel like a babysitter."

Matt smiled and responded," Just kidding! I've got a lot to do and I won't be bored. I'm just giving you a lot of shit. You seem real serious too; we all have to lighten up."

They all laughed as José left the conference room. The two men started back to their suites.

Matt asked Frederic, "How are you doing under all of this?"

"Man, it's been an unbelievable ride," Frederick answered. "I'm just going to sit down and write up some of this stuff. It will give me a clearer picture of everything we've done. I really need some time to reflect on this to be able to sort out the different things I've seen and put it all together."

Matt said, "You've always been a little bit more intellectual than me. I can't believe I haven't seen TV for a couple weeks, so I'm just going to sit in front of the one in my master bedroom and watch CNN. I haven't seen the news or any sporting events for a couple of weeks. I might even surf the web a little. Like I said, I'll just go back, take a shower and watch TV."

He started to smile, "It's been a great ride. Thanks, not just for the trip, but for everything. I got us into this mess..." and then he stopped. "If you need me I'll be with my three buddies."

As he started to leave the room with his detail of three guards, Frederic said, "I have been in this since the beginning. You didn't get me into anything. We always have each other's backs, so don't say anything else about it. We would have been bored as hell if we didn't do this. We would've found something else. It was just a matter of time. I have this feeling chaos is a friend, so like I said, if we weren't doing this, it would've been something else. I want to go back to my room, work on my journal and immerse myself into what we have done for the last couple of weeks. I feel like Syrial had us running and everything is a blur. I want to try to digest why he sent us to the places we have been and the best way for me to do it is to write it down. I think my feelings about China have changed. I need to figure it out. Even though there is a threat on our lives and I have real negative thoughts about China for being an imperialist nation because of the crap they are doing in Kenya, but there is something attaching me to this place. I have to think things through. I am pretty emotional right now so before I make any decisions about the future, I'll put things in journal form and it will cool me down."

Emotions and tension had a way of making Frederic laugh. He continued, "You know the irony of walking to a restaurant for what might be our last meal and liking this place? Man, that is crazy. I'm going to go back to my room but I have to say," he said as he walked away laughing, "I heard it is a hell of a restaurant." He paused, "If we are still alive to enjoy it!"

Chapter 49

Frederic started to feel the stress of time as his thoughts moved to the mega city of Xi'an. He knew his and Matt's faith were in the hands of Jose and Guzman but he tried to bury his head into his journal. He felt an addiction to journaling his trip. Writing on his laptop was like an opiate. He craved the insights of his thoughts. It was, as if clarity had appeared out of nowhere. He could not ferret out if his focus was insightful because of his desire to hide from his appointment with Chin's men or because of the intellectual high from his newfound knowledge. The whole process was exhilarating because it was totally different than anything he had anticipated. Sitting at his desk for hours without taking a respite went by in an instant. His cell phone suddenly rang. It was Gisele.

"Frederic, how are you holding up? I tried to call earlier but I could not get through. I was really frightened. How are you? I miss you."

She was nonstop. Frederic tried to get a word in edgewise.

Gisele, he said in a raised voice, "I am fine. Really, everything is under control. How are you and BiBa now that you are out of Kenya?"

She said, "We are in the air right now on our way back to New York. As soon as we get there, security will be in place. Malique doesn't want us to think this thing with Chin is over. He said until Chin is dead we have to look at this as a failed assassination attempt and he will try it again. We have to find out who is behind Chin. Whoever he is, we have to give him a reason to call off his men. Before we can relax, we either have to kill Chin's boss or negotiate a peace with him. BiBa and I feel a lot better now we have left Nairobi but we know it is not over. We are both okay but tired of people trying to kill us. I didn't call about myself; I called because I'm worried about you. Tell me the truth, are you all right? A minute or two ago I got off the line with Guzman. He laid out what you guys are up against. It sounds like you're okay but I needed to hear your voice. He made it sound like a waiting game and that can't be much fun. When are you guys going to venture out and start this thing?"

Frederic said, "I guess we will get out of here at maybe 9 or 10 o'clock. He hasn't totally filled us in but that's my guess. I'm just sitting here trying to pass time by journaling our trip. It is kind of like therapy. If I start writing, I won't have to think about the next few hours. So far, time has passed by pretty quickly. I'm hiding in my thoughts. I know it is an escape but it is a hell of a lot better than the stress of worrying about being killed by some Chinese assassins."

"You have to trust Jose and Guzman," she said. "If they say it's safe for you to venture out of the hotel then it is. I understand all too well, what it feels like to have no control. But believe it or not, it will be over soon and Jose wouldn't put you in a dangerous position. My phone is starting to fade out. Malique got us out of Nairobi by private jet to Cairo. The co-pilot has informed me that we are entering an area of atmospheric turbulence and I am going to lose you. Before I do I just want to tell you, don't worry. I don't think I have ever said this before and meant it, but I do love you. Tell Matt that BiBa I will call as soon as we get better reception."

The static on the line increased and she hung up. He put his cell phone back on the table and started to type on his laptop once again. Xi'an was only an hour and forty minutes from Beijing but they were worlds apart, wrote Frederick. Xi'an was a mega-city of more than 20-million people but it was totally different than the capital. They landed at its international airport that was small in comparison to Beijing's. As per Syrial's itinerary, a limousine driver and a guide met them and showed them the great city. The surroundings near the airport were totally unexpected. High-rise apartments as far as the eye could see were under construction. The colossal buildings, or apartments as the Chinese called them, were built to house up to 20,000 people. Leaving the airport and looking on either side of the freeway he felt like he was driving by tract homes built by speculators during California's real estate boom in early 2,000's. The difference was the size of these projects and the enormous infrastructures needed to house so many people were quantumly bigger than any thing he had ever seen. Rows of 30 to 40 story apartments flooded the sightline. Each of the mega structures had anywhere from 100 to 120 rooms per floor. Taking into consideration the height of each building, it was possible for the structures to have anywhere from 3,000 to 5,000 rooms. Each unit by American standards was small. The apartments ranged 500 ft.^{2} up to 1,000 ft^2. Frederic estimated each of the buildings ranged anywhere from 2-1/2 million to 3,000,000-ft.^{2} and there were hundreds, if not thousands, of apartments under construction between the airport and the city center. In juxtaposition to the new housing developments were brand-new coal firing power plants right in the middle of these newly developed high-density neighborhoods. Bellowing plumes of gunboat gray and dark black smoke poured from the chimneys of these power generating behemoths right into the newly constructed homes. The air smelled of sulfur dioxide and a gray haze blocking the sun was a product of China's new industrialization. The apartments were for a new wave of agricultural immigrants who left the farms for higher paying jobs and economic opportunities. Progress had its price, Frederic thought to himself. The environmental damage was beyond belief.

The limousine drove by hundreds of new apartments under construction. Each structure was surrounded by bamboo scaffolding. The freshly poured cement constituting the fascias of the buildings took up to two weeks to dry and for that purpose the multistory buildings were wrapped in a green plastic to allow for the even curing of the cement. Hundreds, if not thousands, of green structures coupled with cranes raised into the sky 40 or 50 stories, following the frontage road that ran parallel to the freeway.

Thousands of trucks and earth moving machines augmented the thousands upon thousands of laborers who would complete an apartment's construction in less than three months.

Frederic noted in his journal, "I have never seen such a display of productivity but how could they put all of this physical mass into a limited area without it collapsing under its own weight?"

He felt he was not smart enough to foresee all of the unintended consequences of China's growth. He knew that bringing 2,500,000 new people into a city would cause its collapse. The mental gymnastics of extrapolating Xi'an model to the rest of China whose population was estimated to be 1,400,000,000 people was mind-boggling. He wondered if Syrial brought them, there to show the Chinese drive to their rightful place in history was unattainable. Any negative implications in China's movement towards world dominance seemed out of character for Syrial. Frederic was uneasy about his own interpretation of the country's ability for growth. What Syrial was trying to say was written in capital letters next to the word Xi'an in his journal. He continued his journaling of the city.

"We arrived at the five-star Shangri-La Hotel right in the middle of the financial district of the city. It was designed in a splendid Western fusion architecture. By standards in any other country, it would have been considered a Marquis hotel. It stood over 20 stories tall and had 4,000 rooms and its interior design was magnificent. From its restaurants, to its gym and indoor pool facility, to its gardens, and its first class business center, the hotel facilities were five-star by any measurable standard. The rooms and the hotel staffing met the highest quality of the finest hotels in the world. Frederic marveled at the Shangri-La and compared it to the MGM Grand Hotel in Las Vegas, but the realization that this was built in less than 4-months was incomprehensible to him. Walking through the hotel lobby and viewing its grandeur made Frederic reflect upon the hundreds and hundreds of apartments of equivalent size that he saw under construction from the airport. Obviously the interior design and its artwork and furnishings of the hotel were different than the apartments, but the backbone of the hotel, the building itself, wasn't much different in cost nor scope to the physical structures of the apartments that he had seen on the side of freeway. The amount of labor and resources needed to bring

Xi'an, may it be for apartments for the new working class or grand hotels for business and tourism, were probably equal to the total level of construction activity in the United States. For him to comprehend the total level of construction in China and its magnitude, he would have to multiply the phenomenon of Xi'an by a factor of more than 100. He knew he did not have the ability to comprehend all he had seen with any accuracy. He wondered if anyone in China had the ability to piece all of this together with enough clarity to make it work.

When they arrived at their hotel, he and Matt cleaned up and had lunch. Then they made ready for their afternoon visit to the national Museum. Going to the exhibition of the terra-cotta warriors of the Qin dynasty was an unexpected treat. It featured the terra-cotta marvels and the craftsmen who produced them. They molded more than 7,000 statues without repeating the same face. In the two years they took to craft the warriors, the more than 5,000 skilled workers also built a tomb fit for the afterlife of the Emperor. The project drained the treasury of the ancient empire. More than twenty per cent of the country's skilled work force was engaged in the endeavor. The empire came to a standstill but the needs of the Emperor were met. Still a farming area, the Lintong District, where the tomb was built is 45-km outside of Xi'an, by China's first great Emperor, Qin Shi Huang. The museum had a model of the site. Its construction was at the foot of Mt. Li. The underground pyramidal shaped structure consisted of halls and stables placed around a courtyard housing the Emperor corps and the

7,000 ceramic life-sized replicas of Chinese warriors. The Warriors were fitted with armor, there were archers and there were calvary men with horses and chariots. It was laid out so the Emperor's army could protect him from the East where the Mongols had invaded for centuries. The guide at the Museum said this was a precursor to the following day's outing to the actual tombs. He just wanted to put things into context so Frederic and Matt would not be overwhelmed by the actual site and all of the labor and effort expended to protect the Chinese deity after his death. They took the 45-minute drive the next morning out to the tomb after viewing a ceramic factory that produced twenty first century copies of the warriors. The guide wanted to show Matt and Frederic in 4,000 years mankind had lost many of its skills with the passing of its craftsmen. The ceramic pieces in the tomb, as exemplified by the warriors, could not be reproduced today. The skills of yesteryear were burned with the Emperor.

Frederic found himself in a hurry. He started to jot down simple ideas rather than descriptive analysis. The next morning - archaeological site - great museum - a tourist trap - 5,000,000 ft.^{2} complex - museum is rival to the Archaeological Museum in Athens. Terra-cotta warriors not that impressive – Tremendous sacrifice by masses for ruler’s desire for immortality. – Sacrifice for all, gain for one.

MAIN POINT. The new apartments encircling Xi'an were a deviation from China's past. The laborers making all the sacrifices for the common good were finally getting an increase in their standard of living.

Frederic interpreted this to be the beginning of a populist movement.

SEA CHANGE. The fruits of Chinese labor would benefit the workers, not only the ruling elite. That is what Syrial was trying to convey.

THE MASSES, producing for their own benefit, would once again move China into its rightful position of being the strongest nation in the world.

WORLD IN A POSITION OF NORMALCY WITH CHINA AS ITS LEADER. Frederic struggled with all of the interconnecting linkages of wealth distribution and China's massive labor force and its ability to produce. The need for Kenya's rare earth and heavy metals was part of a process to build Xi'an and other cities. Creating chaos to control markets was a tactic for growth. The exploitation of underdeveloped countries in the 21st century was the equivalent of waging war in China's past to foster a higher standard of living.

NEW APARTMENTS COULD NOT BE BUILT WITHOUT KENYA. Exploitation was a stepping-stone to world domination and the populist movement in China. Instead of killing people and extending its land mass, China used trade to gather resources for world domination. The only difference in its 5000 years of history was the new wealth created would be distributed more equitably to the people who created it. Syrial made his point.

DON'T KNOW ABOUT ENVIRONMENTAL PROBLEMS -- MAYBE THEY CAN GROW THEIR WAY OUT OF THEM?

Jose knocked on the doors of Matt and Frederic's rooms. Both men were still trying to pass time.

"Let's go into the conference room for a few minutes guys," he said.

The three men entered the room where five other men were already seated at the long mahogany table. Jose introduced everyone to Frederic and Matt.

"Okay, I just want to let you know the Eagle has landed. That's an old military phrase, saying the operation has begun. The enemy has arrived. In this case, it meant Chin's men were on scene. Let me give you some information on what's going on. If you have any questions, feel free to interrupt me. We have some time, so I don't want you to leave this room with any questions. It is pretty simple. Chin's men are directly in front of the hotel as we speak. They are right outside the entrance of the hotel. They are posing as maintenance workers on the street repairing a water line. Chin got to the head of Shanghai's Street Maintenance Department, his name is Wo Li, two hours ago. They closed the right lane of Nanking Boulevard. That is the street right out in front of the driveway where all of the taxis pull in and out of the hotel. They started ripping up the street right here in front of Starbucks. Only the right lane is closed. They have a crew of six men working on a water main. Their inventory of equipment is a dump truck filled with asphalt, a steamroller and a bobcat. The crew is made up of three men who are digging and paving the street and three men who drive the trucks. Like I said, six men in all. The only thing distinguishing them is their bright orange street maintenance vests. Our intelligence tells us, they are going to try to run us over on the sidewalk on our way to the restaurant. It will be staged, as an accident. One of the drivers will lose control of a runaway truck or bobcat that jumps the curb and killed some pedestrians, is how they want to play it. They have three large spotlights to illuminate the area for night maintenance. As far as we can tell, the purpose of the lights is to impede people's vision on the sidewalk by shining the halogen lights directly on the site of the accident. With those lights in people's eyes, nobody on the sidewalk will be able to see what actually takes place. Even if the accident is right in front of them, they will be blinded by the lights. No one will have a clear view of what went on. Our people have checked all of the surrounding buildings. Their roofs, windows, the bushes and the trees are all clear. We have men commanding those positions right now."

Jose pointed to the two men sitting directly across the table from Frederic and said, "Charlie and William are their American names. They will be wearing masks," as each one held up a perfect replica of Matt and Frederic's faces.

"They will be walking out of your rooms here on the 37th floor and going directly to the lobby downstairs. We have seen some of Chin's men in the reception area of the hotel. They will certainly take notice of Charlie and William as they approach the double doors at the front of the hotel. After they exit the hotel, Charlie and William will follow the driveway past Starbucks and make a right turn to walk down Nanking Bouelvard to the restaurant. Chin's men in the lobby will communicate their ETA to the crew on the street to set up the kill. The first thing we will do is take care of the three guys here in the hotel and then it is up to us to take out the other six men on the street. In general, this is how it's going to go down. When Charlie and William are walking down the driveway towards the street, they will walk past a busload of Chinese tourists that will be let off the bus exactly as they pass its mid-door. Charlie and William will now be in the middle of the 22 tourists who will turn right onto the sidewalk of Nanking."

He pointed to a real-time satellite picture of the front of the hotel showing the construction site. All the pedestrians without notice will walk right in between the steamroller and the dump truck as if they're trying to cross the street. They will be in the middle of Chin's men's ambush. The first thing our personnel will do is take out the three assassins who are standing up working on the water main. Then one by one, they will take out the three men on the vehicles. We figure this will take less than 45-seconds. Six of our men have vests and will put them on and replace the assassins. Everything will happen so fast, coupled with the blinding lights, that it will make it impossible for anyone on the sidewalk to fully understand what took place. Our men will take the dead assassins and throw them into the dumpster. You can see it right there in the street" he said, pointing to the reconnaissance photo. "Like I said, the whole thing shouldn't take much more than 45-seconds."

"The reason we are going to use Charlie and William is because they are professionals this is what they do. They have gone over this drill for the last hour. Guzman calls this precautionary redundancy. We don't want to take any chances after what happened in Nairobi. While all this is happening in front of the hotel, you guys will be ushered down to the street in the service elevator. You will be escorted across Nanking Boulevard and co-mingled with the men and the tourist group. We will be walking directly towards the Bali Lagoon restaurant as if nothing happened. We have total control of the street past the construction site. You will be safe. From there it shouldn't take more than 10-minutes to get to the park where the restaurant is located. Once we're inside and seated in the main eating area, you will place a call to that son of a bitch Chin. He is real predictable. He always does the same thing. He will leave whatever he is doing behind and go to the café on the plaza near his office. He will sit there in a manic crazed state until he hears from his men. By now, he probably has left his office. In front of the World Trade Center where his office is located, we have men on the street waiting for him to appear. He will go by himself to sit in front of the Chin Yuan café to wait for the call. When you call, he will think it's his men here in Shanghai. This is exactly what he always does. It is like clockwork, but this time when you will call him," he says as he points to Matt, "it will be different. You will turn his world upside down. All you will say is, look to your left, you son of a bitch."

"He will have a feeling of pure disbelief. He will be so jacked up he won't know what is happening.

Your voice will be the last thing he hears. We have two Kenyan assassins that are already in Chongqing. Neither of them have anything to live for. They are both HIV-positive. Their immune systems are shutting down and neither one will live more than 30-days. The only thing holding them together is drugs. We devised a meth-patch, to slowly release the drug. They will do anything to stay high. Because they are so sick and so high, they don't give a shit about anything except the money they will make to feed their drug habit. Like all meth-heads, they will think they are invincible. They will think they are so smart they can get away with killing Chin in public. They got into the country with Kenyan diplomatic passports. We have leverage with Kababi so it was easy to obtain them. No questions asked. When they are arrested, it will signal to Chin's brother-in-law he was killed because of his activities in Kenya. I am getting a little ahead of myself. The Kenyans are sitting in the Lotus restaurant on the second floor of the Bank of China building, in the middle of the financial plaza right this second. Chin is downstairs at an outside table of the café waiting for all of this to go down. By the time, you call him the two Kenyans will have come down the escalator and they will have walked through the café to the tables where Chin is sitting. We have two of our people at a table next to Chin right now. They will leave as soon as the Kenyans get there. Chin is so amped he won't notice the two black Africans sitting next to him. They will both be wearing business suits and blend in with the rest of the professionals in the financial district. When you call, he will look to his left and be shot in the head and the balls, to make a statement. The Kenyans won't try to escape. They are so screwed up they will probably think it's funny. There are surveillance cameras all over the financial district that will video the assassination. We have two of our men across the street. They will tape the whole thing and in real time send it directly to Chin's brother-in-law, Li Xueming.

Matt had a question. "How do you know the Kenyans will follow through with the assassination?"

José answered, "We have given them $50,000 up front and their families will receive another hundred thousand dollars upon completion. They both know they are dead men because of HIV. The meth-patches are strong enough to motivate them to follow through on the contract. They are both religious in their own ways. They know by killing Chin they are taking care of their families and that is important. Remember, I said we have precautionary redundancy. Well, we have a shooter across the street posing as a maintenance worker right in front of a Cartier store. He is directly across the street from the café. One way or another he's a dead man. As soon as he answers his phone, either the Kenyans or the Chinese shooter will take him out. He is a dead man."

Waiting to go downstairs, Frederick still had a few more moments to reflect on his journaling of China. As a seasoned traveler, he was familiar with assimilating every event of a trip. Visualizing ancient ruins, the magnificent wonders of nature, the motion and power of an animal, or any combination of olfactory simulations and sounds were part of conceptualizing an adventure. Putting together this mosaic with China's culture and its political landscape gave him an understanding that broadened his knowledge of the world. To objectify his experience he would have to rule out the physical threat they were under and cast off any preconceived notions of China's history. He would have to view his and Matt's experiences in a condensed timeframe. For some reason he felt he had to compartmentalize Hong Kong from China. He felt it might have something to do with Syrial but he was not sure. He did not have a clear understanding of Syrial but he felt he was the most impressive person he had ever met, other than Guzman who had physicality and violent nature that was intimidating to him. Frederic tried to put the trip in the context of what message Syrial was trying to convey to him. He would lay out the itinerary in chronological order and piece together the picture that his Chinese cohort was trying to put on canvas. He told himself he would try to follow the clues that were put on his path while he visited places of interest on his sojourn.

He started by analyzing Beijing first. In retrospect, the great city seemed like a world away from his suite in Shanghai. With a laptop computer sitting in front of him, he started to type, some brief observations. Initially all he came up with were the names of some major tourist attractions. The hotel they stayed at was the Grand Hyatt Hotel next to Tiananmen Square. The huge open area was contiguous to the grounds of the Forbidden City. It was the world's largest public square and was the scene of China's great social unrest in the middle 1990s. The vast size and openness of this area, surrounded by the People's Hall and ministerial buildings of Defense, Commerce and Culture, was a sensory overload for Frederic. Comprehending the amassing of more than 1-1/2 million, people and the attendant violence that led to dismantling the Communist Party stronghold on its citizenry was mind numbing. He felt like he was in a cocoon or bubble of comfort looking down at the multitude of people from a high. He was a spectator and wondering if his assessments, of what was taking place in front of him was a true measurement of reality. He and Matt were staying in the best hotel in the city. They were eating in the best restaurants that Beijing had to offer. Their chauffeur driven limousine and their access to historical sites and people was not in keeping with the common person. They traveled with the best guides and experts and had access to political dignitaries and the emerging capitalist elite. It was like being an editor of National Geographic magazine, never having put a foot in the country or speaking to its people. He and Matt were spectators not participants in China's wonders. Their views of the Forbidden City and Summer Palace, their journey to the Great Wall, and their visitation to the Ming Tombs were all sterile. The Forbidden City, one of humankind's remarkable construction achievements rivaled that of the great pyramids of Egypt. Frederic thought it remarkable that it only took 40 years to construct the 4,000 room walled city. It was mind boggling to him the number of laborers on site were more than 1-million. He couldn't comprehend the logistics of feeding, housing, and managing that many people. He tried to grapple with the idea of the valuelessness of human beings. It was estimated more than 200,000 people died in the construction of the Emperor's palace. What kind of society was China that it placed the whims and extravagances of a godlike person over the well-being of its people? What type of society was China that it could marshal vast human and physical resources for projects that were so capricious? What type of society was China that its will and direction from an Emperor or despot was accepted with virtually no dissent, no matter what the human costs? There had never been democracy in China and what made it more unacceptable to Frederic was that the life of the common person had no value. He grappled with the question of how much of a carryover existed today. Staring at his computer for more than 15 minutes without typing a word, he came to the realization that it was China's history and its rulers, may it be an Emperor, or a Communist Party president, or even a present day Chinese entrepreneur, that the masses would sacrifice life or limb for in an unrequited gesture of loyalty. What made China powerful was its oneness to task without questioning from its people. Visualizing walking through the tourist attractions, Frederic and Matt being virtually the only Caucasians in the masses of humanity gave him a perspective of China's history. The Forbidden City was a Chinese cultural attraction visited by more than 40 million Chinese a year. It was their historic Disneyland. It wasn't so much for foreigners. It was opened to the public to reinforce

China's greatness and single purposefulness to its own people. Millions of Chinese tourists went through the Great Hall of the Emperor's palace, which at one time in their history would have caused their death if they had merely laid their eyes upon any member of the ruling family. For security and loyalty reasons, men were castrated into eunuchs to lessen the suspicion of palace intrigue for the Emperor. The royal family had thousands of slaves. The Emperor had an Empress and a concubine of up to a thousand secondary wives. The labor of the common person, the taxes derived from the common people, and the liberties taken from the common person were all tribute to a godlike deity that ruled and lived only for their own selfish well-being. The propagandized public display of yesterday's way of life. Most disheartening to him was Chinese tourists did not decry but embraced them. It was a glaring depiction of China's glorious history struck Frederic as transparent social engineering of the highest degree. The Forbidden City was a symbol of China's glorious past and a precursor for its future. China was defined by its ruler's visions and its masses ability to sacrifice. Its people, as if they were soldier ants, were programmed to construct great edifices and to pay great tributes to the ruling class. The masses that created societies' wealth and received nothing in return for centuries made great sacrifices without question. To Frederic it seemed little different today. China was only different in the fact it colonized the poorer countries of the world, the Kenyans, to exploit them, not its own people to the extent they were exploited in the past. The aggregate power of China wasn't its visions, but it was its ability to exploit labor. What created its greatness then and now was its selfish ability to harvest labor for a national goal. Individuals were programmed, as if it were written in their DNA, to submit to the direction of their power elite. No other country in the world has the labor resources and direction of China. Coupled with its new ability to extract factors of production from third world nations and China's destiny would be world leadership again. Syrial gave Frederic the clues of China's 5,000-year domination. Except for the period from 1850 to 1990, the Chinese had been the strongest and most important of the human species. Sending Frederic and Matt to Beijing was Syrial's way of expressing China's greatness of yesterday and more importantly their vision for tomorrow. Its oneness of direction would make it the greatest nation on earth again. From its ashes in the early 1900s, when its people were starving and its lands carved up by the Europeans, to today when it's again moving into its rightful position of world dominance made total sense to Frederic.

Frederick closed his laptop. He sat there for a few minutes staring into space. He did not want to leave the mental rush of his new understanding of China. His mental focus gave him the clarity and perspective of China's determination to be the world's dominant culture and dominant economic powerhouse. Now he and Matt had to leave the conference room and venture out of the hotel to the Bali Lagoon Restaurant as Jose's men attended to their enemies.

Chapter 50

Once seated in the restaurant long room, it didn't take more than 60-seconds for Matt to place a call to Chin and instruct him to look to his left. Soon after, José's cell phone rang.

Over the noise of the restaurant both men could hear him say, "I'll tell them."

He looked at both Matt and Frederic, "He's dead. It's all over."

Jose handed the phone to Matt, "Guzman wants to talk to you."

"He is dead, my friend," announced Guzman. "So are the Kenyans. They were gunned down before they could even leave the café. I'll take it from here. You guys can rest, you're safe now. I just have to make one call, and trust me, then it is all over. I am sending a file of all our intelligence to give to our friend Li Xueming.

It contains copies of his e-mails and tapes of his calls to Chin. I will get back to you as soon as I have talked to him. I want to tell you that BiBa and Gisele have safely landed in Cairo. They will be on a plane for London, and then to New York within the hour. It is over my friend. I just have to clean up a couple of things."

He hung up and then placed a call to the Vice Chairman of the Communist Party. Li answered his personal phone. There were less than ten people in the whole world that had the personal number.

"Mr. Vice Chairman, this is Roberto Coto, the president of Costa Rica and the new head of the non-aligned nations at the UN. You have a problem my friend. I sent you two communications in the last ten minutes that are valuable to your very existence."

Li broke in, "How dare you?" he said in very clear concise English. "No one blackmails me or my country!"

Guzman shot back, "I killed your brother-in-law. That's right, I ordered his death. This is no loss to you. He beat your sister and fucked little boys and you still used him to do your bidding. I did you a favor, you miserable fuck. I didn't call to talk about him. What I can do to your family should be important to you. I have them. That is right, my men have them and you have my word they will be released as soon as my men have IEDs planted into their shoulders. You have already seen what these explosive devices do. I have killed your brother-in-law. You will receive a package shortly. In it will be the heads of Chin's assassins, and I have your family's fate in my hands. Is this all clear to you? That's right; you saw what I did to your man Moi in Nairobi. Well pal, that is what is going to fucking happen to your family if I have any problem with you."

The Vice Chairman tried to speak. Guzman cut him off, "I have your wife and kids and both of your parents as well as a couple members of their staff. So shut the fuck up. Look at the e-mails and calls you made to Chin. That's right; the file I just sent you has all of your communication with that baby fucker. I have you by the balls. What you had him do for you was treason my friend. The ruling party does not take kindly to people like you. For a guy in line for the chairmanship of the Communist Party, and ultimately the presidency of China, you are an arrogant sloppy fuck."

"Here is my deal. The Politburo meets in three months to elect a new leader. As of now you if you don't screw up, and my information doesn't come out to the public, you are the presumptive nominee for the presidency. If you want to keep your meeting with destiny, you do what the fuck I say. I'm willing to endorse you at the UN when you are there to speak to the General Assembly late next month. I have all of the nonaligned nations' votes committed to whoever I back. That can be you. I'll give you international accessibility ushering China into the 21st century. You will personally get the recognition for bringing China to its place of dominance in the world body. I have the votes to make you the head of the Security Council and displace Nationalist China from any seat on any commission in the UN. That will dissolve its relationship with the US. Once that is accomplished, mainland China, that means you, will represent all of the Chinese people. It is a stepping-stone for effectively removing the United States from its role as world leader. On my end, it is a done deal. I have the votes. It's what you are going to give me that will save your ass. You are a dead man if you refuse my demands. What I will ask is very little, compared to what you and China will gain. It is a matter of time before China gets its rightful place as the most dominant player in the world. That tide cannot be turned. I will just move the timetable up 20-years and include you as its new ruler. Refuse me and it will be your death."

Guzman continued to lay out his demands. "When you are the newly elected head of the Politburo, you will stop destabilizing the Third World for the purposes of extracting cheap mineral resources. Financial exploitation will no longer be acceptable as the main driver to Chinese economic expansion. To feed your industrial furnaces, you will employ a model of shared ownership when it comes to purchasing raw materials for your people. No more exploitation of the Third World, the matrix developed by William Nakruru of Kenya will be implemented, throughout China's industrial complex. You will help Nakruru in his run for the presidency of Kenya. You will do the same in Somalia, the Ivory Coast, Liberia, Sierra Leone and all of the African Horn. For that matter, you will change Chinese foreign investment all over the world and make it more populous and friendly to poor people. I call it, shared democracy. China's days of cowboy capitalism are over. What I'm demanding will facilitate more opportunity and fairer distribution of wealth. It won't even significantly slow down China's economic growth. Our analysis shows it will decrease China's GDP by less than one-half of a percent a year. Up to this point, what has moved China towards world dominance is your ability to harness and direct labor, and your colonialization of third world nations to purchase minerals at deflated prices. We both know that its exploitation has made you and your ilk mega rich. It created men like Chin and hundreds of others who brought China into the 20th century from the depths of poverty in a few short decades. People like you and your brother-in-law are moving China into the 21st century at a faster pace than anyone could have ever forecasted, but the costs are enormous and unacceptable. The inequity of wealth, pollution, excessive exploitation of the poor, all your tools to drive China to prosperity are no longer acceptable. The only alternative to saving your life and China's future is what I offer you. You will accept shared democracy for your people or you will die. It will no longer be acceptable to exploit the productivity of labor for the power elite. Take my offer, and move China into its rightful position as the most dominant country in the world. The only condition is it must be done in a populist movement. I will kill your ass and have someone else do it. What I have on you makes you a dead man, if you don't meet my demands. I will find someone else."

Li started to argue. "Shut the fuck up before I pull my offer from the table! I mentioned your family. I want you to call your mother. Get her on the phone and make it a conference call." Guzman gave him a number and said, "I know you have a computer in front of you. Do it on Skype. Call her right now!"

In the kitchen of their Beijing home, his parent's computer phone rang and was answered by his sobbing 78-year-old mother. She was terrorized.

"My son, my son, there are many men in the house who have taken us and our staff. They knocked down your father and placed something in his shoulder. They did the same to me. They hurt me and they hurt your cousin, Mi ling. She is hurt badly."

Guzman looking at events as they played out in front of him on his computer said to his men, "Pick up the guy on the ground in the corner. The cook or whoever he is, tie him up in the chair next to the table."

The next thing that came out of Guzman's mouth was, "Do it." One of Guzman's men pulled out a cell and dialed a number. The man's upper body exploded into hundreds of pieces throwing carnage across the room. Li's blood soaked mother fainted.

His father started yelling, "What is happening? What is happening?"

Li yelled at the screen of his computer, "I will kill you!"

Before he could speak another word, Guzman said in the cold tone of a pathological killer, "Don't fuck with me. You have a decision to make."

Guzman called Matt. "It is over my friend. I talked to that fuck Li Xueming and believe me, he sees our ways. The big stuff has been worked out. He bought into what we want to do. It will take some time to develop some rules for him to live by, but like I said, it's over. You know that I am not good with words, but this is over. I have to go. I have some things to do. I have to prepare a speech for the UN. Be sure to tell BiBa and Gisele that they are safe. I know Frederic is there, tell him I will be in touch next week. Both of you have dinner on me. Let me talk to José before I hang up. I will call Malique and fill him in. Thank you my brother."

Epilogue

The head of the nonaligned nations of the United Nations, Roberto Coto, the president of Costa Rica, was introduced to the General Assembly. He delivered a much anticipated speech to the world body about the widening gap between rich and poor nations. Coto represented the interests of billions of poor and disenfranchised in the third world. While the more flexible and nimble wealthier nations were seeing economic growth and higher standards of living, the income gap between developed and underdeveloped nations followed old lines of the north versus the south, exacerbated by worldwide economic downturn, environmental damage caused by global warming impacted the underdeveloped nations negatively.

Coto pushed for a change in the global financial structure that allows currencies to be pegged to a collective basket of nonaligned nations' currencies. He argued it would promote economic growth in the south. He asked the world body to address trade policies favoring the underdeveloped and subsidized by developed nations, i.e. the G20. He wanted greater transparency and participation by third world nations in the World Bank and the IMF. He advocated a new world order that tempered the arrangements that were historically one-sided in favor of European nations.

At the end of his speech he surprised the assemblage of delegates by advocating for an economic baron to oversee the changes that would right the wrongs of 19th and 20th century colonialism. He introduced Li, the new president of China, as a technocrat who would oversee the transformation of the global economy. Li would be asked to usher in a more balanced approach to world trade that would help facilitate redistribution of wealth from the north to the south in an orderly fashion. It would allow the developed nations natural resources and markets for their finished goods, while they paid higher wages and created better working conditions for the world's working poor.

Trade no longer based on financial exploitation, but driven by comparative advantage of freer markets, would be an advocated by Li for fair trade agreements ultimately lead to greater democratization of the third world.

Guzman's alter ego, Roberto Coto, had done his job, and left the stage to thundering applause as President Li walked across the large stage. The two men shook hands and Guzman exited the auditorium. Upon reaching his waiting limousine, he sat in the back and reflected for a moment before giving the driver an address.

BiBa and Matt were in the throes of making dinner for their friends Frederic, Gisele, and Jose, whom they had not seen since Matt and Frederic had returned from China. This would be the first meeting of the group in over two months. BiBa finally felt up to entertaining and moving ahead with her life, and thought dinner would be a good beginning. She and Matt were in the kitchen at the front of the brownstone when the electronic butler announced an unidentified guest was approaching the front door. BiBa looked down from the second floor through the massive bay window to see a man dressed in a suit with an attractive woman on his arm.

"I don't know him, come take a look," she said to Matt. "Did you invite anyone else and forget to tell me?"

Matt walked over from the other side of the room and looked down, He could not believe his eyes. It was Jose Guzman. Without saying a word he ran down and opened the door. Both men were frozen in time and just looked at each other without saying a word.

Guzman spoke first and introduced his executive assistant, Maria Gomez. "Maria, this is a good friend of mine," he said as he introduced her to Matt.

"I will call you when I'm ready to leave. Have the men," referring to his security detail, "discreetly stay on the street and cover the sides and back of the house."

Matt was stunned. All he could say was, "Ms. Gomez, it is a pleasure."

He looked at Guzman, in his role as the president of Costa Rica, and continued. "Mr. President, please come in," as he let his friend play out his role in front of his executive assistant. The door closed as she walked down the steps and the two men embraced.

"Shit, I can't believe this," Matt said. "I don't know what to say. We have so much to talk about, but first you have to meet BiBa. She is in the kitchen preparing dinner, you won't believe this, Frederic, Gisele and Jose!"

They walked up the stairwell and entered the kitchen where Matt introduced BiBa to the president of Costa Rica. Matt did not know Jose's agenda and played as if he really was Roberto Coto.

Guzman looked at her and said, "I have heard much about you," and extended his hand. His handsome features and physical presence were not lost on BiBa. She felt awkward because there was a stillness to their conversation. It was as if he stopped talking and reflected before he would utter another word.

He looked deep into her eyes and said, "I am Jose Guzman, and it is my pleasure to finally meet you."

She was at a loss for words and impulsively put out her arms to hug him. She was amazed at the deep emotionality of the meeting.

Matt never envisioned this day. He didn't know what to say and the two men hugged as only two brothers could. After their manly embrace, Guzman again turned his attention to BiBa and said, "You are everything I imagined, and my friend, yes, my best friend, is a lucky man. After seeing what you are capable of, I am fortunate to have you as a comrade."

He looked at Matt and said, "Treat her well. It is evident she is very special."

BiBa could not express herself and felt sophomoric. "I feel funny," she said. "When I saw you on the stoop I should have known. I just should have known. You looked like Jose Guzman to me and what is more unbelievable is that I felt I knew you. Jose, I never thought we would meet. It is truly a good day for Matt and me."

Within twenty minutes Gisele, Frederic and Jose arrived. They had come together. The night would leave Ms. Gomez and her associates guarding the house until nearly 2:30 am. Before drinks were even in hand, the six warriors rehashed the Chin Affair, China and Kenya. Li's name came up and Guzman said, "He is in our pocket," and everyone knew that to be the case.

The talk of their particular brand of warfare and Matt and Guzman's transformations, changed to pleasantries and the rest of the night became social.

Early on Matt pulled BiBa into the kitchen and said, "You have to listen to me...I was truly sorry for getting you into this mess, but to be honest with you, I am really glad I did. All of this feels right to me. These are my friends, shit, they're my family. I don't know what to say except I hope you feel the same way."

She knew he was right, and told him she felt the same.

No one really came out and said it, but everyone knew The Papaz Group would fight for a new cause in the future. No one knew where or why, but they were brought together for a reason, not only to enjoy the company of comrades in arms, but they would function as and have the feelings of an extended family.

Frederic said, "It is good to have us all together without all the killing and mayhem. Let's hope it lasts for a while."

The world would not need them for another year, and then all hell would break loose.

Those People

BY RUSSELL C. ARSLAN

David Russell arrived in Africa to share experiences with his grown sons. After clearing customs, the boys waited for David outside the airport terminal. By the time their father arrived with an old Land Rover the boys were wondering why he had brought them to this horrid 'other world' place. The people seemed different. The place stank to high heaven.

When dad rolled up in the Rover saying how beautiful Africa was, they looked at each other thinking he must be delusional.

As they drove to the hotel both boys realized not only was this place different than anything they had ever known, but so was their father. They were introduced to David Russell a Kenyan revolutionary, they saw 'those people', a strange unemotional, brutal, other kind of person. But this was just the beginning. They had encounters with 'those people,' found the loves of their lives, establish a new business, and realized their lives could expand beyond even their expectations.

-----o-----

"HIGHEST STAKES, ALL IN"

BY RUSSELL C. ARSLAN

Matt Papaz goes *All In* to prove his innocence, after being charged with crimes Homeland Security has contrived to entangle him.

This Russell C. Arslan mystery grabs you and makes you a part of Papaz' quest for survival.

Matt Papaz's life depends on the intelligence and strategies needed to win Texas Hold'em or any card game of skill. Going full throttle, *All In*, means take a commanding position, based on odds and the reading of your opponent's hand. Papaz plays from the game's power position rather than from weakness. Taking an aggressive stance gives him the edge in life and death situations.

The best players' template, acting from strength *All In*, becomes Papaz's pattern for dealing with forces more powerful than himself who are bent on his elimination. *All In* uses gambling tactics and strategies as a guide for Matt Papaz dealing with adversaries. His ability to read danger, adapt and overcome all odds is a successful trademark in the world of national security gamesmanship and professional poker.

-----o-----

Leopard Directive

By Russell C. Arslan

The forward thinking nations had freed billions of dollars from policing narcotics. Prisons were no longer overcrowded with drug dealers and addicts. Violent acts monopolizing production and drug distribution were curtailed. Taking drugs was legalized in all but a few isolated countries. Drug cartel's business practices was no longer perceived as a government threat. Their monies and personnel could now be used for the betterment of society.

Roberto Coto, the new democratically elected Costa Rican President with his Chief-of-Staff, Matt Papaz and his old friend, Frederic Valance carefully circumvented the usual money laundering techniques infusing millions of dollars from the notorious Tijuana cartel into the Latin American country. His political and personal persona manufactured after the Porter affair was clean and impervious to public scrutiny. His identity for the entirety of the past four years had been safe.

An email from their old friend Frederic Valence broke three years of silence. In their new identities, as President of Costa Rico and Chief-of-Staff Jose and Matt were appalled. It would be life changing.

-----o-----

Russell C. Arslan, a retired university economics professor with entrepreneurial portfolio describes himself as an internationalist bent on geopolitical and environmental issues. Just as importantly, he is a storyteller who will entertain you. Having traveled extensively in Asia, Europe, Central and South America and Africa for more then five decades, he brings his knowledge and experiences into his writings. His genre is political and scientific themes as contentious as global warming and nuclear proliferation, or as threatening as terrorism.

During his university career, his vocation was teacher; not impersonal academic professing subject material knowledge. His writings display a passion for political economy.

"The factors limiting your success are the limits of your own experiences and knowledge." This postulate threads its way through his writings.

"You cannot teach or write what you do not know or feel." His books are filled with information and an agenda for attacking social ills.

He lives with his wife Janis in Bel Air California. His quest for adventure and insights for his novels have them traveling all over the globe for story lines. At the first printing of You Are Safe they are in Istanbul doing research for another book. Upon his return, he will continue his writings, entrepreneurial activities, sponsorship of students and mentoring endeavors.

www.ingramcontent.com/pod-product-compliance
Lightning Source LLC
Chambersburg PA
CBHW051444260626
47162CB00001B/246

9780985769598